The Samurai's Garden

by
Patricia Kiyono

The Samurai's Garden
by Patricia Kiyono
Published by Astraea Press
www.astraeapress.com

THE SAMURAI'S GARDEN
Copyright © 2012 PATRICIA KIYONO
ISBN: 1482389436
ISBN 13: 978-1482389432
Cover Art Designed by For the Muse Designs

For Mom.
I've always been proud of our heritage because you made it
fascinating and alive through your stories. I hope this story brings
honor to our family.

Prologue

Aomori Prefecture, Honshu, Japan, 1872

So it had come to this.

Hideyori Kato paced the dirt floor, his face wrinkled in a frown of disgust. Unprotected by *tabi*, the silk stockings he was accustomed to wearing, his feet bled from the coarse straw of his sandals. At his palace, he would not have been wearing shoes at all, but the creatures scurrying about in this hovel had forced him into the unheard of habit of wearing shoes indoors.

Kato, the great and once-powerful *daimyo*, was reduced to living in a mud hut on the outer pasture of what had once been the lands surrounding his castle. He should never have surrendered to that child-emperor, Meiji. He should have rallied his army and fought. His treasurer had given him some drivel about the coffers being empty, but he could have promised them riches, and they would have fought for glory, or whatever their silly *Bushido* decreed. Maybe he could have convinced the neighboring *daimyos* to join their armies with his, so he could have overtaken the emperor's forces. And then he, Hideyori Kato, would have ruled all of Japan. The thought of all that power made his mind spin.

His grumbling stomach reminded him he hadn't eaten yet that day. He clapped his hands impatiently.

A wrinkled old man, toothless and bent, hobbled into the hut. He bowed with difficulty and spoke from his lowered position.

"Yes, Master?"

"Where is my meal? I am starving!"

The old man's emaciated figure shrank back. "Chu-san has not returned from hunting for today's food," he began.

The crack of Hideyori's walking stick on the man's back ended the servant's reply.

"Fool! If there is no meat, find something else! I cannot function without food. I smell something cooking outside. Bring me some of that."

"Yes, Master." The old man grunted as he crawled backward out of the hut, his face etched in pain. A moment later he returned with a bowl of steaming liquid.

"Take care! You are spilling the soup on the floor," Hideyori complained. He grabbed the bowl from the man's shaking hands and brought it to his mouth. He blew on the broth to cool it and drank. A moment later, he threw the bowl at the already battered man.

"This is horrible! It's just boiled weeds! How dare you serve such garbage to me?"

"Master, there is nothing else—"

"Use your head and find me something decent to eat. I can't eat this slop!" He emphasized each word with another blow from his stick.

This just wasn't fair. Not only had his lands been confiscated, the government had taken away his title. The *daimyos* who had cooperated with the government had been awarded a new rank in the emperor's court and allowed to keep their lands. Since he'd resisted, he was banished to this hovel. Only the servants too weak or too old to find other jobs had stayed with him. Too bad they were also idiots. Hideyori took out his frustration on the crouched figure before him. With every blow, he shouted another grievance against the Meiji government.

Twenty minutes later, the walking stick broke from its use. The servant's lifeless body lay in a heap, blood streaming from his nose and mouth. Hideyori stamped out of the hut, resigned to the fact that the boiled weeds would have to satisfy his grumbling stomach for now.

But things would change. Somehow.

Two hours later, he sat on a rock outside the hut, still waiting for someone to bring him more food. The weak soup had done little to satisfy his hunger. The old man inside had said someone named Chu-san had gone hunting. Where was the fool? He had a vague memory of a young man, the son of one of his former servants.

He really needed to get better servants. Boiled weeds, indeed! How was he supposed to eat that? If only he had some money, he could buy some decent food. Or better yet, hire someone to prepare it for him.

The sun beat down, and he started to sweat under his thick robe. Reluctantly, he took the robe off, revealing the stained cotton *yukata* underneath. He hated to be seen without his full dress—he had an image to preserve—but it was too hot out here. And it was even worse inside the hut, especially with the servant's body lying there. Chu-san would have to remove the body when he finally returned with something to eat. His servants were totally useless. Where were they when he needed them?

Disgusted, he removed his robe and threw it, not caring where it went. The garment landed on another rock with a "clink."

Clink?

Out of habit, he turned to call for a servant but realized there was no one to hear his summons. Grumbling, he rose from his seat and took the five steps to his robe. It was heavy, made of thick brocade, and the long, hanging sleeves were lined with several layers of silk. He picked up the robe, checking under it. Finding nothing there, he inspected the robe itself. The brocade was worn, the fraying threads a testimony to his dire financial status.

Turning the garment inside out, he frowned at the dingy color. When he had a full staff, his court seamstresses would keep track of these things and replace the linings at regular intervals. But there were no more seamstresses. He was stuck with this lining. There were holes here and there, and the seams were worn. He smoothed the lining down. When he regained his fortune, one of the first things he would do would be to order some new clothes. No one would take him seriously as a leader if he had to wear rags like this.

His hand ran across a hard bump in the fabric. Were the holes so large that a rock had lodged in between the layers? He inspected the bump more closely. No, it wasn't a rock. Eagerly, he picked at the fabric, trying to scratch a hole in the weave. No luck. He needed something sharp. Casting a look around, he spied a short branch under a nearby tree and hurried over to retrieve it.

Ten minutes later, the robe was in tatters, but Hideyori didn't care. His hands cradled a beautiful hand-painted fan, its bamboo frame embellished with finely detailed carvings. For once, a servant had actually followed directions. He remembered the day he had instructed the little maid to "hide the valuables somewhere the emperor's men will not find it." The girl must have hidden the fan in the lining of his robe. *Clever girl.* Too bad he hadn't been able to keep her.

His growling stomach was forgotten as he went back into the hut to look for other hidden treasures in his clothing.

Chapter One

Hokkaido, Japan, Spring, 1874

Hanako Shimizu tightened her lips, struggling to maintain a measure of decorum and respect toward the unkempt man before her. The buzz of springtime activity in the marketplace faded to the back of her mind. She had work to do.

Sato-san peered down at her, a menacing scowl adding more wrinkles to his sagging jowls. Drawing himself up to the fullest extent of his limited height, the livestock merchant looked down his nose and deigned to speak. She managed not to cringe outwardly from the stench of his stale breath.

"And why is your husband or father not here to purchase this livestock himself?"

Hanako ground her teeth to prevent herself from lashing out at the pompous merchant. She curled her fingers into fists, lest she should give in to temptation and claw out his eyes. Sato-san knew very well why her husband was not here to purchase his own livestock. But she needed his cooperation, so she answered.

"The men in my home live no more," she replied. "My father has been gone these past five summers, and my husband perished during the raid of the *ronin* last year."

"Then you must take a new husband." Sato-san grinned widely, displaying the few brown crooked teeth remaining in his mouth. "You are still fairly young. Perhaps I could be persuaded to give up my bachelor ways. A beautiful widow should not be left to fend for herself on a lonely farm. Even though the *shoguns* have declared peace, there are still dangerous men roaming the countryside."

Hanako knew all about the dangers. The memory of last summer's attack still haunted her dreams. Still, the thought of becoming Sato-san's wife was even more repulsive than the bloody memories. She willed herself not to shudder visibly. It wouldn't do to irritate him. Sato-san's livestock wasn't prime grade, but it was reasonably priced, and she needed these animals to help turn a profit from her shabby little farm.

"Please, Sato-san. It has been scarcely six months since I was widowed. I need time to grieve for poor Kenji." She lowered her gaze, projecting the image of sorrow and tragedy.

"Six months is a long time for a fertile young woman to be without a man in her bed," leered the portly merchant. "I think Shimizu-san would not want you to be alone."

I was alone even when he was with me.

"I am not alone. I have his spirit with me in the *obutsudan*." The tiny wooden box in which her husband's ashes rested hardly resembled a true shrine, but it was enough to satisfy the proprieties of a grieving widow. Reminding herself of her mission, she faced Sato-san with resolve, but kept her gaze focused on a point just below his chin. She knew he would not welcome direct eye contact with a woman.

"You flatter me with your attention, Sato-san, but for now I must concentrate on rebuilding my farm. After all, I wouldn't be able to bring a respectable dowry into a marriage with the present state of my property. Now, I have offered a fair price for this cow and those two chickens."

Sato-san was not fooled by Hanako's gentle rebuff. His lips pressed together and he scowled. "I deal only with men," he finally responded as he turned away from her.

Hanako chewed her lip and took a deep breath, admonishing herself not to lose her temper. No matter how unreasonable Sato-san chose to be, she couldn't hope to conduct business with him if she lost control of her emotions.

She opened her mouth, ready to present another argument, but another voice, one with deep, melodic tones, made all her thoughts disappear.

"I see you have chosen well, my little flower. What price have you and this gentleman agreed upon?"

Hanako's mouth closed as she tried to put a face with the voice. It was deep and rich, full of confidence and strength. It belonged to a man of power. The man's speech was much more formal than the casual dialect used by locals.

"Who are you?" Sato-san demanded.

Hanako wondered, too. She turned to look at the mystery speaker. He stood head and shoulders above the unsavory Sato-san, with muscles born of hard physical work, but his facial features radiated intelligence, and his bearing hinted at an aristocratic upbringing. Two swords hung at his side, a testament to his position as a samurai. She'd heard rumors of new laws eliminating their powers, but knew no one in this sleepy village would dare argue with this man's right to carry his swords.

"I am Hiromasa Tanaka. I am not familiar with the merchants in this area, so I sent my intended to find the livestock and supplies we need. If all is ready, I will pay you, and we will be on our way."

"Your intended? But Shimizu-san just told me she still grieves for her late husband."

"Yes, she still grieves. It is normal. But her husband was a cousin and a longtime friend, and I promised him I would care for her. When she is ready, we will marry. Until then, I will take care of the business of the farm."

Before Hanako could blink, the stranger had made the purchase and had turned to lead the cow out of the stockyard. He indicated with a regal nod for her to pick up the cage of chickens, ignoring her frustrated glare. Without a word, he started down the road leading away from the village. Helpless to do anything else, she followed at the customary three paces behind him. He had the animals she wanted, and nothing would be gained by making a scene here.

Trudging silently behind the stranger, Hanako's mind raced. *Who is this man? How dare he step in and purchase the animals I spent so much time choosing? Kenji had never mentioned a cousin. Besides, it's inconceivable for a samurai, especially one so tall and—virile, to be a relative to Kenji, who was smaller than average and—not so virile. And why would he pretend to be my fiancé?* She gathered her thoughts, but before she could deliver her tirade, the stranger stopped, turned around, and held the cow's lead rope out to her.

"This is yours. I only made the purchase because that idiot would not deal with you. I made up the story about being your husband's cousin, and I thought you could just repay me after we were out of his sight."

Hanako tilted her head, confusion lining her face. She took the rope, but couldn't stop herself from asking, "Why would you do this for me?" She narrowed her eyes in suspicion. "What do you want from me?"

The big man shrugged. "Nothing, except repayment for the animals you are holding."

She felt her face burn. "Mmm, that might take a little while. I hoped Sato-san would sell me the animals and let me make payments later." Her embarrassment turned to anger as Hiro burst into laughter. "What's so funny? Do you doubt my ability to work the farm and turn a profit?"

"I don't doubt your ability at all. But I can just imagine what kind of payment that vermin would want from you," he rasped. "I heard some of the things he said." He took her arm as she turned away. "If you don't have the money, then perhaps you could give me a place to stay for a while. The inn here is full, and there are no other accommodations in town. I've been traveling a long time and I'm tired."

Hanako looked closely at the stranger. Her sharp eyes took in the rich fabric of his *obi*, the fine craftsmanship and fit of his clothing, and the bejeweled hilts on both his long and short sword. "I can't offer fine accommodations like you are accustomed to having." Her eyes narrowed as another thought occurred to her. "And why should I believe you would not expect the same payment as you suspect Sato-san wanted?"

Hiro drew himself up. "I have taken the oath of the *Bushido*. You are not an enemy, so I would not harm you or anything that is yours."

It was Hanako's turn to laugh. "It was a band of your honorable men who came and raided my home, killed my husband, and burned my crops last fall. I do not have much faith in your code."

At the mention of the masterless samurai known as *ronin*, Hiro's lips curled in disgust. Though many former samurai had taken positions in the Emperor's army or had found new careers, a few wandered the country aimlessly, causing havoc. Now, Hanako wondered if her insult had pushed the stranger too far. If he chose to punish her for speaking to him so, she would have no defense against his strength. She watched his expression, wondering if she should try to run. Finally, he bowed stiffly and spoke. Hanako braced herself for the worst. But her jaw dropped in surprise at his words.

"I apologize for the actions of my fellow samurai," he began, "and you may consider the animals partial payment toward retribution for your loss. In addition, I will work for you this season so your lands may be restored to their former value."

****

Hiromasa Tanaka studied the tiny woman before him. Instead of the elaborate hairstyle or wig worn by the women in his world, Hanako's hair was scarcely visible. A faded scarf held it off her face and under a wide-brimmed straw hat, but a few stray tendrils had escaped, gently framing her delicate features. Her complexion, though tanned, was not as rough as many of the farmwomen he had seen. Perhaps the straw hat she wore protected her somewhat. A cheap linen kimono hung loosely on her slender frame. The faded brown fabric had no embellishment, and an equally shabby strip of fabric wrapped around her middle was her *obi*, or sash. A coarse rope tied over the *obi* served as her *obi-jime*, holding everything in place. The top of her head barely reached his shoulder, but she held herself with dignity and pride, giving her the illusion of height.

"What is your name?" he asked when she didn't respond.

She peered up at him curiously. "You know my name. You called me 'Little Flower' in the marketplace."

"It was simply an endearment, the first that came to mind. Your name really is Little Flower?"

"I am called Hanako—Flower Child." She turned her face and her cheeks pinked. "My mother loved flowers, and I was born in the spring when her garden started to bloom."

"I see. So, Hanako-san, will you allow me to work in exchange for lodging?"

She bit her lip and looked down, and he guessed at the reason for her hesitation. "I am accustomed to simple accommodations. After all, a soldier must learn to sleep wherever he is at nightfall, whether he is in a cave or under the skies. If you accept my offer, I will do my best to be of assistance to you. Which way to your home?"

She hesitated another moment, and he realized he had been holding his breath when she finally nodded and indicated the direction they would take.

They followed the road until the sun began its descent. The long walk gave Hiro plenty of time to think about his new employer. From his outdoor seat at the tavern, he had noticed her arrival in the village. Marching into the stockyard, she'd made her selections with knowledgeable assurance. Despite her delicate appearance, she had demonstrated experience and a firm hand with the animals. However, the antics of the slimy Sato-san had disgusted him. The merchant's refusal to deal with her had prompted Hiro to step in.

He hadn't intended to do more than help her make her purchase, but the chance to get acquainted intrigued him. Working on her farm would allow him to pass the time while he decided on his life's course, as well as pay penance for the wrongs done by his former comrades.

Finally, they reached a pair of dilapidated huts. From this point, the road curved and disappeared in the woods. He stopped on the road, turning to her and raising his brow in a silent question. When she simply nodded toward the larger one, he walked to the doorway and entered it.

The evening's dim light made it difficult to see inside, but when his eyes adjusted he could tell the woman kept a tidy home. The shabby contents were clean, and arranged comfortably. While Hanako dealt with the animals, he took stock of his new temporary lodgings.

A simple wooden box to the right of the stove held two rusty urns. A bowl of rice and a few berries had been placed in front of the urns, along with a stub of candle. A man's garment, made from cheap coarse fabric, had been draped on the wall behind the box. This must be her *obustudan*, the home for the spirits of her husband and father. It was a far cry from the elaborate, lacquered wood and gold-painted arrangement holding his father's ashes. Yet, the simple tribute was equally profound.

Her entrance into the room interrupted his perusal. She lit a lantern, further highlighting the shabbiness of the hut's furnishings. "I will prepare the evening meal. Will you have some tea?" Her voice, though marked with the accent of a peasant, was lyrical.

"I would enjoy some refreshment. Thank you." He sat on one of the threadbare cushions in the seating area and watched, fascinated, as the young woman performed her task. Her motions were fluid and economical as she prepared tea and a meal of soup and vegetables.

"Does someone live in the other building?" he asked.

"When my father lived, he slept there. I hope it will be suitable for you. It's dusty, so I'll clean it for you while you eat."

"I am certain it will be satisfactory. Thank you for your hospitality."

"I apologize for the lack of substance in our meal," she said as she set the fare on the floor in front of him, "but I left early for the market and didn't go fishing today. I'll be sure to have a better meal tomorrow." She bowed respectfully and turned to leave.

"Please sit with me." The words came from his mouth without warning. She froze in mid-step and spun back to stare at him. *She may be a simple girl, but she has some manners.* It would not be her place to be seated with a man as he took his meal. "I have some questions, and since I am quite tired and would like to sleep after eating, I want to speak with you now."

She hesitated another moment, and then nodded. She knelt demurely, keeping a respectful distance, and folded her hands on her knees. He noted her hands trembled slightly, despite her expressionless face.

"Do you not have any relatives to help you?" he asked.

"No," she replied. "My mother died in childbirth when I

was young. My brother was sickly and lived only two years. My father and I lived here until he passed away three years ago. I have no aunts, uncles, or cousins who will acknowledge me, and my husband never talked about his family."

"How long were you married?"

"Six years."

"So your husband took over the farm when your father died?"

She took her time answering him. A series of expressions swept across her face: frustration, sorrow, defeat. He hadn't meant to evoke painful memories. Finally, she sighed and squared her shoulders. Her eyes still downcast in respect for his gender and rank, she answered in a clear, firm voice. "Father was—ill—for a long time before he died. My husband wasn't raised on a farm, so he didn't really know what to do. I—helped him with the work and the management."

Hiro's compassion for the young widow grew. Apparently her father had left her to make all the arrangements and decisions, and now that her husband was gone she was left with all the physical labor as well. He would need to work hard to help her get back on her feet. But he knew nothing about agriculture, and even less about farm animals. He'd have to observe and take his cues from his hostess.

He finished his meal then set the bowl down. "Thank you for the delicious meal. Are there any duties you wish for me to complete before I retire?"

Hanako shook her head. "The animals are settled for the night, and since the light of day is gone, we can't do any work in the field. As soon as I have prepared your room we should sleep, and begin our work early in the morning." Since he had finished, she rose, bowed, and took his bowl. She placed it in the cooking area and hurried outside.

Hiro took out his pipe and went out into the night. His years of warrior training had taught him to familiarize himself with his surroundings. The road to the village marked the northern edge of Hanako's land. Open fields lay to the east and west. To the south, dense woods guarded the fields. A narrow stream gurgled as it cut a path out of the woods toward the house then curved and returned back into the trees. Hiro examined the earth, digging at it with his toe. The cold harsh winter had left it hard-packed. It was no wonder Hanako wanted livestock to help with the plowing.

The soft rustle of Hanako's kimono told him she had finished cleaning out his hut and returned to her own. Through the open doorway, he saw her scoop out her own meal and sit down to eat. If the thin soup was all she'd had to eat all day, it wouldn't do much to fill her. He would have to do all he could do to help.

Chapter Two

The bright morning sun woke Hanako from a deep slumber. She chided herself for oversleeping. There was so much to do, now that she had the animals. The chickens needed to be fed, the field needed plowing, and —

She sat up, suddenly wide awake. Her guest! He would need something to eat before working outdoors all day. She scrambled to her feet, deciding what to do first. She would not have time to catch fish, but maybe one of the hens she brought home yesterday would have an egg or two.

She stopped suddenly at an unfamiliar sound outside her hut. Who or what would be making that noise? The road was not well-traveled, and it was not the sound of an animal foraging for food. She peeked through the doorway, and her jaw dropped as she realized what she had heard.

Hiro stood at the edge of the clearing, swinging an ancient axe in a deadly arc at the trunk of a thick tree. A loud crack preceded the thunderous boom as it crumpled to the earth. The axe continued its work as limbs and branches were separated from the trunk.

Hanako's mouth went dry at the sight of her handsome guest. He was stripped to the waist, his tanned and muscled arms glistening as they swung rhythmically. She couldn't resist leaning out of the doorway to get a closer look. Mesmerized, she stared at the rippling muscles on his back. Kenji had never stirred such feelings in her. Of course, Kenji had never subjected himself to hard physical labor. He was an artist and an intellectual.

Thinking of her husband brought memories of him cowering in a corner, pleading for his life. A big, muscular soldier stood over him, his sword raised...

Memories of that dreadful time brought a dull ache to her heart. She lifted a hand to her breast as if to massage the ache away. Remembering her guest, she turned from the doorway. She couldn't think about such things now.

She lit the fire and put on water for tea. The little earthen jar held enough rice for one healthy serving, so she washed the precious grains and set them aside to soak. A quick trip to her garden produced a radish and some herbs. After a moment's hesitation, she picked a few blossoms from her flowerbed. Such a fine gentleman was probably used to having lovely things at his table. She didn't have much, but her flowers would have to do.

She found a thin wooden board and cleaned it as well as she could. Remembering an old bottle of cheap *sake* her father had left behind, she dug it out and pulled out the stopper. The rancid odor nearly made her swoon. The fancy gentleman would definitely not drink this concoction. But the decorated bottle gave her an idea. After dumping out the contents, she arranged the blossoms in it and set the arrangement on her makeshift tray.

The rice was boiling in the pot, and she had just finished seasoning the chopped radish when Hiro entered the hut. His face and torso gleamed from his morning exertion. Hanako forced herself to look away.

"Thank you for cutting up the firewood. I didn't realize the woodpile was so low." She continued to look away as she prepared his tray. If she gave in, she would subject herself to longings she had forgotten. It would not do to wish for the attentions of the wealthy traveler.

****

Hiro put the axe away and walked back to his hut. He made use of the tiny washbowl and returned to Hanako's hut to find out what the day's work would be. She was still busy cooking, so he sat down on the cushion to watch her.

He hadn't expected to be comfortable here, but he had slept soundly and awakened full of energy. The air here seemed cleaner, everything looked brighter, and he had tiptoed past her hut to investigate the surroundings in the light of day. Noticing the nearly depleted woodpile, he imagined her struggling to chop the wood for her fire. The thought distressed him so much he chose the tallest tree he could find, cutting it down and chopping it into pieces so that she wouldn't have to worry about the chore for a while.

Watching her now, as she worked on the simple meal, he compared her to the women he had known. Embodying the traditional concept of beauty, their smooth, uncalloused hands held delicately painted fans in front of their powdered faces. Hanako's fingernails were lined with dirt, and her face was tanned from working outdoors. Her clear eyes shone with intelligence and sincerity. Yet in her simplicity she was as elegant as a *geisha*.

Hanako's breakfast preparations were interrupted by a strange bellow from behind the hut. Hiro looked up, uncomprehending, while she jumped up and ran outside. He got up to follow her.

The cow had broken her lead rope and had begun to trot away. Hanako ran after the animal, but the kimono she wore didn't allow her to run very fast. She could only move her legs from the knees down, and the cow got farther and farther away.

Hiro knew he could overtake the animal more easily and raced after the errant cow. Charging past Hanako, he finally reached the animal and grabbed what was left of the lead rope. Then he slowed his steps, gradually bringing the cow to a halt. The massive animal resisted his pull, but Hiro managed to turn her around.

A flash of gray to his right caught his attention. A wolf? Was that why the cow had run? Perhaps he'd better go hunting later.

Before Hiro had the cow back to the hut, Hanako was already hard at work digging a hole. A sturdy pole and a thicker rope lay on the ground nearby.

He admired her athletic movement, as well as her fine form, as she set about her task. She was such a hard worker. A sudden thought entered his mind, startling him with its intensity.

She is a strong woman, worthy of a strong warrior.

He wondered again about the husband who had been fortunate enough to claim her as his own. Had he been strong? She had said that he had not been interested in working the farm, but he must have helped her with the hard physical labor.

His heart had never known jealousy. If a woman preferred not to respond to his advances, it was of no consequence to him. But the vision of this particular woman in another man's arms brought an unfamiliar ache to his chest.

He reached for the shovel. "I will take care of this. You'd better tend to your animals."

She opened her mouth as if to argue but closed it and simply nodded her assent, handed the tool to him, and walked toward her charge.

By the time he finished, the sun was high in the sky, and

his stomach reminded him that he hadn't eaten yet. He remembered the breakfast Hanako had prepared for him. *Would it still be edible?* He doubted it.

He returned to the hut, finding the planned morning meal covered with scavenging insects. He noted the care with which she'd set the makeshift tray and had arranged the flowers. She'd really made an effort to serve him. Gingerly taking the bowl with his fingertips, he disposed of the mess and looked around for her food stores, intending to start over. There were none. Had she really planned to give the last of her food to him?

Remembering the stream behind the hut, he lifted his sword and went in search of some nourishment. The stream, as he had hoped, was clear, and he saw he would be able to make a fine catch.

He found a sturdy old tree with a thick branch overhanging the stream. Carefully inching out on the branch, he found it could accommodate his weight, and lay face down along its length. His hand gripped his sword and he waited, poised and ready for his prey. The rippling water played a calming melody, and the shade from the higher branches enveloped him in a blanket of security he hadn't experienced in years.

As a warrior in the elite forces of his *daimyo*, he had not known serenity, only anger and death. What would it be like to live in peace and beauty, instead of constant pain and needless bloodshed?

A splash in the water below reminded him of his task. A school of carp, making its way upstream, swam into his vantage point. Drawing on his survival training, he lowered his sword, spearing the largest of the group. Quickly he raised and lowered the sword again and again, until the still-moving fish covered half his blade.

The water beneath him turned murky, and his arm froze as the haunting memory of another time, another knife, overtook him. His stomach churned as he remembered a man he had known like a brother, one he loved and revered, dying by his own hand. Though Hiro had fought nobly and had observed the death of many, this time it had brought him to his knees. It was then that he knew he could not continue as a warrior.

He shook his head, bringing himself back into the present. He had a marvelous catch, so the two of them would eat well tonight. Slowly, carefully, he backed off the branch. Carrying his quarry back to the hut, he looked around for his hostess. Apparently, the cow's anxiety had passed, and she grazed contentedly. Hanako was still hard at work, tending the chickens. Hiro felt a moment of guilt, having spent time fishing in the cool shade while his hostess had been laboring.

"I brought some fish from the stream. I'll prepare them for a meal."

Hanako straightened, her eyes taking a moment to focus on him. Her face brightened with pleasure as she eyed his catch.

"That's wonderful!" Her cheeks turned pink and she averted her face. "I had forgotten about preparing a meal. Please forgive me."

"You had other concerns." Hiro shrugged away her apology. He carried the fish into the hut, intending to filet them. She followed him. "Is something wrong? Would you prefer not to eat these tonight?"

"Oh, they will be wonderful! I just thought—well, you have more than we need for a meal, and if you don't mind, I could trade one or two for some rice."

So, this is how the woman has survived. He nodded his assent, and she took two of the larger fish, wrapped them in a clean cloth, and bundled them in a carrier to take to a neighbor. He watched her hurry across the field then set about at his own task.

****

The meal, though simple, was delicious. Hiro stood outside the hut and smoked his pipe, surreptitiously watching as Hanako dug into her nutritious meal with relish. He had eaten earlier, consuming much less than his usual hearty portions, highly aware of the very hungry woman waiting for him in the opposite corner of the room. She was practically fainting away from hunger, and he could not bear to make her wait longer for her own meal. He could always go into the village later, he thought. There was bound to be a place where he could get more food and spirits. And perhaps some companionship.

Watching her devour the simple meal—the fish he had caught, the rice she had bartered from her neighbor, and some spring greens from her garden—he was struck again by her inner strength and resolve. She was a survivor, and yet he sensed a fragility he wanted to protect. She was a woman who would love with her whole heart, not just her body.

He would seek his temporary pleasures elsewhere.

****

Hideyori Kato knelt on the threadbare cushion, struggling to ignore the itchiness from the coarse clothing he wore. He would not submit to such base actions as scratching, especially in front of his company. Once his army was assembled and his fortunes regained, he wouldn't have to resort to wearing such inferior clothing. But the treasures he'd found hidden in his robes weren't enough to hire his servants, make improvements to his home, and purchase fine silk. He'd had to cut corners, and the robe he'd found in the market looked regal, even if it was made of rough linen. He needed to project an image in order to be taken seriously.

The two gentlemen kneeling on the cushions in front of

him wore expressions of curiosity and skepticism. Like him, they were former *daimyos*. Unlike him, they had relinquished their power voluntarily, so they were allowed to keep their homes and much of their lands. Their way of life had not suffered. But careful inquiries had revealed that these men had regretted their decisions and were interested in regaining their power. He needed to convince them it was possible to overthrow the emperor's army and return to their former feudal way of life.

"It is necessary for us to combine our resources," he told them. "None of us, alone, could hope to overthrow the Imperial Army. But together we could restore this country to the *Bushido*—the Way of the Warrior."

"But we are only three," Togashi-san inserted. "How could we hope to overcome the emperor's resources?"

"There are thousands of displaced samurai roaming the country," Hideyori explained. "With the Meiji government's orders, they no longer have their exalted place in society. We just need to convince them to fight for us, so they can resume their rights."

"But many of them have joined the emperor's forces," Akamatsu-san observed.

"True, but once they see we are guaranteeing them a better life, they will join us. And if we can gather enough *ronin*, they will have no choice but to defect." It was rather like the choice given to the *daimyos* once Meiji declared an end to the feudal system.

He raised a finger, signaling the maid in the corner to refill the sake cups. He could see some of the doubt dispelling on the faces of his guests. If he kept them well-fed and the sake flowing, perhaps by the end of the night he would have some partners in his quest. He would have help financing an army. Of course, some of the army's wages would go into his own pocket. He had to get some better clothing.

Chapter Three

Hiro was accustomed to hard work, but nothing in his experience as a solider had prepared him for the labor involved in running a farm. His respect for the people who made their living working the earth rose each time he lay his aching body down on his threadbare *ofuton* at night.

Despite the hard work, Hiro found contentment in the routine. He adopted Hanako's habit of arising early, marveling at the freshness of the morning air. While she attended the animals, he went to the stream to fish then helped prepare a morning meal. In the late afternoon, he would return to the stream a second time or hunt for small game in the nearby woods. He kept the woodpile supplied, mended holes in the shabby roof, and fixed the ancient tools used in the field. Each evening, he thanked her politely for a calming, restful vacation, and then slept soundly until the next morning.

After only a few weeks, he could see her tiny frame begin to fill out, and her face glowed with color and vitality. Hanako was a good teacher, and each day he learned more about the challenges she faced.

He quickly found other things he could do to make things easier for her. The chickens produced eggs, and he learned how to gather them. Even though her farm was small, the work in the field was endless and grueling under the hot sun. Hiro wondered how she had managed alone. When she needed supplies in the village, he accompanied her, not forgetting her difficulties with Sato-san.

"Why did you come here?" she asked one day as they returned to the hut after a trip into the village.

"I felt I needed to pay a debt incurred by my brothers in war."

"No, I mean why were you in our particular village? I understand many of the samurai are finding other uses for their skills. Did you truly expect to find anything suitable here, so far away from the capital city?"

Hiro took his time answering. After his best friend had died, he had lost his will to fight. When the Emperor Meiji put an end to the samurai class, his duty there had ended, and he had traveled north, farther away from the capital and the political wars. He'd wandered across the countryside, watching people, sleeping wherever he could find shelter, and working when he needed to. The money he had used to purchase Hanako's animals had come from a wealthy merchant who'd been grateful for Hiro's temporary services as a bodyguard.

"I was ready for a change from my life in the city. I needed to find another path, one with more peace and harmony. I have grown to appreciate the life you lead, the way you supply most of your needs from the land around you."

There was much more to his story, but thankfully, Hanako seemed to accept his answer.

"Don't you have responsibilities to your family?" she asked.

"I am the second of four sons. My eldest brother is now a member of the Imperial Guard. He has primary care for my mother, now that my father is gone."

"Will you return to the city after the harvest?"

"I am not sure about my future. I think I would like to stay here for some time. If you will agree to teach me all you know, I will continue to stay and help you with your farm."

She regarded him thoughtfully. "The life of a farmer is difficult. It is hard physical labor, and one is always dependent on the weather. Many other things can go wrong, destroying all your work. Fire, drought, disease, and of course—" she swallowed convulsively before continuing "—invasion by *ronin*."

Hiro had taken seriously his vows of samurai ethics, and he was repulsed by the antics of the *ronin*. "The emperor's men are clamping down on them," he began.

"The emperor's men cannot be everywhere," she argued. "The *ronin* travel at night and take people by surprise. No one is exempt from the terror they impart."

He stopped walking and turned to face her, but waited until she met his eyes before he spoke. "They will not harm you again. I swear it."

****

The bartering economy was a fascinating change for Hiro, who had been raised in a monetary society. He found it satisfying to be able to survive on what could be produced or traded. Here, a man earned respect for his own hard work, not for the size of his inheritance or the destruction he could cause. There was no room for vanity or trying to outdo one's peers. He became comfortable wearing the crude cotton clothing of the locals, and his taste for the simple fare he ate at Hanako's table replaced his previous penchant for the elegantly prepared dishes he had enjoyed in the city.

His esteem for his lovely hostess-teacher also grew. She constantly surprised him with her resourcefulness. Though she lacked the education and training of the women he knew in Tokyo, her eyes shone with intelligence and common sense. He bought books to learn what experts had to say about agriculture, and together they would discuss what he had read. She amazed him with her understanding and practical knowledge.

Hiro was planting a row of radishes when his thoughts turned to her. A vision of the two of them together, older, surrounded by children, flashed in his mind. He quickly shook the vision away. He was not looking for a wife, certainly not here, at the edge of the known world. Hanako was simply his mentor, as well as his temporary landlord. He needed to remember that.

While they toiled in the field one day, an unexpected visitor came to call. Hiro noticed him first. The man stood at the end of a row of beans, watching them work, and waited for them to reach the edge of the field. His fine silk robes and aristocratic bearing, as well as the servants waiting with his sedan chair, were markedly out of place. Touching Hanako on the shoulder, Hiro nodded toward the stranger.

"Do you know him?" he asked.

Hanako squinted at the lone figure. "I don't think so," she began, "but he reminds me of a character in some stories my father used to tell me when I was young. He was the evil man who could cast curses and create storms." She shuddered as if a chill had overtaken her.

Hiro chuckled at her colorful description, but sensing her discomfort, he walked with her to greet the man.

As they reached the edge of the field, the stranger bowed low. "Greetings, Shimizu-san. I am Ishikawa, and I come from the Office of Finance in Hakodate."

Hanako's face paled, and she seemed to shrink as the man continued speaking. Hiro reached out to put a reassuring hand on her back, but then realized the man was speaking to him.

"...and the Office of Finance has come to the realization that this farm has not been registered properly in the court records. You are thereby required to pay the fine, plus the taxes due for the past five years."

He heard Hanako's gasp of dismay, and gave her shoulder a squeeze before bowing to the man. "Ishikawa-san, I am afraid there has been a mistake. My name is Tanaka, and this is the widow of Shimizu-san. I am sure that she was unaware of the registration requirement, as well as the taxes."

Ishikawa was undeterred by Hiro's pronouncement. "Nonetheless, as the widow, she is responsible for the debts incurred by her husband. She must pay the fines and taxes, or the government will take ownership of the land."

"How is it that Shimizu-san was not notified of her husband's oversight?" Hiro persisted. "She cannot be held responsible for fines of which she was never made aware."

"She was notified by courier last fall. The missive specifically told her she would have six months to pay all debts."

Hiro turned to Hanako, who seemed to have shrunk even smaller. "Do you remember receiving this message?"

She turned sad eyes up to meet his. "I remember a courier came with a message, but I had no idea that it was a demand for money. It was—just after Kenji was killed in the raid, and all our crops were destroyed."

Indignation erupted in Hiro, and he breathed deeply to keep his composure. When he spoke, his words whipped at Ishikawa like steel shards, and the courier stepped back as if to avoid their sting. "How dare you come here, demanding so much from a woman who has nothing? Has she not suffered enough?"

Ishikawa trembled and backed up to his waiting chair, but delivered one last blow. "She can have four more months, but the debt must be paid." Then he scrambled into his chair and squeaked a command to his lackeys to return him to the city. His head appeared through the window as he issued a parting threat. "I will return after the harvest."

Hiro waited until the man and his entourage were out of sight before turning to Hanako. The sight of her made him forget every thought, every feeling except compassion for her. Never had he seen such dejection, such defeat. He lifted her chin until his gaze met hers. He wanted to reassure her, to protect her from the pain Ishikawa-san's visit had caused.

"Do you still have the message he sent?" he asked quietly.

Hanako nodded mutely, and scurried into the hut. A moment later she returned with a rolled up document tied with a gold silk ribbon. Hiro raised a brow at her. "This looks unopened."

She bent her head. Hiro was about to ask why she would have ignored a directive from the government when she finally spoke.

"I can't read, and I didn't want to ask someone else to read it for me. I thought it was about Kenji, and since he was dead, I hoped it wouldn't matter." She gazed back to the fields she had so diligently cultivated all her life. "In the end, I guess it really doesn't make any difference. Even with the extra four months, I can't possibly earn enough money to pay the fines and taxes, whatever the amount. I'll be lucky to grow enough to live on through the winter."

Slowly she plodded back to her work.

Hiro tore the ribbon away and opened the document. His eyes opened wide at the amount named. Surely this was a mistake! His estate in Tokyo was not taxed this highly, and his lands were far more expansive than this plot. Something was not right. He would have to investigate the origin of this "official" document. In the meantime, he needed to offer comfort and assurance. Tucking the paper into the folds of his *yukata*, he rejoined Hanako in the field.

****

Hanako didn't dare look at Hiro for the rest of the afternoon. How he must loathe her for her lack of responsibility! Even though the missive had arrived at a difficult time in her life, she should have realized that it was something she needed to address immediately. Now she would certainly lose her home. She would have to sell the farm in order to raise some of the money she owed, but where would she go? She had no family to take her in. No one in the small village would hire her. Perhaps she could go to Sapporo and find work as a servant. For now, she needed to bury herself in work. She had a four-month reprieve. Perhaps the profits from a good harvest, along with the sale of the farm, would be enough to pay the debts.

In addition to her ignorance of financial matters, Hiro was probably disgusted by her illiteracy. A part of her realized most people in her station could not read, but in the presence of an intelligent man like Hiro, her lack of knowledge embarrassed her. Any time now, he would leave. After all, what could he possibly learn from a naive, illiterate, downtrodden female farmer?

She would miss his presence on the farm. Life had been so much easier since he came. Having a willing pair of hands—strong hands—had greatly increased productivity. More of her fields had been cultivated and cared for than any other season in her memory. Not only did her fields look better, her home was more habitable. The roof no longer leaked, and there was plenty of good food to eat. She had her "guest" to thank for all this.

Now he knew how sadly she lacked intelligence. He would soon be bored of her presence and move on. She would be alone again. It was her lot in life—first her father, then her husband, and now this gentle stranger would leave her. But this separation would be far more painful than either of the others.

In the evening, too restless to sleep, she went back outside and started digging the earth around the hut. Hiro found her there, meticulously turning the earth with her spade.

"What will you plant here?"

"I'm going to plant some flowers. The widow Nakamura gave some seedlings to me in exchange for some radishes."

"What will they look like?"

"I'm not sure, but the blossoms around her home always look beautiful. I thought I would try to make the place presentable if—if—" She held in a sob, unable to go on.

She felt his large hand, warm and reassuring, on her shoulder. "Do not think of that. You will continue to work here, as you always have, and you will have a good harvest this fall. Tomorrow morning, I must make a short trip to the city. I will return as soon as my business is completed."

Her eyes flew open, and she looked at him for the first time since Ishikawa's visit that afternoon. "You're leaving?"

"Only for a short while." His eyes twinkled and his lips stretched into a grin. "I still have much to learn from you."

****

Hanako woke early the next morning, intending to prepare a fine breakfast, but Hiro had already left. She supposed it was for the best. It would have been more painful to watch him leave.

The morning's chores were completed automatically. The animals were fed. The eggs were gathered and brought to the market. She came home and tended her fields. Though her hands kept busy, her mind was elsewhere. And then it was dinnertime. She watched the sun dip in the western sky, wondering where the day had gone.

Hiro had snared a wild rabbit the day before. He had wrapped the leftover meat in layers of cloth and had stored it in the cool shaded waters of the river. A heavy rock had kept it from floating away. Unable to summon an appetite for more than a few bites, she forced herself to eat. Then what to do? There were a few more hours before sunset. She went outside to tend to the flowers she had planted outside the night before. Standing in her flower garden, she remembered the reassurance she had received from Hiro while out here. Gentle warmth stole over her, as if Hiro was standing next to her. She kneeled down and began to dig.

For the next two weeks, she kept the same routine. She would wake with the sun and tend to her animals before working in her fields. At the end of the day she would drag herself back to her hut and make an effort to eat. Much of what she cooked was fed to her animals, and she would spend time in the flower garden before collapsing on her *ofuton* for a night of sleeplessness. So many times she found herself wanting to tell him about small things, like the pesky birds that irritated her by diving into her beans, or the visible growth in the other plants. And when the seedlings in her flower patch began to bud, she nearly wept, wishing Hiro was there to see them.

Her weight dropped again, and her *yukata* hung in folds. She found it difficult to summon the energy to go into the fields. Sometimes the effort seemed too great. But she reminded herself to care for the growing plants and the animals she, or rather Hiro, had purchased. Perhaps he would demand payment for the animals. She would need a good crop in order to repay him.

She crouched in the flower garden, staring at the growing buds with unseeing eyes, when a large shadow loomed over her. She took a deep calming breath, trying to think of a way to defend herself, when the shadow moved to her side, and the figure crouched beside her.

"I see the flowers are almost ready to sprout. They have grown much since I left."

Hiro has returned! Hanako placed a hand over her rapidly

beating heart. She fought to contain the squeal of joy threatening to escape her lips. She simply nodded, not trusting her voice. Finally she composed herself enough to look up at him. He was as handsome as she remembered. His clothes and sandals were dusty from the walk, and he seemed thinner. But despite the dust, he was the most welcome sight she could imagine. His lips were moving—*what was he saying?* She forced herself to concentrate on his words.

"If you are working out here, then you must have had your dinner. Would you have any left for a hungry traveler?"

"Oh! Forgive me. You must indeed be tired and hungry from your travels. I will prepare something—" Standing quickly, she felt the earth tilt, and fade away.

When she opened her eyes, she was lying on her *ofuton*, and an anxious Hiro was bathing her face with a cool cloth. She heard water boiling on the stove. Embarrassed to see him preparing his own tea, she tried to sit up, but he pushed her gently back down.

"Rest," he commanded her. "It seems my absence has caused you to work too hard. And you have not eaten well. I could not even find a cup of rice to boil."

His comment brought her further embarrassment. "I'll go to Nakamura-san and ask if she has something I can trade."

"No. It is not necessary. I made some purchases in the market, so I will prepare something for us to eat."

He got up and sprinkled some tea leaves into her ancient, cracked tea kettle. Then he poured the boiling water over them and put the lid on top. While waiting for the leaves to steep, he took his purchases from his pack. Fresh beef, large mushrooms, and onions tumbled out. She watched in amazement as he skillfully trimmed the fat from the beef and put the chunks in a skillet to melt before pouring the green tea into two cups. And she was even more amazed when he brought one of the cups to her. Never would she have dreamed of being served by a man, especially one as powerful and masculine as Hiro.

As she drank the light green liquid, she watched as he made himself at home in her kitchen. How had he learned to cook with such mastery and flair? He again reached into his bag and pulled out an enormous knife, with which he carefully sliced the vegetables. They were placed in the hot grease to cook. When the food began to sizzle, he told her about his mission in Hakodate, the island's capital.

"I visited the Office of Finance in Hakodate. They were very interested to hear about your visit from Ishikawa-san." He paused as he concentrated on cutting a slab of beef into paper-thin slices. "It seems he did work for their office, but he was dismissed from his position more than a year ago."

"A year ago? But the message only came last fall."

"Yes. Apparently he took several items with him when he left the office, including an official signature stamp, some forms, and the enclosure ribbon. He has used them to send tax notices to people who will not question authority—widows, small business owners—anyone he thinks will take him seriously. The directives instruct the poor victims to send the 'taxes' to his own address." He took the vegetables out of the pan and added the meat to the sizzling fat.

"He kept the money himself? How terrible. But how did you know that the bill was not official?"

"I wasn't sure, but I became suspicious when I read the message and saw the money was to be sent to him, at an address that was not near the government offices. I paid a visit to my cousin, who is with the Department of Justice. He was able to get an edict for Ishikawa-san's arrest."

"So I don't have to pay the fines and taxes? What a relief that would be!"

"You do have to pay some taxes, since your husband did not pay them before he died, but they are not nearly as high as the amount Ishikawa demanded of you."

"How much will I owe?" A knot of unease started to

grow in the pit of her stomach.

"The amount was so minimal, I paid it. It will be easier for you to repay me than to send the payment to them." He tested the vegetables to be sure they were done, and then added the beef.

Her unease flared into irritation. *How could he be so arrogant as to pay her bills and demand payment?* "Repay you? How can I do that? You know I won't have any money until the harvest!" Agitated, she rose and paced the short length of the hut. "I already owe you more than a year's harvest for the animals. And you've been working for no wages. Now my debt is increased even more!"

He waited patiently for her tirade to end. He answered in a voice so deliberate Hanako felt he was treating her as an impatient child. "You don't owe me for the animals. They were given to you as compensation for your losses from last year's raid. As for my wages, you are paying me by teaching me a new profession, as well as feeding me and giving me a place to stay." He pulled a bottle of dark brown liquid from his bottomless pack and poured some of its contents over the mixture.

"Nonsense. You could afford to stay in the finest hotels and learn about farming from a wealthy landowner."

"But the wealthy landowner would not be able to show me the pleasure of working with the soil, of creating something from nothing. He would not show me the beauty of the sunrise, the wonderful fresh smell after a spring rain, or the musical melodies of the insects in the evening. If I stayed in a fine inn, I would not understand all the difficulties you face, and see how you manage in spite of them. You are a far better teacher than any moneyed landowner, and your lessons are worth far more than the money I have paid for your livestock and taxes."

He stopped speaking then, as if he realized he had said more than he intended. He stirred his culinary creation, pulled two new bowls from a package she hadn't seen and scooped a generous portion into one. Then he brought it to her, along with a pair of chopsticks.

Hanako was stunned, both at the novelty of having a man serve her, as well as the poetic way Hiro had described her life. Could it be he understood why she stayed here, despite all the hardships and advice against it? Was it possible a man who had been raised to destroy could actually embrace a life celebrating growth? Could she trust him? But no, he wasn't offering a lifetime. His stay here was only temporary. Soon he would pack his swords and leave. If he wanted to continue farming, he would purchase his own land, and she would go back to her dreary existence.

She simply nodded and said, "I'm glad you're pleased with your experience here. I will work hard to make sure you learn enough to make it worth your investment. But I insist that when the harvest is in, you must share in the profit."

He regarded her silently for a moment then turned to fill his own bowl. He took his time pouring himself some tea, and carefully brought his food and drink to her futon. Then he settled himself on a cushion and began to eat. Hanako wondered if he planned to ignore her and was about to repeat herself. Finally, he answered.

"There is one way we can settle the matter of money owed and profit shared."

"How is that possible?"

"We could marry. Then our possessions and our fortunes would become one."

Chapter Four

Hiro saw his suggestion had caught Hanako by surprise. Turning an honest look inward, he had surprised himself. He had been reluctant to pledge himself to any woman. Remembering the pain in his mother's eyes when his father had been killed had always been enough to make him avoid that complication in the past. But now his life as a samurai was over, and if he wanted to be a farmer, he needed a strong farmer wife. Who better than a woman who was already accustomed to that life?

Marriage to Hanako would certainly be pleasant. He had long ago admitted to himself that he was attracted to her natural beauty. But he had been unwilling to give in to that attraction because of his respect for her. Several times he had gone into the village, with the goal of releasing that pent-up longing, but although the women in the tavern were willing, they did not interest him the way the beautiful woman at the farm did. If they married, he would not have to hide that attraction.

But perhaps she did not see him as a suitable husband.

She had not said a word since he uttered his suggestion. Was it because she did not trust a man who had once been a samurai? Did she require more stability? Perhaps she saw him as a threat to her way of life. He remembered his mother declaring that she would never remarry because she was too set in her ways.

The meal continued in an uncomfortable silence. Without a word, Hanako rose and took their plates to the washbowl, never looking at Hiro, never giving an indication of her thoughts.

Unable to bear the tension, Hiro went outside. He needed to do something to get his mind off his obsession. The woodpile was low again, so he decided to release some of his energy by replenishing it. He had purchased a proper axe on a previous trip to the village, and now he swung it with vigor. The tree he had selected came down with a crash and was soon cut up into pieces for the fire. How he wished he could mow down all of Hanako's reservations so easily.

He had bent to gather the wood into a neat pile when he heard the singing. An unsteady voice, rendering a wobbly version of an old drinking song, came from deep in the woods. Occasionally the voice would stop, as if unsure of how the song should continue. Hiro stood still, watching the woods, trying to place the voice. It was a familiar song, sung by someone he felt he knew. Finally he saw him—a bent, haggard shadow of a man, weighted down by his pack and his swords. Judging from his posture, it seemed he also carried the weight of his world. He staggered along the path, losing his footing and bumping against a tree. The offending tree was duly cursed and punished by an ineffectual swipe with the short sword.

Hiro grimaced.

Ginjiro Yamada had fought with him in many battles, but his weakness for drink and women had prevented him from becoming a samurai of the first rank. When the feudal system was discontinued and samurai were forced to find other careers, Ginjiro had limited choices. The older man had not been a great scholar, and his unfortunate habits prevented him from succeeding in business. Hiro suspected Ginjiro had become one of the *ronin*, the displaced samurai. While some *ronin* had found respectable new occupations, many wandered the country and caused trouble for innocent citizens.

Ginjiro's winding path took him past the woods where Hiro stood, and he teetered as he noted Hiro's presence. His eyes scrunched as he tried to focus. "Friend, could you help an old soldier?" he slurred.

"You are not so old, Ginjiro, and I see your habits have not changed. Why do you continue to drink yourself into a stupor? You can hardly walk. Sit down and stop weaving about before you hurt yourself."

The inebriated man started in surprise. "You know me?" He tottered forward and squinted again. "Tanaka-san, is that you? What are you doing so far from the mainland? I thought you would have a successful career as a merchant or a politician in Tokyo."

"We will not talk about me. You need to sleep off your drink."

"No, I need to fill myself with the ale. It will dull the pain."

"Why are you in pain? You don't appear injured."

"I'm talking about the pain of my sword when I perform *seppuku*."

Hiro's eyes widened, and he stepped toward his former comrade. "No!"

"Yes, my friend. You are smart. You have the mind and the money to become anything you choose. But I am a warrior. Perhaps not a very good one, but I am a soldier. It is all I know. I cannot do anything else. I have looked all around trying to find a noble to take me on as a guard, but I am too small, too weak, too—stupid. I even worked for some disreputable men, but I was not able to stay. I am a failure as a samurai. I must die."

"Ginjiro, do not speak of yourself this way. You can find honest work. I can help you. Please—you must not kill yourself."

Hiro had fought in countless battles, but nothing had brought him the horror he had once experienced watching a childhood friend disembowel himself in the name of honor. Hiro himself had taken the code of the *Bushido*, but he failed to understand the need for the awful ritual required of the samurai soldiers for crimes real or imagined. It was the primary reason he had left the mainland in search of another calling. He could not face his former comrades who had become politicians and merchants, vocations as cutthroat as the life of a samurai. He needed to find a more peaceful life. Ginjiro's words had recalled the violence he had tried so hard to escape. He could not bear to watch another comrade take his own life.

Ginjiro ignored Hiro's pleas. "I left the tavern to find someone to be my second. Now that you are here, I can finish the job. At least I can die with honor."

He took out his dagger and raised it. Hiro reached him in an instant and grabbed his arm before he could lower it. With his free hand, Hiro disarmed the man, tossing away the dagger, and unsheathing the larger sword before Ginjiro could react. The older man struggled ineffectively, weakened by his drink, until his limited strength ebbed, and he slumped to the ground, sobbing.

"How can you dishonor me like this? I cannot even kill myself properly!"

Hiro took a moment to catch his breath, making sure Ginjiro would not try again to harm himself. He took both blades into one hand and held the other out to Ginjiro. "Come with me. We will have some tea and some decent food, and when your mind is clear we will talk."

****

Hanako knelt at her wooden basin, rinsing the new dishes and cups Hiro had brought. Never had she held such lovely things before. She was afraid of handling them, knowing how easily they could break. Rather than chance washing the delicate dishes in the stream, she had carried the water back to the hut.

What had made Hiro purchase such finery? He claimed he was happier here than in the city, but perhaps he missed some of the niceties there. Her crude wooden bowls and utensils looked so shabby next to the finely painted china, and she felt some embarrassment seeing them.

Long ago, when she was very young, she had found an old trunk hidden in the back of the hut, behind her father's *ofuton*. Overcome with curiosity, she had opened the trunk and found a treasure chest of memories. A tiny silk purse, a beautiful silk fan, two golden combs inlaid with coral and a pair of china teacups. The items must have belonged to her mother. Delighted with her find, she had taken the teacups out, wanting to use them with her father. But she had tripped, dropping the delicate cups on the hard wooden floor. One cup had shattered, and she had moved quickly to sweep up the mess and dispose of it before her father returned home. The box had been replaced in the corner, and for months, Hanako had lived in fear that her father would open the box and discover the missing treasure.

She was never sure if her father hadn't ever looked in the box, or if he didn't want to confront her and admit to harboring the keepsakes, but he had not mentioned the missing cup. After he died, she took the box out of the dark corner, and found another hiding place for it. Her husband would have had no use for the keepsakes, but she suspected his consuming need for alcohol would have led him to sell the treasures.

If she were to marry Hiro, he would probably expect to use finery like this every day. She would have to learn to behave like a lady, perhaps learn to walk and speak like a noblewoman. Could she live up to such expectations? Or would he tire of her clumsiness, the rough accommodations, the quiet pace of life in the country?

She finished cleaning the china and carefully set them in a lacquered box Kenji had once used to store his art supplies. Looking out through the lone window in the front of the hut, she saw Hiro making his way back from the woods, half carrying and half dragging someone she didn't recognize. The other man was much smaller and older than Hiro. Hiro carried two weapons in his free hand. Samurai swords. Her heart stopped. Had Hiro and this other samurai been engaged in a fight? Was he injured?

She hurried out of the hut. "What happened? Who is this man? Are you hurt?"

Hiro shifted his load so he could greet Hanako. "This is Ginjiro Yamada, my former comrade. He is in need of a place to rest and some food to eat. May I bring him in?"

Hanako took a closer look at the smaller man. He opened his brown eyes and made an attempt to focus on her. The fuzzy look became an appreciative leer, and she cringed inwardly.

"Tanaka-san," he slurred, "you did not tell me you had taken a wife. You are luckier than ever; she is a beautiful woman. How did you manage to talk such a fine lady into coming to live here, in the middle of nowhere?"

The man's speech revealed the true nature of his condition. Years of depending on no one but herself told her that she should block the door and keep him out. But Hiro had said this man was his friend. It would not do to refuse him hospitality. Hopefully, the newcomer would not take advantage of her if he thought she belonged to Hiro. She looked back at Hiro and bowed. "Certainly, a friend of yours is welcome here. I will serve what is left of this evening's meal."

She backed into the house and sighed with relief when Hiro took the man into his own hut rather than into hers. She reheated the water and the food, then reached for one of the china cups Hiro had brought. Before she could fill it with tea, she felt his warmth as he came up behind her.

"It is not necessary to use good china for Ginjiro. He is in no condition to safely handle such finery. A wooden teacup and bowl will be sufficient."

The warm breath on her neck and the deep, resonant voice, so close to her ear, sent a shiver down her spine. She felt his solid presence and again, she caught a glimpse of what it would be like to be protected and cherished. Her heart pumped soundly against her ribs, and she put a hand to her chest to calm the chaos there. Never had she experienced such a reaction to a man's nearness.

The dream ended when Hiro backed away and returned to his friend, leaving her to complete her task. Apparently, Yamada-san was not an important visitor who needed to be impressed by nice things. Setting the china cup back down, she scooped the leftover food into a wooden bowl and took it to Hiro's hut.

Hiro sat on the edge of his futon, talking quietly to Ginjiro. Hanako was struck by the contrast between the two men. The newcomer had carried the two swords of the samurai class, and his clothing was similar to what Hiro had worn when he first appeared in the village. But there the similarities ended. It wasn't just the obvious difference in size. Hiro's bearing and confidence made him a man who demanded and received respect.

Hiro thanked her graciously and took the bowl from her. Ginjiro refused at first, but finally accepted the meal and tore into it enthusiastically. *Another difference between the men*, Hanako noted as she returned to her place. When Hiro ate, he did it quietly, sitting upright, and he displayed manners she had seen in people of wealth and nobility. This comrade of his crouched over his food and reminded her of the unkempt men in the taverns her father had frequented. Hiro kept himself clean and well groomed; this man looked as if his last bath was a distant memory.

She wondered why Hiro had brought him here, rather than simply giving him money to buy food. Did he owe the man a debt of honor? Were they somehow related? She would have to wait for her answers.

Hiro brought the dishes back to her hut when his friend had finished eating. She washed them and finished tidying the hut and prepared for bed. Her mind was brimming with questions about Hiro's friend. They had probably not seen each other for a long time. Perhaps Ginjiro had come bearing an important message.

Surely Hiro would tell her eventually. Meanwhile, she needed her rest. The sun had set, and thanks to Hiro's wonderful food, she could sleep soundly. She ignored the nagging voice in her head telling her the real reason she would sleep well was because Hiro had returned. He had suggested marriage, but did he mean it or was it a passing notion? The men in her life did not stay permanently or, if they did, they could not be relied on. She warned herself it would not be wise to depend on him.

****

Morning brought dark, dreary skies and driving rain. Hanako awakened to find several freshly caught fish cleaned and ready for cooking. Apparently she had overslept, but Hiro had been busy for quite some time. She wondered why he and his guest had not stayed to eat the fish. She looked outside and nearly chuckled at the sight of the two men, dripping from the rain, erecting a crude shelter for the animals.

His presence was reflected in every corner of her life, from the sturdily repaired home to the manicured fields. She had more energy than she remembered ever having before, due in part to his contributions from hunting and fishing. His willingness to share in the physical labor around the farm took much of the burden off her shoulders, and she slept better, not overwhelmed by exhaustion and hopelessness. She was ashamed by her reaction to his short trip to the city, her appetite plunging, her attitude becoming lethargic. Now that he had returned, so had her appetite, not only for food, but also for life.

The men would be hungry for the fish they caught. She lit the fire in her stove and seasoned the fish with herbs from her garden. In the past, most of her herbs went to the market to help pay for necessities until the fall harvest was in. But since Hiro had begun to share the workload, she was able to spend more time preparing nutritious and filling meals. She chose a few spicy greens she hoped Hiro and Ginjiro would enjoy, and prepared a salad. There was no rice, but finding some leafy spinach and green onions near the hut, she decided that a robust soup would complement the fish.

As she worked, she pondered again his proposition of marriage. Should she take a chance? Hiro was not the man her father was, nor was he like her husband.

Her introspection stopped when the men dragged themselves inside, their clothing soaked from the rain. Hanako stopped them at the doorway, bringing her threadbare blankets to stem some of the dripping and prevent a chill. They both thanked her before sitting at the table.

Hiro's friend looked better now the effect of the alcohol had passed. The rain had washed off some of his dirt and grime, too. He was still considerably wrinkled and worn, but the eyes that regarded her today were bright and friendly. There was no trace of the ashen-faced helplessness she had seen the previous day. She wondered what Hiro had done or said to give the man hope.

The herbed fish and spinach soup was consumed with relish and pronounced a culinary delight. Hanako blushed with pleasure at their praise and retreated to eat her own meal. After she rinsed the plates, she donned her straw raincoat and hat and headed outdoors. The fields would get their nourishment from the rain, but her animals needed food. Both men moved to follow her, but she insisted they had done enough for the morning and told them to rest. Feeding her few animals wouldn't take her long.

The cow had settled comfortably in the shelter Hiro and Ginjiro had built. The beast nodded her greeting but didn't move from her shelter. The chickens had taken refuge under the old cart Hanako used for bringing her vegetables to the market. They clucked furiously at her, seeming to scold her for the lateness of their meal.

Returning to the hut, she hung the wet straw garment on a hook and turned to find the two men waiting for her. Hiro wore an expression of excitement and anticipation. Would he leave soon with his friend on a new adventure? Had he forgotten his proposal of marriage? She prepared herself for disappointment. Now that she had healthy animals and a field full of crops, she would survive alone—somehow. She silenced her fearful thoughts and realized Hiro had been speaking.

"...so if it is acceptable to you, Ginjiro also would like to stay and learn the business of farming. With both of us working here, the farm will certainly prosper."

Hanako's eyes widened. He wasn't leaving! She reached for the wall, fearing her knees would buckle in relief. She would not have to return to her solitary existence, eking out a meager existence from the land. At least not immediately.

She pressed her hand to her heart and took a deep breath, bringing her focus back to Hiro's request. Ginjiro wanted to stay as well. Though she trusted Hiro, she was inwardly cautious of his friend. But an extra pair of hands would certainly make the work even easier, and as Hiro had pointed out, production from her tiny farm could be increased even more. She could perhaps afford to make some much-needed improvements on the farm.

When she looked at the men, she found Hiro regarding her patiently, while Ginjiro looked anxious. She realized they were waiting for her to make a decision. The idea of two men waiting for her approval spread a warm feeling through her. Unlike many of the men in the village, these two respected her and accepted her as the mistress of this home and the farm.

She bowed regally. "I would be honored to share my farm and my home with a friend of Tanaka-san."

Chapter Five

Hideyori sipped on the fragrant tea and closed his eyes, savoring the aroma. He set the cup down and adjusted the folds of his new silk robe. After their initial doubts, Togashi and Akamatsu had finally come through and advanced him the funds to start recruiting and training an army. He had assured them he would be the muscle, the brains, and the military strategist behind the operation. He knew how to lead people, even if he had never led an army. He would find strong samurai to fight. And they would win back all he had lost. But first he had had to improve his own standard of living. New clothes, a better home, good servants, and good food. He couldn't lead an army on an empty stomach, wearing nothing but rags.

His campaign for soldiers had brought a handful of applicants so far, but he had yet to meet one worth his time. There were numerous reports of *ronin* roaming the countryside, leaving fear and havoc in their wake. Former samurai, fierce enough to level entire communities, could surely be convinced to use their strength in the name of an esteemed *daimyo*. There weren't many soldiers guarding his lands—and they were definitely his lands, no matter what the emperor said—so a small but powerful army would be all he'd need.

When he took back what was rightfully his, the victory would attract more warriors to join him, and he could begin taking over more and more of the country. He smiled inwardly, contemplating the possibilities.

"Excuse me, are you the *daimyo* looking for soldiers?"

Hideyori's head snapped up at the question. The speaker had used correct grammar and had phrased his question using the appropriate amount of politeness due to one of his rank. This was promising. It showed the speaker had an education and had learned court manners.

He hid his eagerness. It would not do to appear desperate.

"I am his—representative. Who are you?"

The soldier replied by presenting his identification papers. Hideyori's hands nearly shook with anticipation as he pored over them. The applicant, Masao Akira, came from an established samurai family. He had been employed by a *daimyo* in the south; however, the last few years were unaccounted for.

"What have you been doing since the Meiji government took over?"

The man shifted, obviously uncomfortable with the question.

"I have been—traveling. I was not interested in working for the emperor."

Hideyori's brows rose at the hesitation in the man's response. Had there been bad blood between Masao and the emperor's forces? This could be an advantage. He would have motivation to fight against them, if necessary.

"If you were not interested in serving the emperor, why would you be interested in working for m—for Kato-san?" he asked.

The man straightened. "The emperor's forces are far too complacent. I read Kato-san's recruitment advertisement. He is looking for forces to stop the troublemakers in the area. If the emperor's forces aren't able to do that, more force is needed. It has been far too long since I have been part of that kind of action."

Hideyori noticed the gleam in the younger man's eyes. He was indeed a warrior. Bloodthirsty. Eager for a fight. This was a good sign. *I need to find more men like this one!*

****

Hiro fed the chickens, his mind on his journey to this place. It had been a wayward path, one he had not expected to take. Only a few years ago, he had been a soldier, a member of the elite fighting force feared and respected by all. And now he was here, laboring in the hot sun, in a place where his fighting skills and tactical training were of no use.

After Hiro's final break with the *daimyo*, his older brother had encouraged him to return to Tokyo and join the Imperial Army. Taro's letter had been the last communication he'd had from his family:

We would be a strong force for the emperor. Like our father, we would be able to represent and defend a leader, one we can be proud of. Please come back to Tokyo and join me. I would be proud to serve with you.

Instead, Hiro had gone even farther north. Taking a ferry to the island of Hokkaido, he had walked aimlessly for days, until he had reached the village of Furano. And now he was here, on Hanako's farm. Instead of being paid to take lives and use his strength to suppress lives, he earned his way by nurturing life. What would his father, the great Yukio Tanaka, think of his son now? Would he be embarrassed to know his second born had chosen to live as a simple farmer?

He was certain his family and friends would be amazed to see him working like this. The Tanaka family had wealth and social standing, and even though he was a second son, he had the benefit of the finest education and training. His father had hired tutors in music, literature, mathematics, and science, as well as the physical training necessary for a samurai. Hiro had enjoyed his studies and had endured the physical training as a necessary part of his regimen.

Now, Hiro used his strength to spread the grains from his sack over the ground, chuckling at the way the birds raced around to snatch them up. The chickens now numbered four, and a rooster had joined the menagerie. The hens' combined output of eggs now exceeded what three people could eat, and Hanako sold the excess during her weekly trips into town. Hiro was trying a new combination of grains to feed the flock. Lately, he'd read whatever he could find about the science of agriculture, and had persuaded Hanako to let him experiment with different types of feed to see if it would improve the hens' size and output.

Across the yard, Ginjiro milked the cow. When finished with his task, he covered the bucket with a cloth, and carried it to the stream, where the milk would stay fresh for a day or two in the cool shade. Farm life seemed to suit the former warrior. His eyes were now clear, his step lighter, and he stood straighter, having a purpose in life.

"I think I'm getting used to this," Ginjiro bragged. "I managed to keep my head away from the hooves this time," he added, pointing at the nasty gash on his forehead. "I've had my share of injuries, but I've never been attacked by a farm animal." He glanced around the yard. "So what's next? Shall I go to the field and help Hanako?"

"That's fine. I'll join you in a moment," agreed Hiro.

Ginjiro nodded and turned toward the field. After a few steps, he stopped and turned back to Hiro, a question in his eyes.

"What happens to these animals in the winter? They aren't going to live in the hut with Hanako, are they?"

Hiro stared at his friend. "I hadn't thought of that. The hut is too small for her, let alone all her animals. We will need to build something."

"If we're going to build something, we should build a home for her, and turn the hut into a barn. The place we sleep in would make a nice chicken coop, but then we would need to build two structures."

Hiro nodded in agreement. "Good idea. I'll discuss it with her."

Ginjiro regarded his friend shrewdly. "Would you share this home with her?"

Hiro hesitated. "We have not agreed to that," he hedged.

His friend grinned. "She's afraid of you?"

"I'm not sure. Perhaps she's not ready to marry again."

Ginjiro's eyes widened and his jaw dropped. Hiro almost laughed at the comical look of surprise.

"Marry? Why would you want to do that? Just build her a house and live in it with her. You would be her protector. No one would expect you to do more."

Hiro knew this was true. Many of his fellow samurai had concubines. But the idea did not sit well with Hiro. Hanako deserved to be treated with respect, and reducing her to the role of mistress would not do. His friends always teased him about his soft heart, his penchant for healing lost souls. Was Hanako a lost soul in need of protection? Was that why he was so concerned about her feelings, her needs, and her reputation? How had the son of a samurai become such a bleeding heart? His father had been known for his strength, but there was one summer long ago when he'd shown another side of his personality. Hiro had been on his way home from school when he'd decided to take another route...

****

The tiny kitten lay on the roadside, injured and abandoned. Ten-year old Hiro couldn't leave the animal in the road to die, so he brought her home, cleaned her up, and nursed her back to health. He found an old basket, lined it with a soft blanket, and hid the kitten in his room. Each day, after completing his studies and exercises, he sneaked back to his room, gently petting the fur ball and crooning to her softly. Always a dutiful son, he was careful to complete his tasks before indulging himself in the luxury of cuddling with his pet.

One day, the kitten fell ill. Hiro's heart ached for the tiny being as she lay listlessly, refusing to eat, not wanting to play. He feared for the kitten's life, but didn't know how to help her. Chores were done quickly, and he hurried back to his room to check on his charge. He sat on his *ofuton*, gently petting her, when the *shoji* screen opened and his father walked in. In his hand was a piece of armor. Hiro had been instructed to polish the headpiece, but the lack of shine attested to his carelessness. Hiro looked up, up, up at the man he loved and feared more than any other. Not only had he failed in his duty, he was harboring a pet. What would the great samurai do? Could he stand by and watch his father callously discard the kitten?

He clutched the kitten to his chest, trembling. The pet squirmed, but thankfully remained quiet, as if understanding that her fate lay in this powerful man's hand. Hiro struggled to contain the tears that filled his eyes and fought to keep from pleading for the mercy he knew would not come. Duty came first to a samurai. There was no time for the frivolity of pets.

And then the great warrior spoke. Hiro mentally prepared himself for the lashing he knew would follow.

"I wondered about the noises I heard coming from this room when you weren't home. But you have not come here during the day before now. What caused you to abandon your duties today?"

Hiro's heart held to a thread of hope. Was it possible that his warrior father understood? He struggled to find his voice. "F-forgive me, *otousan*. She—she seems ill. She is not eating."

Otousan said nothing, but one brow raised. He held out his hand and waited.

Dutifully, Hiro handed over the kitten, though his hands trembled, and he feared he might drop her. *Otousan* took the tiny bundle in his large hands and examined her closely. "It appears she has a cold. See, her eyes are watering, and her breathing seems labored. Let's see if we can help her." He turned and strode to the *ofuro*, the bath area, with Hiro following closely on his heels.

In the hot, steamy room, *otousan* lay the kitten on a soft, clean towel. Gradually, the kitten settled in, her breathing calmed. Hiro's anxiety also eased as he realized she was going to be all right.

Father and son brought the pet back to Hiro's room to rest. "You should bring her back to the *ofuro* three or four times each day to clear out her lungs." He turned a stern eye toward his son. "Of course you will do this in between your chores and lessons." Hiro nodded in understanding. "And now that she is resting comfortably, you can return to polishing this armor properly."

Hiro bowed low, thanking the gods he would not be punished today. "Yes, *Otousan*. I will polish until it gleams."

The beloved pet had lived until her master left for the university, and Hiro never forgot his father's compassion that day. He had learned it was possible to be both a fierce samurai and to have a tender heart. And he realized that strength used to care for a weaker being showed a greater nobility than strength used to take from those who could not fight back.

****

Now, Hiro leveled a steady look at his friend. "Hanako

would make a fine samurai wife. I would be honored if she agreed."

Chapter Six

"Ginjiro and I would like to build a house for you."

Hanako nearly dropped her rice ball. "Build a house? Why?"

"Consider it payment for our room and board. Or a payment for you teaching us these new skills and profession. Or..." He leaned toward her and lowered his voice, eliciting a chill in her spine. "...consider it an early wedding gift."

Heat flooded her cheeks at the mention of a wedding— their wedding. She cast a quick glance at Ginjiro, who lay snoring under another tree. The three had taken a lunch break from their farm work. She and Hiro hadn't really discussed marriage. He had not brought it up since the day he had first dropped the suggestion, and she had wondered if he had regretted the impulsive offer. But she wasn't ready to discuss it now. She tried another line of questions.

"What would happen to the house I have now?"

"You could tear it down—or perhaps keep the animals in there during the winter. They would not be able to survive outdoors in the snow."

She hadn't considered that problem. Hokkaido was famous for its pleasant summer breezes, but winters in Japan's northernmost island were brutal.

"Where did you keep the animals in the winters before the raid?"

Before the raid, they'd had a barn for her larger animals and a coop full of chickens. The *ronin* had slaughtered the animals, eaten a few, and left the rest to rot. The outbuildings were burned to the ground. How could she have forgotten about building permanent shelters for these new animals? Her shoulders sagged as she realized the implications of what was needed to keep her farm afloat. In order to make the needed improvements, she needed money. What was she willing to do to get that money? Hiro had offered a solution. Would it be wise to accept his offer? Or would she be selling her body and soul?

And what was Hiro's motivation? What did he stand to gain by marrying her?

Long ago, when she was about eight years old, she'd gone to Sapporo with her father. It was one of the last times she remembered her father with fondness. They went to visit a relative, a cousin of her mother. Her home had tatami floors, unlike the rough wood planks at home. Flowers, artfully arranged, graced brightly lacquered tables. But what had impressed Hanako most was the aura of tranquility. Servants came in and out of the rooms, their steps muffled by the *tatami* mats on the floors. Sitting in the courtyard with a tiny cup of tea, she heard nothing but the rippling of water in the pond.

The lady of the house greeted them with smiles. She had no children, she told Hanako, and was so happy her cousin's daughter had come to see her. "Please call me *obachan*, since I am like an aunt to you."

This aunt, though older than her father, showed none of the signs of aging so evident on farm women. She wore her hair in a pretty style, and she smelled so nice. Her voice was gentle, reminding Hanako of a soft, comforting voice from deep in the recesses of her memory.

The pleasantries ended when her *obachan's* husband came home. Hanako remembered a big man with a big voice. The servants dropped down, their faces touching the floor in a deep bow, and the temperature seemed to plunge considerably. The man reminded her of a bear, the way he stormed into the house and roared at everyone. *Obachan* stopped what she was doing, rose shakily, and bowed. Her smile disappeared, and she remained silent, her eyes remained downward as her husband frowned at Hanako and her father.

Hanako was sent to the servants' quarters to wait while the adults conducted their business. She never knew exactly what her father had hoped to accomplish on this trip, but suddenly the voices in the sitting room were raised, and the sliding door opened. Her father was pushed roughly out of the room, and the magistrate was heard to say, "Do not come here again! I have already loaned you enough money to buy and supply your farm four times over! You have nothing to show for it. You are no longer family."

With sharp instructions to a servant to see Father out, the door panel slid closed with enough force to rattle its bamboo frame. A moment later, a maid came to escort Hanako outside, and the visit to the lovely home came to an abrupt end.

The walk home had been even longer than the trip there. After they returned to their hut, her father had been a changed man. Though he had once been a kind, loving man, he'd become distant and preoccupied. He no longer seemed to care about the farm or about his child. His only concern had been getting his next drink.

The experience had taught Hanako about the dangers of being in someone else's debt. Allowing Hiro to build her a new home would put her deeply in his debt, unless they married. Her farm would be her dowry. Could she do it?

She snapped out of her trance and realized Hiro was still

waiting for a response. "We had a barn over there," she answered, gesturing toward an empty spot near the hut, "but it was burnt to the ground. I was fortunate the house wasn't destroyed, too. Forgive me," she continued. "I must think about rebuilding and—about all this."

Hiro grinned, and her mutinous heart zinged. He simply nodded and rose to return to work.

****

Hanako frowned as she prepared the evening meal. When the three had returned from the fields that afternoon, the two men had gone into their hut and engaged in an intense conversation. She had gone into her garden for some herbs, pausing to peek into the other hut. The men hadn't noticed her. Hiro wrote as he spoke. She had no idea what the brushstrokes meant, but it sounded like they were talking about money. She crept away before they could notice her.

When she called them to dinner, the men ceased their conversation and came into her hut with smiles. Dinner was relatively quiet, although the men seemed to be quite cheerful. As had become their custom, Hiro and Ginjiro insisted she eat with them, but she didn't have much of an appetite. What had their conversation been about? Were they pooling their resources so that they could leave and start over somewhere else? Perhaps they felt they knew enough about farming to start their own. Perhaps—her heart froze at the thought— perhaps they wanted to buy her out!

As soon as the meal was finished, Hanako rose on her knees and reached for the plates to clear them away, but Hiro caught her wrist and stopped her. Her skin warmed at his touch, and the warmth spread up her arm straight to her heart.

"The dishes can wait. Ginjiro and I have something we want to share with you."

Hanako sat back on her heels, apprehensive of the change

that she knew would take place. Perhaps she would now know about the mysterious document Hiro and Ginjiro were working on in their hut. Sure enough, Hiro pulled the roll from inside his *yukata.*

"Ginjiro and I have discussed the matter of wages and benefits."

Hanako's heart sank. *Wages? Benefits?* She had not paid either of them, and they had received no benefits other than the food from her lands and stream.

"We have agreed we owe you much for what you have given us."

They owe me? What I have given? What does he mean? The questions raced through Hanako's mind.

"We were both in need of a place to stay and a purpose to our days. You have given us that, and excellent meals."

"But—"

"Your accommodations are clean and comfortable, and much more suited to our needs than an inn. The air here is cleaner and the surroundings much more peaceful."

"But surely—"

"In addition, you are instructing us in a new skill, a noble profession so basic that no one can exist without people like you. In our former profession, we knew nothing of the work you do. Now, no matter what we choose to do with our lives, we will have the skill to provide ourselves with food. So we have figured out what we would have had to pay for an apprenticeship in addition to our lodging. It more than equals the cost of a new home."

Hanako barely glanced at the paper Hiro held. The figures would have no meaning for her. She recognized a few slashes as numbers, but had no idea what they said. Numbers meant little to her, other than the general cost of her needs and knowing which coins would pay for them.

"What is this?" She gestured toward the document.

He angled it toward her so she could look at the figures.

She was too ashamed to admit they meant nothing to her. Even the calculations were foreign to her, because they included numbers far greater than any she had ever used. She felt small, so small.

"We have added together the amounts we owe you for our lodging, as well as tutoring in our new profession. And there is a modest retribution for the damage brought by the *ronin* last year."

"I can't believe you would want to pay me enough for a new home. Besides, you need to subtract what I would pay you in wages for your work on my farm."

Hiro opened his mouth to refute her, but this time Ginjiro intervened.

"Shimizu-san, I owe you my life."

Both Hanako and Hiro turned to him in surprise.

"It is true, Shimizu-san. When I first came here, I intended to commit *seppuku*. I was unable to find a position as a warrior, the only life I have ever known. I felt I was of no worth and was about to end my life. But you have given me a new purpose, a reason to wake up in the morning. For that I owe you a far greater debt than the figures on that document. I have not much money to offer, but I am honored to work on your farm and will gladly assist in the building of a new home for you. It is the least I can do."

****

Hanako clutched the rolled paper to her chest as she made her way down the dusty road. The sun had barely made its appearance, but Hiro and Ginjiro had already started the work in the field. Hiro had been concerned about her going alone, but she had assured him she would be quite safe walking to her neighbor's home.

The Nakamura home graced the land to the east of hers. Since the Nakamuras were her closest neighbors, she had gone there many times to barter for her needs. But in the past, she had dealt mainly with the servants. It was they who traded the fish in her stream and the vegetables from her fields for rice, tea, or other needs.

She made her way to the doorway and greeted the maid who answered her knock. When the maid turned to lead her to the kitchen where she normally met with the cook, Hanako's voice trembled as she blurted, "I need to speak with—the mother of Nakamura-san."

The maid turned in surprise but quickly masked her expression as she nodded and took her instead to an elegant sitting room. Hanako's heart pounded as she waited for the Widow Nakamura.

She had met her neighbor, but only in passing. Reiko Nakamura was the daughter of a wealthy noble family and had come from Mutsu, on the main island of Honshu. She was an educated woman, and though her son now headed the family business, Reiko continued to hold a great deal of power and influence.

"Good morning, Shimizu-san. What a lovely surprise." Reiko Nakamura glided gracefully into the room. The woman's fluid movements reminded Hanako of the nice *okasan* she had met so long ago.

Remembering to keep her mind in the present, Hanako bowed low. "Thank you for seeing me, Nakamura-san. I am honored."

The widow made a slight bow in return. "You honor me. Please have some tea with me." She gestured toward a low table, surrounded with beautiful silk cushions. When Hanako knelt on one, the widow clapped for a servant and gave instructions for the beverages to be served before joining Hanako at the table.

"Now, as much as I am pleased and honored by your visit, I know you are far too busy to pay a social call merely to socialize. What can I do for you, Hanako? Has my kitchen staff not cooperated with you? Have they perhaps traded inferior foods in exchange for your crops?"

Hanako felt her face warm. Though she had rehearsed her request, the words came out with difficulty.

"Nakamura-san, I need your help. I—I have a financial agreement, and I wanted to be sure it says what I was told. I heard you are able to read, and—"

"Of course, I would be happy to read it for you. What kind of agreement is it?"

In answer, Hanako pulled the document from her *yukata* and held it out to her neighbor. It embarrassed her, showing her neighbor the details of the agreement. But after the incident with the so-called "tax collector," she had to be sure she understood what this agreement entailed before she could consider signing it. And though her heart yearned to trust Hiro, her head told her she needed the advice of a woman.

Nakamura-san unrolled the paper, smoothed it out on the table, and read.

Hanako fidgeted, waiting for the widow to finish. *What will Nakamura-san think? Will she consider me nothing more than a mistress if I were to accept this offer?* The maid's entrance with the tea was a relief, because it gave her something to do with her hands.

The older woman's expression gave nothing away. Occasionally she would nod, as if agreeing with whatever the lines and swirls told her. Once or twice she looked up from the document, frowning in thought. She called for her maid to bring a *soroban*, which Hanako recognized as a tool used by several merchants in the village to calculate their sales. The clicking of the beads as the widow pushed them up and down their spindles made the only sound in the room.

When Hanako thought she could bear the suspense no longer, the widow finally looked up. Hanako braced herself for the widow's interpretation of Hiro's proposal.

"Tanaka-san and his friend have been very thorough. He

has listed each item for which he will pay you, the amount per day, and multiplied that by the number of days he has been here."

Hanako nodded. "That's what he told me. Do you think his rates are fair?"

The widow regarded her closely. "They seem fair. And his calculations are accurate. But this is—most unusual."

Hanako knew the underlying question was reasonable. The man was offering her huge sums of money. It was only natural Nakamura-san would want to know the reason for the necessity of a contract like this.

"Tanaka-san offered to build me a house," she began. "He said it is because the animals need a shelter for winter, and it would be better to build a house and convert my present home into a barn. When I didn't agree right away, he and his friend came up with this—agreement."

Nakamura-san's eyes widened. "He offered to build you a house? Would this house be for the two of you to occupy together? Is that why he's proposing to give you all this money?"

Hanako felt her cheeks burn. "He said the house would be—an early wedding gift, but I—"

To her surprise, the widow's face broke into a wide smile. "That is wonderful! You have indeed made a most advantageous match."

Hanako was stunned at the widow's enthusiastic response. "I—I haven't agreed."

"Why not?" the widow asked.

"I'm not—not worthy of marrying a samurai."

"Of course you are. You are more than worthy. You are a landowner. Moreover, you are the daughter of the first rank."

"What do you mean? My father was the town drunk."

"Yes, that was—unfortunate. He was not always that way. Before your mother died, he was a good man. He was not from a wealthy or noble family, but he was hardworking and honest. And your mother loved him so. She defied her father to marry him. And until she died, he did his best to keep her from regretting it."

"You knew my mother?"

"Yes. She was a bit older than me, but we came from the same city. We attended the same classes in *ikebana* and calligraphy."

Hanako stared at her neighbor in stunned silence. Flower arranging and elegant character writing were subjects studied only by women who came from wealthy families. She knew her mother had no contact with her family, but never knew the reasons for the rift.

Reiko continued. "The girls my age were in awe of your mother. She was the finest student in all our classes. We all knew she would attract the attention of someone significant and influential. But once she met your father, a gardener at the castle, she had eyes for no one else."

Hanako finally found her voice. "So, my mother was from an important family?"

Reiko laughed. "Important? Hanako, your mother was the eldest daughter of the head of the Nanbu Clan, the most powerful samurai family in the province of Mutsu!"

She leaned toward Hanako. "There is no question in my mind you are worthy of the samurai's interest. The real question is whether or not *he* is worthy of *you*."

Chapter Seven

Hanako pulled the weeds growing among her beans, trying to ignore the sounds of construction. However, it was hard to dismiss the activity of a dozen men as they pieced together the lumber for the framework of her new home.

Her visit with the Widow Nakamura had been a turning point for Hanako. She had taken her time walking back to her own farm, her mind reeling with the new knowledge of her own ancestry. Her father had never talked about his wife's family, other than to say they were selfish, vindictive people, and that he and Hanako were better off without them. Growing up, she hadn't even known their names or where they lived.

Now she had a name and a place. She had never heard of this clan, and had no idea where Mutsu province was other than it was not on the island of Hokkaido. But Nakamura-san had said they were important. And Nakamura-san was the most intelligent woman Hanako knew.

The conversation still hadn't convinced her she should marry Hiro. Even if her mother had been a member of the

Nanbu Clan, Hanako had no idea how to speak or how to act if she were to meet them. Her rough speech and manners would surely be an embarrassment to a man like Hiro. Perhaps Nakamura-san might agree to coach her in some of the ways of a lady.

But her discussion with the Widow Nakamura had given her the confidence to accept Hiro and Ginjiro's proposal to build a home in exchange for their food, lodging, and "instruction". She knew this agreement would be followed by a hard decision about marriage, but practicality was behind her decision to accept the offer to build. No matter how successful the harvest, she still would not have enough money or time to build a barn for her animals. Taking the offer would ensure her animals would have protection from the harsh winter.

She had not told Hiro or anyone else about the amazing discovery of her mother's family. After all, the Nanbu Clan had disowned her mother and would probably not acknowledge her. Hiro would not be impressed at her noble lineage, especially since her mother had chosen a nobody, who had not been able to keep up this small farm. No, if Hiro really wanted to marry her, he would have to accept her lowly status.

For now, she would concentrate on getting her farm up and running to the point where she could go on alone. Nakamura-san had told her that the agreement Hiro and Ginjiro had drawn up was fair, and she trusted the woman. The agreement gave her the means to build the structures necessary for her animals, and a warmer, safer home for herself.

This would be enough. For now.

"Hana-chan."

The deep voice never failed to excite her. Hearing him shorten her name with the endearing "chan" suffix sent warmth down her spine. She rose and turned to see him, his hair tousled and his chest gleaming with sweat. She quickly turned her gaze downward. Another mistake. The rest of him was just as appetizing.

"What is it, Tanaka-san?"

She saw his body tense, as if insulted by her formality. His broad chest expanded as he took a deep, calming breath. Fortunately, he chose to put her response aside and go on. "Come with me, please. The builders need your opinion on something." He turned and strode away, leaving her to follow.

For the next hour, she followed him around the site, listening to explanations as the head builder related the choices to be made. Hanako was lost. She had absolutely no understanding of what she was asked to choose. What did it matter to her whether the panels on the shoji screens were decorated with cranes or plants, or whether the weave in the tatami mats went in one direction or the other? She had never lived in a home with either luxury.

Seeing her distress, Hiro asked, "What would *you* recommend?"

The craftsman, obviously pleased to have the customer defer to his expertise, made recommendations. After thoughtful consideration, Hiro nodded in agreement.

The experience gave her further proof she was not fit to be a wealthy man's wife.

When the outer walls of the new home were erected, Hanako insisted the two men should move to the larger structure. Since they did so much of the farm work, she felt guilty about them staying in the tiny hut. If and when she and Hiro married, she would move to the larger home. If not, Hiro would leave eventually, and the home would be hers anyway. Now plans were drawn for another house, this one for Ginjiro.

She had expected the progress on the buildings would be slow, since her "apprentices" continued to spend a considerable amount of time in the fields with her. But each day, a crew of men arrived, checked in with Hiro, and went to work on the new structure. Instead of the circular, reed-covered walls common to the area, straight walls of fine lumber were erected, higher than she had ever seen except in pictures of the great temples. The interior was divided into sections. Having lived in a one-room hut all her life, she wasn't sure she could become accustomed to so much space.

Hiro said they needed room for their children. *Children.* She would love to have children. A little boy, a strong, miniature version of Hiro. Or a little girl she could dress in lovely clothes. She would sing lullabies to them and cherish them. There would be happiness, and laughter.

But what if she were barren?

Her heart clenched at the possibility. She and Kenji had never conceived. What would Hiro do if she were unable to give him a son? Would he go elsewhere? Would he divorce her? Or would he turn to a concubine and bring home another woman's son for her to raise?

She decided to bury her worries in work. Despite the distractions from the builders, the threesome got a lot of farming done. Hanako continued to be amazed at the amount of produce that came from her tiny farm. Each week, she and Hiro would go into town with a cart piled high with vegetables and herbs. At the end of each trip, she tried to share the earnings with Hiro and Ginjiro, but both men steadfastly refused to take anything but a mere pittance, insisting that she set aside the majority of the cash for the winter months, and for purchasing additional livestock and supplies in the spring.

The Widow Nakamura had invited her to tea, and Hiro insisted she go. "You should become friends with your neighbors," he advised her. "There may be a time when you will be of great assistance to each other."

So Hanako accepted, bathing in the stream and dressing carefully in her better kimono. She brushed her waist-long ebony hair until it shone, and then tied it carefully behind her neck with strips of fabric. The dusty road and the long walk nearly negated her attempt at tidiness, but she wanted to look her best. Her apparel was not as nice as the widow's lowest servants, but the widow always received her with a warm smile, making her forget her shabby clothes. The older woman, though obviously well-educated and high-born, had a down-to-earth manner and outlook on life. Reiko was definitely in charge of the house, but treated her children and her servants with kindness.

Just like Hiro.

The thought came to her as she trudged along the road to the Nakamura home. Hiro and the Widow Nakamura had much in common. With them, she never felt small. She was treated as an equal. And this was why she trusted them, and why she was able to voice her thoughts with Reiko.

Today, the widow waited for her in the lush gardens beside her home.

"Good morning, Hanako," she called.

"Good morning, Nakamura-san," Hanako replied, stopping to bow respectfully.

"It is such a lovely day. I thought we would have our tea out here in the garden."

Hanako nodded her assent, and Reiko led the way through the garden to an open structure about the size of Hanako's hut. Under the roof, a small, low table held a plate of appetizing treats. Reiko gestured toward one of the silky cushions beside the table. "Please sit down. Chidori-san will bring the tea shortly."

Hanako knelt on the cushion, looking around her at the colorful garden. It was such a peaceful spot. Her mother had grown flowers like these all around their hut. Hanako remembered the colors, the fragrance, and the brightness they had provided to their drab surroundings. Had the castle in Mutsu boasted a large garden, with a place to sit and entertain guests?

Reiko settled herself on the cushion opposite Hanako,

smiling serenely as she poured the tea. Hanako reached out to pick up the fragile cup, carefully lifting it to sip the fragrant brew.

For a moment she remembered Kenji's mocking words when she had wanted to purchase a tea set in the marketplace. "Why would you need something like that? You don't need nice cups for the slop we drink. It would be a waste!"

If only you could see me now. I am drinking fine tea out of a lovely cup while seated on a silk cushion in a beautiful garden.

"How is the construction of your new home coming along?" The widow asked.

Hanako didn't know where to begin. "It seems very large," she managed. "I don't know why I would need so much room."

"A wealthy samurai and his wife should live in a home befitting his station."

"Wife? But—" Hanako struggled to voice her thoughts. How could she explain her hesitation to marry? Any other woman would not hesitate to accept the advances made by a man like Hiro, whether or not they included the offer of marriage. But Hanako wasn't any other woman.

"Are you afraid of marriage to the samurai?"

"No," Hanako admitted. "Actually I was afraid the home is large so I would agree to—" She gasped as she realized what she was about to say.

The older woman waited patiently, her eyes full of understanding. She grasped Hanako's hand, encouraging her to continue. When it was apparent that wasn't going to happen, she squeezed her grasp.

"You don't want to be bought, to be kept as a concubine. Even when your father and husband were with you, you were independent and made decisions that kept your family fed. It goes against your nature to allow someone else to share the burden of the work and the financial worries, because it also means you would give up your freedom."

Hanako gazed in shocked admiration at this woman who had pinpointed her feelings and articulated them so clearly. How had she known?

Nakamura-san smiled in understanding. "We are kindred spirits, you and I. I have not struggled financially, as you have, but like you, I fought to be heard in a man's world. My father despaired of my ever finding a husband because I was too outspoken, too independent, too opinionated. But there are men who appreciate those qualities, and I believe Tanaka-san is one of them."

Hanako beamed with happiness. Her neighbor understood her so well.

"But how can I be sure about Hiro?"

Reiko shrugged. "I suppose one can never be sure how things will turn out in the end. I knew my husband would remain faithful and would provide for me and for our children as long as he lived. But I didn't know he would die relatively young. If I had known ahead of time, I may have wavered. But I can't regret the decision I made. We had less than twenty years together, but they were full of joy, and I have four fine sons who bear his name and give testimony to his character."

Hanako thought about that for a moment. Hiro had never given her reason to doubt his character, but she had only known him for a few months.

Her concern must have shown in her face, because Reiko surprised her yet again.

"I hope you are not offended, but since you have no family, I have taken the liberty of standing in as your mother and have sent an investigator to Tokyo to find out about Tanaka-san's family and his character."

Hanako sat up in surprise. She felt her jaw drop and her eyes widen in disbelief. Remembering her manners, she quickly averted her gaze away from direct eye contact with the older woman.

"I—I am honored that you would be so concerned for

me."

The widow leaned toward her, with a maternal expression of concern. "I never had a daughter, Hanako. If I had, I would wish her to be as strong and disciplined as you. Since your mother and I were acquaintances, I feel she would want to know about an intended husband for you, especially since your first experience was so—painful. Tanaka-san seems like the perfect husband, but we will have to be sure. When my investigator returns, we will talk again."

****

A few days later, the Widow Nakamura made a surprise appearance at Hanako's home. Though the two women had become acquainted, it had always been Hanako who went to visit Reiko.

Hanako was indoors, mending. Rising to her feet, she bowed respectfully. "Good morning, Nakamura-san."

"Good morning, Hanako," the widow returned, nodding her acknowledgement. "I see you are hard at work, as always. I am so glad you finally have some others to share the burden with you."

Hanako blushed, uncomfortable with the woman's concern. "Thank you, Nakamura-san," she murmured. "You have come a long way from your home. Please sit and rest. Could I serve you some tea?"

The older woman smiled. "I would be grateful for a cup of tea."

Hanako ushered the woman into the hut, grateful now for the improvements Hiro had provided. During recent visits into the village, he had purchased a new table and comfortable cushions. Hanako shuddered at the mental image of the silk-clad Widow Nakamura kneeling on the flat, dingy, threadbare cushions that had flanked her crude makeshift table.

She tried not to tremble as she handled the delicate china

cups Hiro had brought back from Hakodate. Quickly, she set the water on her stove to boil. She found some of the fancy rice crackers he and Ginjiro had purchased on their last trip to the village and set a few on a small tray. *A few weeks ago I would not have had anything to serve a guest. My life has changed so much that a fine lady is going to sit on a lovely cushion at my polished table, sip on tea from a fine china cup, and nibble on fancy crackers.* Happiness warmed her.

She brought the tea and crackers to the table and knelt next to her guest. The elder woman nodded her thanks and helped herself to two crackers and took a dainty sip of her tea before clearing her throat and looking into Hanako's eyes.

Hanako studied the widow as she waited for her to speak. A distant memory of her mother came to her. She too held herself like this. So had her mother's cousin, the one who had asked Hanako to call her *obachan*.

"It is fortunate that your late husband made arrangements with his cousin for your protection," Reiko began. Hanako's brow furrowed momentarily. Cousin? Then she remembered her first meeting with Hiro, when he introduced himself to Sato-san as Kenji's cousin. And Sato-san was widely known as the village gossip.

"It is especially fortunate that Tanaka-san and his friend are experienced warriors. I would not wish to see you or anyone else experience more pain like the tragic losses you suffered last harvest."

More pain? Hanako felt her chest tighten. "What do you mean?"

"There have been reports of raids in the villages to the south. The *ronin* have been causing more trouble."

Hanako's heart stood still. The *ronin* had returned? How would she survive another raid like the last one? She had managed to live through the winter only because of the charity of her neighbors. But what if they too suffered heavy losses? What would they all do?

"I know you are still trying to rebuild after the raid last fall. I wanted to warn you to take precautions before they return. I have hired extra field workers, but like most of the people in this area, they are simple farmers who are no match for former samurai warriors. In order to protect our lands, the men and women must be trained to fight. Hiro has this training. We need his expertise."

"You want Hiro to train your field workers to fight against the *ronin*?"

"It is our only chance for survival. Last summer, we were totally helpless. We could do nothing but wait for them to finish their destruction and hope that we survived."

"But if we fight, we could lose even more people!"

"That would be better than waiting to die."

Inwardly, Hanako agreed, though the thought of a battle between the gentle townspeople and a band of former samurai terrified her.

"While he may be a strong and intelligent man, I know that Tanaka-san is learning about this business from you, and I suspect that he will not commit to anything like this unless he knows you approve. I wanted to come to you first so that you would understand why this is necessary. I know you need his help and presence here, but the entire village needs him now. Please, for the good of us all, share Hiro and his skill with us."

Hanako nodded her agreement, but her mind was not on the rest of the conversation.

****

Just outside the doorway, Ginjiro froze in place, listening intently. He'd come to ask for instructions about crops in the far side of the field, but the voice he heard was not Hanako's. Caution had him stopping to assess a possible threat to his mistress, but the cultured, melodious voice was anything but fearsome. Her words were not threatening, and he decided

Hanako was not in danger, but he allowed himself to listen to the mystery woman's voice, letting himself be drawn in by the soothing tones. During his years as a warrior, he had known many noblewomen, but the pampered, empty-headed ladies had held no appeal for him. Certainly, none had held his attention simply with the sound of her voice.

He wanted to see the owner of the voice. Carefully, he bent his upper body toward the doorway, not wanting his sometimes clumsy feet to give him away. The new voice spoke calmly, but directly. Hopefully, her attention would be focused on Hanako, who customarily knelt at the table with her back to the door. This meant that the guest would be facing the doorway.

His upper body was nearly level with the ground, but he couldn't quite see far enough into the room to get a glimpse of the voice's owner. Perhaps if he just took one more step…

Carefully, quietly, he lifted his left foot and moved it toward the doorway. Unfortunately, his right foot was in the way, and his eyes widened in horror as he realized that he was now face down, his limbs arranged in an inelegant heap on the floor. Thank goodness he and Hiro had installed a new tatami mat inside the doorway, or his face would have hit the rough wood planks.

Perhaps his tumble had gone unnoticed. Perhaps he could just back out, and the women wouldn't know…

"Ginjiro!" Hanako's footsteps scurried toward him. "Are you all right?"

Ginjiro nodded, wincing when the motion scraped his face on the dry reeds in the mat. Despite the discomfort, he kept his face to the floor, scooting backward, hoping to leave before she—

"It seems the samurai has injured his head in the fall."

Ginjiro groaned, mortified to be caught in such an embarrassing position. How on earth could he explain his clumsiness?

His groan of frustration was interpreted as a sign of pain.

"Oh, Ginjiro," Hanako cried, "Forgive me! You must have tripped in that trench I dug for the plants outside the door. And now you are hurt!"

"Perhaps we should move him inside so we can tend to his wound." The warm contralto voice that had mesmerized him floated from his other side. He turned his head toward the voice and nearly yelped from the pain of the movement.

A gentle touch—one he hadn't experienced since his youth—caressed his face. Another hand probed his scalp, almost immediately finding the very spot that throbbed from within. He flinched and his eyelids clenched shut.

"Ah, here it is. Fortunately, there is no bleeding, but it is starting to swell. Let's help him get comfortable, and then we can put a cold cloth on his head."

Ginjiro's mind momentarily transported him back to his youth, when gentle hands cared for his boyhood scrapes, when a soft voice helped him relax and be coddled. But the voice he heard now was not his mother's. The women helped him to his feet and led him to the cushions around the table.

Finally, the pain faded enough for him to open his eyes and behold the owner of the intriguing voice. The sight was as stunning as the sound.

The beautiful woman holding the cloth to his head couldn't possibly be the mother of the Nakamura brothers. Her raven hair had only a few streaks of gray, and her face was unlined. She held his head with a maternal touch, but the reaction in his heart was anything but filial.

He heard Hanako's footsteps as she left for the stream and returned with a wet cloth, but he had eyes only for the lovely guest.

All too soon his time in paradise ended, and the widow left. A servant assisted her into a waiting carriage, and she was whisked away. Hanako answered his original question about the western field, and he returned to work. But for the rest of the day and all through the night, images of Hanako's beautiful neighbor filled his thoughts.

****

As soon as he saw Hanako, Hiro realized something had happened. She knelt over a plot of scallions, listlessly pulling out weeds. Sometimes a scallion would come up along with the weeds, but she didn't seem to notice. Worried, he knelt beside her.

"What has happened to disturb you?" he asked gently.

Hanako gasped and dropped the plants as her hand flew to her throat "You—I didn't hear you come." Her eyes widened as she noted the position of the sun, and she pushed to her feet. "It is late! I don't have a meal prepared."

She turned to go into the hut, but Hiro caught her arm before she could escape.

"It is not so late that Ginjiro and I will perish from lack of food. We are accustomed to living without regular meal times. Please, come and sit with me by the stream. Between us, we should be able to catch a fine supper in no time."

Hanako's hesitation worried him even more. "Has someone or something frightened you?" His frown deepened as another thought occurred to him. "Has Sato-san been harassing you again?"

The surprise in her eyes reassured him before her adamant denial. "No, I have not seen him, except when I am with you." Her lips curved in an impish grin. "I am certain he would not dare to trouble me in front of you."

"He would be wise not to trouble you even if I am not with you," he muttered. "But what is bothering you? You seemed to be pulling out as many scallions as weeds. You are normally much more careful."

Hanako stared down at the mess she had made and groaned. Hiro gently turned her away from the garden and led her toward the stream, hoping the serenity of the wooded area would calm her enough to share her thoughts. He did not have to wait long.

He listened intently as she told him about her visitor. His chest tightened at the mention of the *ronin*. But he sensed there was more on her mind than the news of a possible invasion.

"You know that Ginjiro and I will protect you with our lives," he reminded her.

"I hope it will not come to that. I am so glad you are here. But the two of you are the only men who know how to fight against them."

Hiro's senses went on alert. "Wouldn't the rest of the men in the area try to protect their own?"

"Yes, they would, and many women too. But the people here don't know how to fight against former samurai. Nakamura-san said—" She bit her lip as she chose the words to reveal her neighbor's plan.

"What did she say?"

"She said her sons will come to ask you to train them and the other villagers to fight, if and when the time comes. She says it is our only hope."

Hiro digested this news. He would be asked to return to his former life. Not only would he be asked to think and act as a warrior, but he would be expected to help others in this peaceful place to become warriors as well. Everything he had tried to escape was returning to him. Slowly he turned toward the stream. His steps were measured as he approached the water. Finally, he looked up at Hanako.

"Nakamura-san may be right," he told her. "If the villagers do nothing but wait, they will be like the fish in this stream, going about their business without a thought to the danger that approaches them. The *ronin* will descend upon them, and they will be helpless—" He drew his short sword and plunged it into the water, raising it again with two wriggling fish speared through. "—as helpless as these creatures."

Chapter Eight

The summer had brought a good harvest. Hiro felt a sense of accomplishment each time he finished cutting a section of barley, holding a *kama* in each hand. The sickles cut neatly through the stalks as his arms swung to and fro, just as if participating in a military training exercise. Left, right, left, right. Both arms formed smooth arcs across his body, as he stepped in time to an imaginary march, pressing him onward through the row.

A scream pierced the air, turning his blood to ice. Rough male laughter accompanied additional screams. He ran toward the sound, gripping the *kama* tightly. Hanako was not squeamish, nor was she one to needlessly raise her voice in alarm. She had been working at the opposite end of her lands, picking beans to take to the market. *Help me reach her in time*, he prayed.

He entered the clearing around the hut to find her fighting for her life. Three men surrounded her. Two held swords, waving them menacingly about her. Hanako, armed with nothing more than a hoe, held them off with the stance of a samurai woman. The third man stood back, watching the scene with an indulgent smirk.

Out of the corner of his eye, he saw Ginjiro entering the clearing from the opposite direction. Their gazes connected, and they both charged forward. Raising his voice in a fierce battle cry, Hiro focused on the man nearest him. The man turned toward him, surprised at the intrusion, but quickly settled his features in determination and raised his sword.

The *kama* Hiro held were somewhat like the *kusarigama*, a deadly fighting tool he had used in battle. Unlike the *kusarigama*, his tools didn't have a chain and weighted ball, which would have allowed him to snag his opponent's sword. In order to cause injury, Hiro would have to attack from within the sword's striking distance.

The other man was young, and the first swing of his sword betrayed his inexperience. Hiro easily deflected the slashing blade. Time after time, he raised his *kata* simply to block the sword. He knew he had to wait for the right moment to strike.

Eventually, the sword's motions became more erratic, giving Hiro the opening he needed. The younger man swung a wide arc across his body, leaving his torso exposed. Hiro moved in, one kama slicing off the man's sword arm, the other ripping into his body.

Not stopping to look back at him, he charged toward the second man, who was giving Ginjiro a challenge.

The nobleman, seeing his retainers were overpowered, retreated, but Hanako, still gripping her hoe, stopped him with a quick blow to his head. The man's eyes glazed, and he crumpled to the ground.

****

"You are not harmed anywhere?" Hanako fretted as she checked Hiro for wounds. The constable had come with his men and had taken the three intruders away. The man Hiro fought was dead, and the other would be fortunate to survive the night. The third man was a merchant from Sapporo who had seen Hanako in the local market and had decided to add her to his stable of concubines. Taking her for a simple farm woman, he'd decided she would be a welcome addition to his collection. He hadn't counted on the woman having two field hands who had been part of an elite fighting force. He now awaited sentencing in the village jail.

Hiro still burned with rage at the callous way the nobleman had tried to take Hanako. As a member of the samurai class, he had embraced a strict code of ethics. Justice, Bravery, Benevolence, Politeness, Veracity, Honor, and Loyalty were the seven codes of the *Bushido*, or "Way of the Warrior". Taking a woman against her will went against the majority of these codes. The men who had come today deserved the harshest punishment available.

"Are you certain you are all right?" Hanako asked again.

"I'm fine," he insisted. "I'm just hungry."

"Yes, of course. I will prepare your meal," she said as she scurried toward the cook stove. He noticed her hands shook as she measured the rice, poured water into the pot, and attempted to light the fire. The flame would not start for her, and as she tried again and again, she got more agitated. Finally he got up and stood behind her. He reached around her and put his hand on hers.

"You are too distressed from today's events. I can do this."

She dropped the flint and covered her eyes. Great sobs racked her body, and she tried to step away from him, but he gathered her in his arms and rocked her gently.

"You are safe, my little flower. I would not let anyone harm you."

"B-but they could have killed you! They had swords and you and Ginjiro had nothing but farm tools!"

"I could not let them take my future wife."

"You must have been a fierce warrior."

He smiled against her hair. "When I needed to be, I was."

Hiro basked in the warmth of their embrace. He had made the right choice for a wife, he thought. They would make a comfortable life together.

She pushed herself away. Her brows were knit together, her lips pursed in a frown.

"What is it?" he asked.

She took her time answering. "The men who came today—I wonder if they were part of the group who came last fall."

"I suppose it's possible. They seemed quite young, though. They didn't fight like trained samurai."

"The *ronin*—the ones who came last fall—they took the same oath as you, didn't they?"

Hiro froze at the question. His lips pressed into a thin line, his brows dipped, and he fixed her with an icy stare. When he spoke again, his voice was low and menacing.

"Do you mean to say you consider me in the same league as them? Has nothing I have said or done convinced you that you can trust me with your life? Is that why you will not consent to marry me?"

He advanced again, and she stepped back against the wall. Her eyes widened, and Hiro wondered if he'd frightened her. But the eyes shone not with fear, but excitement. She reached out and laid a hand on his chest, and his heart danced at the contact.

"I do feel safe with you. In my head, I know you are not like those men. I have never known such comfort as you have given me these last months. But I am leery of binding my life to another. The last time, I was not allowed a choice, and the result was...unfortunate."

He could feel his anger drain from him, and she continued. "The other men in my life, my father and my husband, were not strong men. And yet they controlled my life. You are so strong I fear your power over me would be much greater. And that frightens me. It's not your physical power—I know you would not hurt me physically—but you might perhaps expect me to be someone I am not."

"Do you fear my power as much now as when I first came here?"

She took her time answering. "I don't think so." She stepped around him and paced, absently noticing this house allowed her to pace farther than the tiny hut she had lived in most of her life. "Actually, I don't think I ever feared you. If you had wanted to hurt me and take my lands by force, you could've done so long ago. It's just that if I marry you, you would legally own all I have—little as it is—and I would again have nothing."

She watched him as he considered her answer. Would he dismiss her concerns? Her belongings were nothing compared to many, but they were hard won. If they were to marry, and then he tired of her, she would need to start over again. How could she not want to hold on to what little she had now?

Finally, Hiro answered. "It is true I would be considered the owner of your lands and possessions. But all I have would also be yours."

"And all of it could be taken away if you decide we don't suit each other."

"Yes, the laws don't protect women. I have seen wives and concubines tossed aside by unscrupulous, wealthy men." He caressed her cheek then lifted her chin, waiting for her to match his gaze with his. "I would not do that to the woman to whom I pledge my life. But I know it would be a lot to ask of you to believe that. What if we were to find a way to legally set your holdings separate from mine? Perhaps we could will them to our sons or daughters. Would that satisfy your concerns?"

Again, she was struck speechless by his generosity. He

had actually listened to her concerns and offered a compromise far beyond what any woman could expect.

"Could—could this really be done?" she asked.

Hiro shrugged. "I don't know," he replied. "But I can find out. For now, I think we should take a break from the hot sun. Let's sit by the river and catch some fish for our supper."

The ordeal left Hanako too drained to argue. She followed Hiro to the stream.

****

Hanako didn't notice the silent message Hiro sent to Ginjiro, or the answering nod. Ginjiro would spread the news of the troublemakers to neighboring farms.

Before leaving on his errand, Ginjiro watched his friend and Hanako stroll toward the stream. How fortunate Hiro would be if Hanako agreed to become his wife. Ginjiro had always thought he would marry and raise a few fine sons, but having passed his fortieth year, he doubted he could find someone to marry.

The last few years had been difficult for Ginjiro. When the Meiji government had abolished the samurai class, he had been left at a loss. He had no family to return to, and his very way of life no longer existed. He had never wanted to be anything other than a samurai, and though his size and skill had not allowed him to rise above the lowest levels of the class, he had reveled in the honor of serving his *daimyo*.

But now he was on his own. His *daimyo* had not been able to adjust to the "new ways" and was unable to retain him in any capacity, so he had spent the past five years looking for work. He had heard rumors about fighting opportunities in the north and had traveled a long way, but had been rejected because of his age and size. It had been the final straw. If Hiro had not found him in the woods, he would have ended his life.

Now, things were starting to look better. Thanks to Hiro

and Hanako, he had a purpose and dreamed of owning his own land. And now his dreams included someone who could make his life complete. He sighed, thinking of Hanako's beautiful neighbor. She was the embodiment of grace and serenity. How wonderful it would be to have the right to protect her, to care for her.

But she was beyond his reach.

Ginjiro scolded himself for daydreaming, reminding himself of his errand. He had a job to do, and useless yearnings would do him no good.

****

The offending missive hit the flames, spraying sparks so high they nearly burned him. Hideyori paced, cursing the sender. *How dare Akamatsu rescind his support? How in the world will I finance this military takeover if I don't have sponsors?* He thought he had talked Togashi and Akamatsu into joining his coalition. It was only a matter of time before the emperor was defeated and the country could return to its former glory.

It was true his army hadn't increased much in size, but he hadn't been able to find enough soldiers to form a decent army. Masao Akira was a good soldier, but he lacked proper respect for his superiors. He argued and spoke up too much. But at least he kept the rest of the troops in line.

If only he been able to keep his army from the old days. There had been some good warriors. There was one who had really stood out. What was his name? Tanaka. Hiromasa Tanaka. Strong and loyal, he was a true warrior. But he'd had that bothersome streak of honor. He'd left after that mess with his friend, but where had he gone? *If I could find Tanaka-san, perhaps he could be persuaded to join my "New Army."* Hopefully, the man hadn't joined the emperor's forces. Yes, Tanaka-san would definitely whip this rag-tag group into shape.

The confident stride of approaching footsteps broke him

out of his reverie. Masao strode into the tent without asking permission and spoke without bowing. Hideyori's eyes narrowed at such rudeness.

"We are out of food. We need money so we can go into the village and buy supplies."

"That will have to wait. Our funds haven't arrived. Go to the farms and get food."

"The farmers have next to nothing. How can they share with us? We took practically everything they had last time we came through. You promised us our situation was temporary. When are we going to be paid?"

"How dare you speak to me this way? I could have you killed for your insolence!"

Masao didn't flinch. "Who would you get to do the killing? I outrank them. They would answer to me." He leaned closer. "They're certainly not afraid of you."

"As soon as the money arrives, you will get your share."

Togashi had been weak and sided with the Emperor. And now Akamatsu had abandoned him. *Bah, I can do this without them.* There were others. Other benefactors with more men, more money. He just needed to convince them.

"The money is coming. In the meantime, we will need to go to the north. I have heard there are more resources, more farmlands. We will find food there. For now, send the men into the woods to hunt."

His second in command cast a doubting frown, but he bowed and left.

Hideyori's feet traced a path back and forth in front of the fire. It was time to make more plans.

Chapter Nine

The sounds of clanging metal and grunting men distracted Hanako as she tended her livestock, settling them for the night. Hiro and Ginjiro led a nightly training session in the wide meadow separating her farm from the Nakamura property. Torches mounted on stakes illuminated the men as they worked through their exercises. The widow's sons, along with twenty other villagers, listened intently as Hiro gave his instructions.

"Always hold your blade toward the opponent. Don't leave yourself vulnerable to his sword," he directed.

It had been three weeks since the widow's visit. As promised, her sons had approached Hiro with their request, and he had readily agreed. Each night for the last two weeks, a ragtag group of men, some with ancient swords handed down for generations, some with nothing more than their farm tools, had appeared in the field for drill and instruction. At first it had seemed an impossible task. These were peaceful farmers and simple merchants. How could they ever be taught to fight against trained warriors?

Rumors of the *ronin's* activities fueled the men's motivation. The renegade band was reported to have assaulted a town not more than ten days south of here. Time was of the essence. Hiro instructed the men to take precautions to safeguard their homes and families as well. An alarm system was set up. Each family was given a supply of flares with instructions to set them off if and when they spotted the intruders. Sato-san had supplied the flares, greatly raising him in the villagers' esteem.

When the training first began, several wives appeared with their husbands. Some actually participated in the training exercises themselves, but most were content to watch from the sidelines, some holding their infants and toddlers. Gradually, all but a few stopped coming along, leaving the men to learn the fighting while they tended to their homes.

Hanako knew she should participate more readily in the exercises. After all, this was her property they were defending. Last fall she'd been helpless to stop them. The image of her husband cowering under the furniture still left a knot in her stomach. Would she be as ineffective if put to the test again?

She decided to listen carefully to the instruction, and practice alone in the privacy of the woods, rather than in front of the other villagers. Perhaps later she could join the others.

Seeing that all the animals were settled for the evening, she picked up the handle to an old hoe, and holding it out in front of her, tried to mimic the movements the group performed with Hiro. Carefully, she sliced a diagonal arc in front of herself. The motion didn't seem quite like the technique Hiro had demonstrated, so she tried again, raising the hoe above her head and bringing it down and across her body with her hands ending near her left knee. She prepared to try the motion again, but gasped when her back connected with a solid wall of muscle. A deep, melodic voice rumbled from the wall at a point above her head.

"Don't bring your weapon down so far. Remember, this

leaves your body open to the opponent's attack."

Hanako's heart stopped at the unexpected contact. Before she could react, two strong arms came around her. Hiro's right hand enveloped both of hers as they gripped the hoe, and the other came to rest on her left side, holding her close to him. Without thinking, she leaned back against his massive chest. Time stood still as she sank into his warmth.

She barely registered his words as he gently guided her through the drill, keeping the weapon in front of her as it sliced through the air. Using a sturdy willow as an imaginary foe, he positioned her so that her right arm extended toward the tree and the right side of her body faced it.

"Turn your body away from your opponent. This gives him a smaller target and protects your torso from his sword." Her arms and legs continued the drill, but her senses were aware only of her body pressing against his. Her back warmed from his solid presence, and her side tingled where his hand pressed gently to guide her. What would it be like to have those strong hands caressing her, guiding her through a different dance, another ritual?

She let herself dream as his arms and body cradled her. They went through the motions, his right hand and arm directing the improvised weapon, his left hand moving her body. It was amazing how their bodies fit together, how their limbs moved in perfect synchronization. His hands switched as he moved the improvised weapon to her other hand and turned her body so her left side faced the imaginary opponent. Hanako knew the movements had been designed for fighting, but the two of them were engaged in a much different, though equally intense, reality.

All too soon, the fantasy ended. The muscular arms left her sides, and her heart returned to earth with a crash. Hiro backed away, taking the comforting warmth with him.

"Are you all right?" he asked, peering at her curiously. "You look pale. Perhaps you have been working too hard. I should end the training sessions earlier so that I can help you—"

"No." Hanako shook her head, her cheeks burning. The physical contact with him had affected her so strongly that he had noticed.

"You and Ginjiro are helping me more than enough. I am simply winded from the drill. I really should practice more, especially since the *ronin* are getting closer." Realizing she was babbling, she waved her hand toward the group in the clearing. "And the help you are giving the village is so greatly appreciated."

Hiro shrugged off her words of praise. "I do not expect thanks from you or the others. It is the least I can do. But you are my main concern. You looked so tired when I first came to the farm. And now you are finally starting to get enough rest and food. I do not wish to see you so exhausted again."

The intensity in Hiro's brown eyes mesmerized her. She felt them pulling her in. *Should I bind myself to him? Can we truly build a good life together? Or would he tire of me some day and wish to return to his old life?*

****

Hiro walked back to his eager pupils, his mind whirling from his encounter with Hanako. Touching her, holding her in his arms, he had felt at peace and yet so alive. Her compact body had felt right in his arms. He'd struggled to keep his mind on the sword drill and not give in to the temptation to crush her in an embrace. It would not do to give in to such a whim, especially with people there who could see them. His strong moral code had never been this sorely tested, not even with the most stunning courtesan.

Perhaps Hanako would soon agree to be his wife. He would have no trouble remaining faithful to her, and he could provide her with luxuries she had never had. She would provide him with strong sons, and together they would raise them to be stewards of the earth. They would be honest, intelligent men, judged by their competence and not by the size of their inheritance, or the strength of their warlord.

He stopped in mid-step. Sons? The vision had played briefly in his mind before, but this time it was so clear. A family. Strong sons and daughters. Hanako was the key to that dream. She must agree to be his wife before the visions would become reality. He needed to convince her to share the dream with him.

For now, he had a job to do. If the villagers could not defend themselves against the *ronin*, there would be no land on which to raise his family. He entered the clearing from behind the group, observing their progress.

Ginjiro had continued the drill, encouraging the ragtag army of villagers while correcting their errors. Hiro was impressed at the ease with which his friend had integrated himself into the community. His genial personality had earned him several friends among the farming community, and when he wasn't needed on Hanako's small plot, he had gone to work on other farms in the area.

Standing at the edge of the clearing, he watched his friend bark instructions. As a samurai, Ginjiro had never been in a position of leadership. His size and easy-going temperament had denied him the promotions his more fierce counterparts had earned. But here, in this small, tight-knit community, he was well-liked, and the men were responsive to his instructions. With each command, he seemed to gain more confidence.

There was no sound, but Hiro became aware of a presence at his side. Drawing on his own training and instinct, his hand quickly went to his sword as he faced the potential intruder. The sword dropped back into its scabbard as he realized the person approaching him was Shinobu Nakamura, one of the widow's sons. The young man paused, eyes wide with fear as he realized his approach had been viewed as a potential threat. When Hiro took his hand away from the sword's hilt, he spoke, though he kept a respectful distance between them.

"Tanaka-san, I wish to speak with you a moment," he began, bowing low. As a former member of the samurai class, Hiro was given the highest respect by even the local village officials.

Hiro bowed in return. "What is it, Nakamura-san?"

One of our men reported the *ronin* have now split into two factions. Part of the group is going to Tokyo, looking for work with the Imperial Guard. A smaller group is staying in the area. It seems the threat of this group is not as great as before."

Hiro considered this development. "How large is the group that stayed?"

"There are about ten men. They have been observed in village taverns each night, loudly bragging about their exploits in other towns. They prey upon travelers. It is said their finances are getting low, and they are waiting for the arrival of a former *daimyo* who will retain them for his cause."

"A *daimyo* is traveling to recruit men? But they no longer need independent armies. Who is he?"

"I don't know. But his delayed arrival is causing the *ronin* to make trouble in the villages."

"Ten angry warriors can do a great deal of damage. We have about thirty men here, but they are spread out, and it would take valuable time to gather us all together. We must continue our training and be on alert."

The younger man smiled. "We were all hoping you would say that, Tanaka-san. We know we are not as efficient as an entire army of samurai warriors, but feel better able to protect ourselves with your training. We all sleep better at night now that we have a plan. We have taught our wives and children how to sound the alarm if needed. Thanks to you, we may have something to leave to our sons." He bowed low again as he backed away then turned around to take his place in the fighting drill.

Hiro thought about Nakamura-san's words long after the drill was over and the men had left for their homes. He had spent most of his adult life fighting for another man's land, for someone else's home. He had fought for financial gain, as well as honor. Generations of his family had been groomed for this life. He had known of no other course.

But these men were fighting for their own homes. Their technique wasn't as polished as the soldiers Hiro had fought with, but they were more motivated, because they had more at stake. They were going against their peaceful natures to protect what was theirs. Hiro admired their tenacity. He, too, was trying to put aside generations of family tradition and take on another way of life. These people were now his people. Their cause was now his. He did not intend to let them lose.

****

From her seat in her rickshaw, the Widow Nakamura watched her sons as they learned and practiced their drills. She was proud of the village men for taking the incentive to guard their homes from the rebel soldiers. Even after a handful of training sessions, she could see a change in the physical strength as well as the mindset of the townspeople. There was a sprig of hope in the air.

A few other women watched, but they kept themselves apart from the widow. She was accustomed to the isolation. It wasn't that the other women disliked her, but her status as the widow of a wealthy landowner and government official set her apart. When passing, the townspeople stopped and bowed, but said nothing unless asked. They were not in her social class.

So the widow watched alone. She loved her family, but

yearned for friends like those she'd had in the city. Her brother, a physician, had recently retired from his practice and lived nearby, but there was no companionship for her.

Though her eyes were focused on her sons, her senses were always aware of another person. Tanaka-san's assistant reminded her so much of the man who had once been the center of her world. Her marriage to Fujii Nakamura had been a love match, and he had been a good provider. Together, they had produced four strong sons to carry on the family name and lands. Fujii had always treated her with kindness and respect. He had been small but wiry, and stronger than one would expect of a man of his stature.

When a farming accident had claimed Fujii's life, Reiko had wanted to throw herself into the funeral pyre. The knowledge that her sons, then ranging in age from three to twenty, still needed her had prevented her from doing so. Since then, she had built a comfortable life for herself, thanks to the excellent managerial skills of her eldest son. Even now, Noburo tried to shelter her from the hardest tasks and decisions, though she had her ways of learning what went on.

Her sons would eventually move on. As the eldest, Noburo and his family would stay, of course, and there was enough room on the estate for any or all of her sons to share in the work and profits of this farm should they choose to do so. She would enjoy seeing them marry and begin their families. More grandchildren would be welcome, and it would be nice to have some young female companionship.

But the former samurai, even in his awkward state on Hanako's floor, had touched a long forgotten chord. Was it because his build was similar to Fujii's? Was it because she missed the companionship? Or was it the way those deep brown eyes had looked into her soul?

It would do her no good to dream. She was a mature woman, not a starry-eyed maiden. She had no business yearning for a younger man. Sighing, she signaled to her servant to take her home.

Chapter Ten

The sun had set, but Hiro was unable to sleep. He sat at the table, reading by the dim light of a lantern. Before him lay a newspaper he had purchased during his last trip to the village. Though some of the news from Tokyo was dated, he could at least get some idea about what was happening in his home city.

His eyes scanned the page, but his mind was on the drill earlier. Seeing Hanako attempt the fighting exercise with the hoe, it had seemed only right to step in and help her perfect the moves. He hadn't meant to hold her so closely, but once his arms had wrapped around her, it had seemed so natural, so right. It had taken all his strength to step away.

He turned the pages idly, without actually reading, when a name caught his eye. It was a name he had not seen in over a year, not since he had left his former life behind. Instantly his blood began to burn, and his hands gripped the paper as he read the article more carefully.

In coming to the rural north, he had wanted to leave behind all traces of his former life, especially the memory of the treacherous *daimyo* for whom he had fought. At one time he and his best friend Kunio Fukada had entered battles side by side, conquering foes in the name of the mighty *daimyo*, Hideyori Kato. But after that final battle, the only reward his friend collected was the order to kill himself in the bloody ritual called *hara-kiri*. Kunio had not deserved to die that way. He had kept his honor and fought bravely. But he was powerless to override the edict presented to him. And so Hiro had watched his best friend die. With his friend's death, Hiro had also lost his trust in the *Bushido*, the "Way of the Warrior".

Now it appeared that Kato-san had found another cause, another reason to send young men to their deaths. The article read the former *daimyo* had declared war on the renegade *ronin* and wanted to recruit "strong, honorable men" to help stop these troublemakers and keep peace in the area. Strong, honorable men indeed! The former *daimyo* had not recognized honor when he had witnessed it. This was obviously a plot to raise his standing in the eyes of the emperor. If the *ronin* could be defeated, a grateful emperor would no doubt bestow favor upon the nobleman who brought this about. Though the emperor and his army had made progress, they were unable to stop the devastation left by several renegade soldiers. Hiro shook with rage as he finished reading the notice. Hideyori Kato must be the *daimyo* Nakamura-san had mentioned, the one the local *ronin* were waiting for.

When Hiro had stopped working for Kato-san, the man had lived in a stone fortress with hundreds of guards and servants to do his bidding. What had happened to make it necessary for him to recruit ruffians like the *ronin* who terrorized innocent people? The offending paper fell to the floor as Hiro rose, picked up his pipe, and went out into the night. Walking always helped him to think and plan. He had to make sure Kato was unsuccessful in recruiting an army for this "honorable" cause.

****

The morning after experiencing blissful warmth in Hiro's arms, Hanako woke to find him gone. Ginjiro arrived for breakfast, but did not share any information about his friend's whereabouts. It was nearly midday before Hiro returned to the farm. He wordlessly joined Ginjiro in the field. At the evening meal, he still had nothing to say about his absence. Hanako wondered if Hiro had been repulsed by the closeness they had shared the night before, but his cool demeanor kept her from asking.

The coldness continued for weeks, and Hiro's disappearances occurred again and again. Sometimes, he would be gone for several hours; other times days would pass before she would see him. If it hadn't been for Ginjiro's continued presence, she would have been frantic with worry. While Hiro was gone, Ginjiro and the Nakamuras would lead the drill group. Hanako noticed their numbers had dwindled, but the remaining core of would-be soldiers stayed committed.

The men had decided to hold their drills in a different location each night to avoid attracting the attention of unwelcome strangers. This decision resulted in a larger number of trainees, though attendance at each session varied. She resolved to attend as many sessions as possible, determined to defend her land if necessary.

During one of Hiro's unexplained absences, Hanako noticed a stranger standing silently at the edge of the field. The last time strangers came, Hiro and Ginjiro had fought them off. But this man looked more dangerous than the two ruffians who had attempted to abduct her. She looked around for Ginjiro, wondering how she could signal a warning to him. Her hands trembled as she attempted to appear unconcerned, continuing to tend to the radishes, but her eyes were not focused on her work. Faster and faster, she moved toward the end of the row away from the stranger. Quick, furtive glances assured her that the man had not moved from the edge of the field. Finally, she spotted Ginjiro, working in the next field with the ox and the ancient plow. She gave up all pretense of calm and raced to him. He looked up in surprise as she approached him.

"What is wrong?" he asked.

Hanako struggled to catch her breath as she gasped out a description of the man at the roadside. Ginjiro's expression tightened, and he checked for his sword before heading to where she had seen him. He trod slowly, looking around for signs of other intruders, until he spied the newcomer. Then his face broke into a wide grin, and he re-sheathed his sword before running to greet the man.

Hanako breathed a sigh of relief. If Ginjiro knew this person, he was probably not a threat to her. But why would an acquaintance of his travel here? Perhaps he was a relative.

Ginjiro brought the silent man to her and introduced him as a former comrade. He had answered a request to come and help the town defend against the *ronin*. The newcomer was immediately invited inside for tea. Since the new house had a larger kitchen and dining area, Hanako usually prepared and served meals there. She got out her fine china cups and special tea. As she worked, she caught snippets of their conversation.

The newcomer, Watanabe-san, was younger than Hiro and Ginjiro. Like Hiro, he walked with a proud, erect posture that bespoke a life of privilege and importance. She suspected that he, too, came from a long line of samurai. She wondered what business he had with Hiro.

Hanako strained to hear the men's conversation as she prepared the tea and a light snack. Ginjiro's voice carried more clearly, and she could make out his words. Being a lower-level samurai, he was respectful as he spoke to the younger man.

"Watanabe-san, we are honored you came here to assist us. The *ronin* have caused much damage here and in other nearby towns in the last year."

"Yes, Tanaka-san told me about their evil deeds," the newcomer replied. "It is a shame that some of our kind have chosen to use their skills in dishonorable ways. It was an honor for Tanaka-san to invite me, and I was intrigued by his offer of payment."

Payment? Hiro was paying men to help fight the ronin? Hanako nearly dropped the teapot.

"I have never owned property, and since I am a younger brother, I will not inherit my family's estate. My older brother would provide for me, of course, but a chance to have my own land was an enticement for me."

Hanako brought the tea in to the men, bowed, and left to complete dinner preparations. But she left the sliding *shoji* screen open just enough so she could hear more of their conversation.

So Hiro has promised land in exchange for fighting power. Such a brilliant idea. But is he purchasing this land to give to them?

"I have spoken to Fukazawa-san and Kobayashi-san, and they should arrive within the week," the newcomer continued.

The rest of the conversation was lost to her. *There are more men coming! He is recruiting an army! The village will be protected!* She let the rest of the conversation flow as she prepared the finest meal she could provide. As she chopped and stirred, she thanked the gods for her short time spent as a kitchen maid in the house of a fine gentleman. She had watched as the cook transformed piles of meat and vegetables into creations she could appreciate through her sense of smell. It was only after the gentleman and his family ate, and then the higher servants, that she was allowed the scraps that remained. But the experience had given her an appreciation for the crops she grew and the knowledge of how to serve them.

"Hanako-san."

She nearly dropped the long wooden chopsticks she used to stir her concoction. "Nakamura-san, forgive me," she cried, quickly turning to bow to her esteemed neighbor.

"Please do not stop your work. I was passing by on the way to the village, and the wonderful aroma from your new home enticed me to investigate."

"Thank you. But—this is actually Hiro's home," she began.

"And you are merely a servant? No, this will be your home soon, when you and Hiro marry. And then you will have servants to prepare your food."

"Servants? No, I—" She paused in her denial, realizing that Hiro, as the head of the household, would undoubtedly hire servants to take care of the housework. The idea was unsettling. After working hard all her life, how could she sit back and let people work for her?

"Have I disturbed you, Hanako-san?"

"Oh! Of course not. Would you like some tea?"

"You are kind to offer, but my son is outside fixing a broken wheel on our wagon. I must be ready to go when he is. But I wanted to let you know—I have heard about the extra samurai Tanaka-san has recruited. You should not have to feed all these hungry men alone. Please allow me to assist you. Since you already have tonight's meal started, I will send food over for tomorrow."

Hanako stared in amazement at the woman's offer. It had never occurred to her to ask for help. "I—I am humbled by your generosity, Nakamura-san," she finally managed.

The older woman smiled. "You are so accustomed to doing everything alone. But these men are helping the entire village and surrounding areas. It is only right we should all help to feed them."

Hanako again stammered her thanks. "But how did you hear about the new soldiers? Watanabe-san arrived only today."

"Tanaka-san is a celebrity in the village. When his friend arrived, asking where to find him, word immediately spread. My sons learned that others are coming. When they arrive, we will all be honored to help feed and house them."

Noburo Nakamura appeared at the doorway. He bowed a greeting to Hanako and then to his mother. "*Okaasan,* the wagon is repaired enough for us to return home. I am sorry to make you wait."

"It is no trouble, Nobu-chan," the widow replied. "I rather enjoyed this opportunity to visit with our neighbor." Turning to Hanako, she repeated her promise to send food the next day, and left.

Hanako returned to her cooking, but as she worked, she marveled at this unfamiliar feeling of contentment. It wasn't from the fact that she wasn't hungry or excessively tired. It wasn't from the fact that she felt safe with three former samurai in her home. It came from her connection with another human being, another woman, who expressed care for her well-being and was willing to help. This must be what people referred to as friendship.

She decided she liked having a friend.

****

Leaving Hiro's house, Reiko covertly looked around for a glimpse of Tanaka-san's friend. When she had arrived, she thought she had heard his voice as he spoke to the newcomer in another room. But she had no good excuse for walking through the house. She would have to find another time and place to speak to him.

It was easy to see why the village women were drawn to Hiro. His tall, muscular build and his noble bearing made him a very desirable man. But though she respected the handsome samurai, it was his friend who intrigued her. He was not formally educated, having instead obtained his learning through life lessons.

But it was his eyes that held her captive. Eyes that expressed every thought, every desire, every defeat. In the years since she had been left a widow, she had learned much about the ways of men, and her ability to judge a man's character through his eyes had been the key to the success of her lands. And Ginjiro's eyes told her he was a man she could trust, a man who would be loyal in every sense.

Since he had arrived in the village, Ginjiro had been a faithful friend to Hiro, an indispensable help to Hanako, and a willing guard for the village. The story of how he had defended Hanako during the attempted abduction had reached Reiko's ears, and she grew more intrigued about him. *Does he have a family somewhere? Will he be free to stay in the area once the threat of the* ronin *is over?*

Noburo helped her into the carriage and climbed up to his perch for the ride home. Reiko berated herself for her childish thoughts. One would think her a silly girl, daydreaming about a man this way. She was a woman of stature, a mother and a widow. She had far more important things to think about.

If only she could remember what they were.

Chapter Eleven

She was watching again. Ginjiro closed his eyes and took a deep breath to calm his racing heart and forced himself to continue the drill. Hiro had decided to focus the drill tonight on using the *bo*, and he needed to concentrate on wielding the six-foot rod with care. He focused on his weapon, not looking toward the doorway where he knew she stood. The landowners surrounding the village took turns hosting the training sessions. Tonight, the exercises were conducted on the Nakamura homestead.

It was so embarrassing, the way he longed for her like a lovesick puppy. She was so far above him, so refined. She would never look at him as anything other than a low-ranking soldier. It would not do to harbor wishes that could never come true.

"Yamada-san."

Ginjiro yelped as his *bo* swung in a crazy arc, hitting his forehead.

"Forgive me. I should not have interrupted you while you concentrated on your drill."

He ignored the throbbing pain in his head, turned, and bowed. "It is I who should apologize for my clumsiness. I might have injured you with my wayward weapon."

"I have more faith in your skill than that. But I did have a purpose for interrupting you."

Ginjiro nodded, keeping his eyes down in a show of respect. Nakamura-san wasn't royalty, but through her sons, she exerted much influence in the village, and the citizens paid her a great deal of respect.

"Surely you don't consider a farmer's widow to outrank you, Yamada-san?"

The question brought Ginjiro's eyes upward. His mind worked feverishly, searching for an appropriate reply. His ears finally told him the incoherent sounds coming out of his mouth were not creating the best image for him. He closed his mouth, irritated he had let it hang open like an inarticulate fool. He swallowed, took a deep breath, and forced himself to speak.

"How may I be of assistance to you, Nakamura-san?" He smiled inwardly, pleased that his voice had not cracked.

"I need your help moving an item of furniture in my home," she explained. "It is too large for my youngest son to move."

Ginjiro nodded and followed the widow into her home. He was instantly enveloped in comfort. The house, though large, had none of the sterile coldness of the last castle he had worked in, or the overblown pretentiousness of the nobleman he had helped to protect. This was a home, a place where a family lived, worked, and played.

Colorful flower arrangements graced highly polished lacquer tables in the corners of the room. The sliding *shoji* screens were painted with outdoor scenes, giving the illusion of an outdoor patio. Plump, comfortable cushions surrounded the low table. A large buffet lined most of the far wall.

"I have decided I want to have the table over there," the widow told him as she pointed toward the far wall. "It makes more sense to have the table closer to the kitchen."

Ginjiro didn't understand why the arrangement made more sense to her, but he nodded and went to work. But once he had the table and cushions moved, the woman frowned.

"Oh dear. This won't do. There isn't enough room to fit six cushions around the table here."

Six? She has four sons, and two of them are married and living in their own homes, so why would she need so many? But what did he know of such things?

"Perhaps it would have been better to have the table back where it was, and move the buffet over to that wall next to it," she said, pointing at one of the side walls.

For the next half hour, he worked, arranging things to suit the woman. Briefly, he wondered what she hoped to accomplish by moving things around. *What difference did it make whether a table was placed here or there?*

It wasn't until later that night, after he lay on his *ofuton* in Hiro's new house, that he realized the beautiful widow had three older sons who could have easily moved her furniture. His lips curved into a wide smile as he drifted into slumber.

****

In the next week, two other strong, able soldiers joined Watanabe-san. During the day, they worked in the fields with Ginjiro, and in the evening, Hanako fed the entire group in the spacious dining room of the new house.

Hiro returned from his latest trip, and held meetings with the men after the fighting drills. Hanako, preparing for sleep in her own hut, heard the voices of the men as they planned. Though she loved cooking in the spacious new home, she still felt the need to return to her own hut at night.

Five strong men sleeping next door provided her with a

sense of security. Her worries about feeding them all had been needless. The men were used to providing for themselves, catching fish from the stream and hunting small game, and true to her word, Nakamura-san often sent meals. During her next visit into the village, Hanako saw a renewed energy among the townspeople. Hiro was treated with even more respect than before, and she knew it was because people appreciated his efforts to help protect them. People stopped him, bearing gifts of food for "the protectors" and sincere words of thanks. Hiro accepted the praise modestly and in turn thanked them for their gifts.

The new developments made Hanako believe Hiro really planned to stay. She still had some doubts about her own suitability, but more and more she contemplated life with her handsome samurai. She would live in the fine house he had built. She could forget about financial worries and backbreaking work. She would have someone with whom she could share her life, her dreams, and her future. Perhaps there would be children—strong, handsome sons, and beautiful, graceful daughters. How she would cherish a child born to her and Hiro. Even if Hiro left, she could go on if she had his children.

****

The sun beat down mercilessly after a long day at the market. Hiro, walking ahead of Hanako as he led the ox and cart, glanced over his shoulder and noted her pensiveness and wondered if she was uncomfortable with the attention they had received from the townspeople. *Is she embarrassed from the attention? Does she resent the time I spent away from the farm? Should I have explained about my visits to the city and my correspondence with my former comrades?* He was glad his requests had resulted in responses. The three men who had come in answer to his request were people he could trust, men who held the same high moral standards as he, men who truly lived according to the code they had sworn to uphold. They all had expressed disgust at the troublemakers roaming the countryside and agreed to help.

The key to bringing them here had been to get the village to agree to provide compensation. He knew monetary rewards were out of the question. Most villagers were barely able to do more than subsist from their earnings. But land here in the far north was plentiful, and since the men of the samurai class no longer received the privileges they had previously enjoyed, many of these men were looking for a new purpose in life. Hiro had found joy in working with the land. Perhaps others could learn the trade, or perhaps find another equally satisfying role in life.

But studying Hanako's pale face and quiet demeanor, he wondered if perhaps he had overstepped his role in her life. His only thought had been to protect her and his adopted town. *Is it possible that such an independent woman would resent my interference?* After all, he had agreed to stay on her farm as an assistant, a hired hand.

"The people in the village were very generous with their gifts of food," he began.

Hanako didn't look at him. She simply nodded. The juices in his stomach turned sour. *Is she angry?* A new thought occurred to him, and his blood began to boil. "Have the new men been unkind or disrespectful to you?" His throat began to close as he ground out, "Have they hurt you in any way?"

The last question caused a quick reaction. Hanako looked up at him, her eyes wide with surprise. "No, of course not! They have been perfect gentlemen. I am proud to have them here. Forgive me for not thanking you properly. We are all safer because of their presence."

Hiro sighed in frustration, turned and walked on. He didn't want her gratitude. But he did want her approval. Her listless manner of the last few days bothered him. It was her strength of character that he had first noticed about her. What caused this sudden lethargy?

He stopped so suddenly that Hanako, walking three paces behind him, nearly collided with his massive frame. He turned, stepped toward her, lifted her chin and waited for her to meet his gaze.

"Do you feel the extra men are causing too much work for you? I know I didn't ask you about housing them here. Would you like them to stay elsewhere?"

"No! I feel safer with them here."

"Would you like extra help with the cooking and cleaning?"

"The other farmers in the area and many in the village have been sending food."

"But it is still extra work to serve it and clean up. Perhaps I should hire a young girl from the village to help you."

"N—" She paused in her automatic refusal. Hiro waited patiently, hiding his amusement. His independent little flower would have difficulty letting someone else do what she considered to be her work.

"Perhaps, later, when the harvest brings more work in the fields. Right now, I enjoy the cooking. I've never had the opportunity to spend so much time indoors during the summer. Thanks to all the help we have here, I am free to do this, and I am grateful for the opportunity to show my gratitude to the men who are helping to save my village."

Hiro studied her as she spoke. She was telling the truth in that the extra work was not bothering her. But he still needed to know what had taken away her fire, her passion. He moved his hand to her shoulder, needing to touch her, wanting so much more.

"Please tell me what has taken the light from your eyes," he asked gently.

She closed her eyes for a moment, and Hiro feared she wouldn't answer. But then her lovely eyes opened, and Hiro felt his heart stir as their gazes met and held. He forced himself to listen carefully to her answer.

"I have been considering your offer of marriage. I am so honored, and yet I am afraid."

Afraid? *Is she afraid of me?* Hiro's quick intake of breath must have alerted her to his question, because she quickly reassured him with her next words.

"I'm not afraid of you. I know you would never hurt me. I'm afraid of not being able to be a proper wife for you. I'm afraid of letting go of my simple way of life. I'm afraid of— change. Until now, my life has been centered on these fields. And now that you and the others are here, I have other concerns. Change is necessary and is often good. If my life is going to be different, I have to change, and that frightens me. I have asked Nakamura-san to teach me about things I should know."

She paused and took a deep breath. Hiro held still, waiting for the words he hoped would follow.

"I thought perhaps we could marry after the harvest, if you still wish it."

Chapter Twelve

The Nakamura brothers stared curiously at the strange device brought by the new samurai. "How does it work?" asked Shinobu, the second eldest.

Watanabe-san patiently explained the mechanism that propelled the bullet. He even took one of the cartridges apart, much to the delight of Takaro, the family mechanic.

"Will you show us?" asked Yoshiro. At ten years of age, his curiosity still caused him to forget traditional rules of etiquette, and the arrival of the new samurai and his exotic weapon were of prime interest to a boy for whom farming was simply endless drudgery.

Propelled by the brothers' interest, Watanabe-san readily agreed to stage a demonstration. Targets were set up by hanging two old ceramic pots from the branches of a tree. Noburo Nakamura, the eldest, brought out his best bow and arrow and aimed at the pot on the left. The arrow flew directly at its target and bounced off. Everyone nodded in appreciation and turned to the samurai, waiting to see if he could outdo the feat. The newcomer raised the rifle to his shoulder, closed one eye as he took aim, and pulled the trigger. The sound of the blast was deafening, but all eyes widened in amazement at the shattered pot on the ground beneath the rope that once held it.

Noboro was the first to speak. "This is truly a deadly weapon," he conceded.

Hiro nodded his agreement. "In the past, *shoguns* used large groups of gunmen, called *ashigaru*, to conquer opposing forces. But after the Tokugawa clan took power over most of Japan, the guns were put away in favor of more traditional weapons. I have read that in the west, gun use is much more prevalent."

"How did Watanabe-san get this weapon?" Shinobu, the second eldest, turned a suspicious glance toward the newcomer.

"The American Admiral Perry brought newer and more deadly versions of these weapons. Some of these were left here. They say some of the *ronin* have them." He looked around at the men assembled there. "If that's true of the *ronin* here, we will be in more danger than I thought."

Takaro suddenly jumped up. "I know where we can get some of these!" At the incredulous stares from the rest, he pointed to a slightly overgrown path leading away from the village.

"A few years ago as I was gathering firewood, I found an old abandoned shack. When I looked inside, I found several crates, with broken locks on them. The crates had strange looking characters on them, so I couldn't tell what was in them. Since the locks were broken, I looked inside, and there were dozens of these. I didn't know what they were, so I forgot about them until now."

He led the group to a dilapidated structure on the edge of the Nakamura property. Overgrown bushes concealed most of the tiny hut. The dusty interior and preponderance of cobwebs testified to the absence of human visitors for quite some time. A dozen wooden crates were stacked in the middle of the single room, bearing foreign characters.

Hiro pointed to the red, white, and blue emblem painted on some of the boxes. "These are from the United States. They manufactured most of the guns imported by the *shogun* many years ago."

Noboru perked up. "I remember hearing about a shipment supposedly lost at sea. When the shipwreck was finally located, the entire cargo had been taken."

"These must have been weapons intended for the *shogun*," Hiro mused, "but they are no good to him now. The question is, do the *ronin* know about these?"

"We must keep them out of their hands," Noboru insisted, and the others agreed. Hiro and the other former samurai brought the crates out of the hut and dragged them to the path, while two of the Nakamuras went to get some horses and small carts. The guns would be stored in a compartment under the floor of the Nakamura house.

"The guns are useless without ammunition," the young samurai reminded the group.

"Yes, that is true," Hiro agreed. I will look into sources. If I get them, would you be willing to train several men to use these weapons?"

****

Sometimes help comes from surprising sources. Less than two weeks after the arsenal discovery, Sato-san arrived at Hiro's home, leading a sad-looking, heavily-burdened horse.

It was after the dinner hour. Hiro and several other men were in the house, putting finishing touches on the new home. His eyebrows rose when he saw his visitor, but he bowed in response to Sato-san's greeting.

After asking the young housemaid to bring tea, he led his guest to a low table and gestured for him to sit. The little merchant shuffled in, staring around him in awe. Stiffly, he lowered his bulk to sit beside the richly lacquered table.

"What can I do for you, Sato-san?"

"I heard about the cache of guns at the Nakamura lands. It is very fortunate, but the weapons are of no use without ammunition. Please accept my humble contribution," he concluded, bowing as he held out a small wooden box toward Hiro.

Nodding his acknowledgement, Hiro pried the lid off the box. Inside were hundreds of metal cylinders, about two inches long and a half-inch in diameter. Protruding from one end of each cylinder was a pointed metal missile. They looked exactly like those Watanabe-san used in his rifle.

"How did you manage this?"

Sato-san's lips curved into a smile that did not reach his eyes. "In some things, it is better if you remain in the dark." He rose and bowed, showing Hiro no more information would be forthcoming. "It was my honor to be of service."

"Wait," Hiro called out. "All this ammunition must have been expensive. Could I assist you in paying for it?"

A slow grin crossed the older man's face. "You are generous to make such an offer, Tanaka-san. But I have as much at stake here as the rest of the villagers. When the *ronin* came last year, we all suffered. I think Shimizu-san perhaps suffered more than most, but we all lost. Much of my livestock was taken for food, some simply slaughtered and left in the streets for no reason other than to cause havoc. I was fortunate I had enough left so I could go on. But the shock was too much for my elderly mother. She—"

He swallowed, closed his eyes, and composed himself.

"She recognized one of her grandchildren in the unruly mob. A young soldier who, until then, had been a source of great pride for her. Before I could stop her, she killed herself in shame." He looked up at Hiro then, determination mixed with grief. "I vowed I would have vengeance for her death. I am not a fierce warrior. But I am a businessman, and I wish to use my resources to contribute to this cause." He bowed again, and left.

This time, Hiro did not stop him.

****

Ginjiro sat on the bank of the stream, soaking in the coolness of the shade. It had been a long day in the fields. Hiro was anxious to get the crops in, because the end of the harvest meant an end to his bachelorhood. Ginjiro had never seen Hiro so happy. Hanako was a good match for him. She was a strong, resourceful woman. They would have fine children.

Once, Ginjiro had thought of marrying. She had been a lovely girl, the daughter of a prosperous merchant. He had brought her lovely things—combs for her hair, lotions, and special sweets. But in the end she had rejected him for a more successful man, a rising politician. A handsome man with a bright future. Ginjiro had never again thought of binding himself to another.

Until now.

But once again, the woman was of a higher station. It would do no good to dream.

A twig cracked behind him. Instinct had him alert and ready to fight. He had no weapon except his walking stick, but he knew how to use it. As soon as he saw the two men walking toward him, he knew they posed no threat.

"Good afternoon, Yamada-san." Noboru and Shinobu Nakamura bowed respectfully, and Ginjiro returned the greeting. He looked up at them, curious to know why Reiko's two eldest sons would be walking along the stream, rather than along the road to the town.

"We wanted to speak with you a moment, if you would be willing," Noboru began. At Ginjiro's nod, he continued.

"We have been looking out for our mother for a long time. Our father has been dead for ten years. She is an astute woman, but I'm sure you understand that the heart knows no reason."

Ginjiro's eyes narrowed. Were they here to warn him against any contact with their mother?

"Our father was a hard-working man. He was not poor, but he wasn't titled. Hers was a wealthy, influential family who disowned her when she defied them and married a farmer.

"She had faith in him and moved with him to the far north, here to Hokkaido, where they started from nothing and built our home. Father wanted to make sure she never regretted her decision—and her trust was not misplaced."

Noboru's eyes met Ginjiro's. "You are much like our father. You may have nothing, but you work hard, and are an honest man. Not only have you taken the oath of the *Bushido*, you live by it. Tanaka-san says he would trust you with his life. And so we have come to tell you that if it is your wish, we would trust you with our mother."

The Nakamuras left, but Ginjiro stood in a daze. He had just been awarded the heavens and the earth. What more could he ask?

Then he quickly sobered. Having the permission of her sons was a gift. But he had yet to gain the assent of the woman herself.

Chapter Thirteen

Hanako knelt on the floor of the hut. With shaking hands she opened the box. It had been years since she had looked inside, but she knew every item in it. It was the box of memories, the mementos of her dear mother. After this day, she would no longer live here in this hut, the only home she could remember. Today was her wedding day.

When she had married Kenji, it had been a hurried affair. Her father had lost her in a card game, and Kenji had been eager to collect his winnings. There had been no preparation, no new kimono, no celebration. This marriage was so different. By mutual choice, she was marrying a samurai, a respected member of the community. Instead of being repayment of a debt, she was a true bride.

Her gown was a simple one, rather than a traditional hooded, white wedding kimono, but it was far nicer than any she had ever worn. Hiro had insisted on buying it for her. She couldn't understand the necessity of purchasing such finery, but had finally relented when Nakamura-san took her aside to give her some advice.

"As Hiro's wife, you will need to present an image of importance and dignity. You must dress accordingly. It would not do for you to appear at a special occasion like your wedding in the same clothes you wear every day," the older woman had told her.

Now, Hanako raised the tiny clasp on the wooden box and lifted the lid. There they were—her mother's finery. One remaining china teacup, two elegant lacquered combs, a silk fan, and a silk purse. She lifted one of the combs out of the box and held it gently. Faded silk ribbons cascaded from it. Hanako closed her eyes and tried desperately to remember what her mother might have looked like wearing it. A vague image of a gentle woman with a kind face floated in her mind, but it was her voice she remembered most.

"Hanako-san?"

Could it be? Had her mother come back to her on this important day?

"Hanako, I thought you might need some help. I hope I'm not intruding."

Hanako opened her eyes. Reiko Nakamura stood at the doorway. Quickly, she rose to greet her neighbor.

"Nakamura-san, thank you so much for coming. I—I don't know how to put this on." She held out the comb. "And I've never worn a silk kimono, so I don't know how to tie the *obi*. Could you help me?"

Reiko came to her and reached for the comb. "This is very lovely. Was it your mother's?"

"Yes, I think so. I found it a long time ago. It was in this box." She stooped to pick up the case. "I would like to use the combs and her other things today. Do you think they would look all right?"

****

Reiko's heart rejoiced at Hanako's request. She loved her

sons, but would have cherished a daughter. The last few months had been a joy for her, meeting with Hanako, instructing her in the etiquette of polite society. There had been lessons on proper grammar, on walking while wearing wooden *geta*, and serving tea as a hostess rather than a servant.

She remembered her own wedding, so long ago. It had been a clandestine affair, as she had married a man her father deemed beneath her. She had taken only the clothes on her back, and a few cherished mementos. But there had been love. Looking at Hanako now, she saw love there, and knew this union would be blessed. Now, she lifted the delicate comb from Hanako's hand.

"Your mother would be so pleased to see you wear these today. They will be perfect with your new kimono." She looked up at Hanako, her eyes wet.

"I would be delighted to help you get dressed."

The white silk was decorated with cranes flying gracefully over a field of lavender. *How appropriate.* Cranes were the symbol of long life and prosperity. Lavender stood for faithfulness. Hiro and Hanako would have a long and prosperous life together.

****

"You are certain about this?" Hiro spoke over his shoulder as they mounted the steps to the temple. She had agreed to the marriage, but now she seemed to have second thoughts. Walking three steps behind him, she looked so pale, so fragile, and her hands shook in her long kimono sleeves.

"I am certain," she assured him, though the tremor in her voice told him she was not.

The gown was new, his wedding gift to her. She was not dressed in traditional wedding finery, but rather in a lovely silk gown that could be worn in any formal setting. Even this gesture had been met with resistance. What was the sense in spending good money on silk, when the garment would probably be worn only once? A good, serviceable cotton gown would be much more practical. Hiro had insisted, assuring her the cost provided no hardship for him. He had appealed to the Widow Nakamura for help. Finally, Hanako had relented, muttering about all the animals that she could have purchased for the price of the silk.

Instead of the traditional wig, she had swept her hair up in a simple hairstyle, held in place with a pair of combs. The coral-inlaid combs looked expensive, but lovely in their simplicity. The women he knew in his other life would have preferred ornate hairdos, but on Hanako's shining hair the combs were perfect. She carried a fan and a tiny silk purse he had not seen before. He wondered where she had obtained such lovely trinkets.

Hiro smiled inwardly as they made their way into the temple. His sensible little flower, he thought. She had not viewed this marriage as a means to financial gain, but rather as a practical arrangement. Merchants in the village were more willing to deal with her when he was along to make the final sale or purchase, even though they knew she was the one who did all the bartering and made the decisions. In addition, she had grudgingly acknowledged his financial resources, as well as his manpower, made it easier for her to get the work done.

He didn't have to remind her that having children would be beneficial for her as well. Sons would mean extra labor, as well as assuring the land would remain in her family. Daughters would be welcome, too. He imagined a tiny version of his Hanako. She would be brave and outspoken like her mother, with intelligence as well as beauty.

With his personal wealth, he could have purchased his own land and hired workers to do most of the manual labor, but it would not have given him the satisfaction he had here. Hanako had taught him well, but he would not want to undertake his own agricultural venture without her. She had become so much more than his mentor.

Since neither of them had any family, The Nakamura family sat on Hanako's side, and Ginjiro and the other samurai sat on Hiro's side. The guests sat along the sides of the temple, facing each other.

Once everyone took their places, the priest, attended by two shrine maidens, entered. The priest began the cleansing ritual by waving his *onusa*, a pole with white paper streamers cascading from the top. The priest chanted, using an ancient dialect. Even though he had studied with Shinto priests, Hiro didn't understand all the words. Still, he took comfort in the solemn tradition. He stole a look at his bride. She knelt beside him, perfectly still, though he noticed her eyes moved constantly, taking things in. She was frightened. Her hands shook, and her breaths were shallow and rapid. *Has she ever attended a Shinto ceremony? Perhaps not.* From what he had heard of her previous marriage, it probably hadn't been performed in the temple. Would she know what to do when it came time for the tea ceremony?

Careful to keep his face forward, he glanced to his left toward the Nakamuras. Reiko sat with her sons, a calm, serene expression on her face. She had spent a lot of time with Hanako lately. Hopefully she would have told her what to expect.

He wanted to tell Hanako not to worry. To promise her he would take care of her and cherish her always. To reassure her that they would work together to make their dreams come true. To show how very much he desired her. Taking care not to move his head any more than necessary, turned his face and saw his bride looking up at him. Their gazes met, and a wealth of communication passed between them.

****

Hanako felt ready to bolt. *What have I done? Is it too late to change my mind?* Nakamura-san had spent hours coaching her on the rituals for the ceremony. But the priest's chants held no meaning for her, and she couldn't remember what she was supposed to do next.

She was about to marry the most highly regarded man in the village. People would expect her to act with decorum. What an impossible task for a simple farm girl! She looked up, ready to beg Hiro to end the ceremony. Their eyes met and all thought vanished from her mind. His gaze conveyed a message, as clearly as if he had spoken the words. *Don't worry. Everything will be all right.* There was something more. A promise of wonderful things to come. She immediately felt calming warmth coursing through her veins, and she took a deep breath. She could do this.

It was time for the ritual known as *San-San-Kudo.* Three cups were stacked on a pedestal. The top cup, the smallest, represented heaven, the middle one, slightly larger, represented earth, and the bottom, the largest one, represented humankind. The shrine maiden poured *sake* into the top cup and presented it to Hiro so he could sip from it three times. He bowed and returned it. The shrine maiden then passed the cup to Hanako so she too could sip from it three times. The same procedure was done with the second cup, and then the third. Three sips from each of three cups. Since three was a lucky number, three times three represented extra good luck for them.

****

Hanako felt a moment of panic as they descended the wide staircase of the temple. She was now legally bound to the tall, handsome man who had mysteriously swept into her life only a few months ago. There had been no go-between, no long engagement. Nakamura-san's investigators had assured her Hiro was indeed from a well-respected samurai family in Tokyo. Though her mother was from an equally high-born family, she and Hiro were raised in different worlds, and he was much more highly educated than she.

Aside from financial security, she now had a partner with whom she could share her burdens and dreams for the farm. He had been a willing and hard worker in the fields, and an eager student in what he called agriculture and animal science. She had been amazed at the speed with which he had assimilated his knowledge.

He'd told her he wanted sons to continue his family dynasty. Her cheeks burned with the anticipation of creating those sons. Kenji had been a disinterested husband and lover, concerned only with his writing. He had come to her home only because it was a place to live, away from the demands of landlords and his many debtors.

A gentle touch at her elbow reminded her that life with this husband would be altogether different. If nothing else, Hiro was much more pleasing to the eye. He was strong and used to hard work, to which Kenji had had a distinct aversion. Hiro was also willing to listen. He would ask questions and pay attention to her answers; this alone was extraordinary. She would be the envy of all the women in the village. Whenever they came into town to sell their crops or make purchases, his tall, graceful form drew stares of interest. A few women even tossed aside convention enough to initiate conversations with him. He always answered them politely, but stayed with her as they completed their errands.

She turned toward her wagon to begin their trip back to the farm, but Hiro put his hand on her back and turned her in the opposite direction. A new wagon, freshly painted and piled high with supplies, blocked their path. Attached to it was a magnificent horse, finer than she had ever seen. She waited for her husband to lead her around it, but instead he led her to the side of it.

"Since we are combining our fortunes, we will undoubtedly increase our profit. I felt it was necessary to purchase a cart large enough to transport our wares to the market. And of course, with a healthy horse to pull it, we will get our goods to the market more quickly." He paused briefly before adding, "And I thought you might enjoy a ride home."

Hanako blinked her eyes rapidly to stem the tears of joy that threatened to spill out. Never had she imagined such compassion! She bowed low to hide her face. "I thank you, my husband, for anticipating my needs. I trust that your prophecy concerning our profit will come true." She began to part the skirt of her kimono so that she could step up into the cart, but found herself airborne as her new husband lifted her up into the seat. She turned before sitting, wanting to avoid catching her silk gown on a stray sliver, and gasped at seeing the thick cushion, upholstered with a rich brocade fabric. Life would certainly be different from now on.

She sat demurely on the edge of the seat, leaving plenty of room for Hiro. He scrambled up to the bench, picked up the reins and slapped them to begin the ride. Knowing that the locals were watching, she sat up straight. For once, she could be proud of the sight she made. So many times, she had retrieved her father and husband from the tavern nearby. The proprietor had helped her to load them into her old cart. What a spectacle she had made then. The rickety cart had not been large enough to completely contain her father's limp body, and the aging mule, barely able to move its burden, plodded so slowly through the streets it would have been faster to walk rather than ride.

Now, she rode proudly next to a fine gentleman, seated with dignity in a new carriage. She wore a gown finer than any she had ever hoped to own. For this privilege, she would have followed Hiro anywhere, but the knowledge that she was entering her new marriage filled her with anticipation.

The ride back to the farm was smooth and uneventful, but Hanako barely remembered any of it. She spent the entire journey thinking about how different her life would be.

The horse would make the field work much more efficient. The cow she had purchased earlier could now graze peacefully, producing milk.

As they came closer to the home she would share with Hiro, she gasped and cried out in excitement. In the pasture, where before a lone cow grazed, a bull and two goats now shared the space. Her ecstatic reaction melted into confusion. *Where had these animals come from?*

"The new animals are a wedding gift from some of the merchants in the village," he told her.

"A wedding gift? Why would anyone give us such extravagant gifts?"

"I have assured them they would receive our business once our resources are combined," he explained.

He drove the cart up to the house, climbed down, and walked around to assist her out. She went inside as he took care of the horse and cart.

Up until now, she had only allowed herself to enter the kitchen and dining area. But now this was her home. With tentative steps, she explored the rest of the house. New *tatami* floors covered every surface. No more hard, wooden floors. She slid open the screens to the living area and gasped.

She had never dreamed she would live in a home like this. Beautiful lacquered tables, plush silk floor pillows, and lovely painted screens graced one room. She went through, marveling at Hiro's good taste. There were several more rooms, each with large closets storing thick futons and bedding. This must be where the new samurai had stayed. She wondered where they were tonight. Should she begin preparing a meal for them?

"Do you find everything to your liking?" Hiro's voice startled her.

"Oh! Everything is so wonderful! The rooms are so large! And there are so many!"

"We will need rooms for our children to grow."

****

Hanako's quick intake of breath and heightened color told Hiro she had not forgotten one of the reasons for their marriage. While he looked forward to being a father, he was even more eager to begin his life as a husband. Slowly, he approached her. She lifted her lashes until their eyes met and held. Now that the time for consummating their marriage was at hand, he was thankful for her reluctance to don the full traditional wedding costume. The many layers of clothing would take so much longer to remove, and right now he was burning with anticipation.

Rather than a large, ornate wig and head covering, her hair had been arranged in a simple knot at the nape of her neck and held in place with the pair of inlaid combs. He reached over to pull them out, wondering if they been a gift from her first husband. But then he chided himself for resorting to jealous thoughts on his wedding day. No matter what had happened between this woman and Kenji, she was his now. The combs came away, and he watched her thick raven tresses tumble down, covering her like a waist-length cape.

The silk kimono was held in place by a brocade *obi*, tied in a knot at her back. Again, he was grateful for his wife's simple style. She had foregone many of the traditional ornaments and ties that usually adorned the *obi*. Never taking his eyes from hers, he reached behind her and pulled down on the ends of the sash, releasing the ends and letting the front panels of her kimono gape open. In a moment, the white and lavender silk lay in a pool at her feet. A layer of cotton remained, and Hiro felt like a child, opening a specially wrapped gift. The undergarment was tied with a plain cotton rope, and this presented a greater challenge. Hiro was ready to tear the garment apart when the knot finally unraveled, and the fabric floated to the floor.

He had often imagined her like this, late at night, as he tried to sleep knowing she was only a short walk away. His mind's eye had constructed the creaminess of her skin, the smooth curve of her body, the warmth of her smile. But the vision before him surpassed all of his dreams. This woman had been created especially for him, and he alone would have the right to cherish her from now to eternity. He would not ever take this right for granted.

Moments passed as he simply drank in the sight of her. She stared back, her lips curved upward in a secret smile. Finally, raw need overcame the awe, and he reached for her.

Chapter Fourteen

Hiro closed the door to the barn, satisfied the animals were settled in for the night. He trudged back to the house, shivering in the cold. Having spent most of his life in the south, he wasn't used to the harsh northern winter. It was no wonder Hanako bundled up in several layers of clothing before going outside.

But now that the day's chores were done, he could relax in the warmth of his home. And that warmth now included a lovely wife who waited for him. He smiled to himself. Married life suited him well.

He had been surprised at the amount of work to be done even when there were no crops in the field. The animals had to be fed and tended to, and there was much preparation for the coming year. Hanako had taught him how to make rope from rice straw, and the Nakamura brothers had taught him how to do some simple woodworking. He took great pride in making things with his hands.

A visit to the bookshop ensured he had plenty to read, and thanks to a successful harvest, there was plenty of food.

He had everything he needed.

The books he chose were about farming, and more than half of them were about flowers. Hanako's gardens had intrigued him. She grew a great variety of flowers, some blossoming early in the summer, others later on. He wanted to know more about them. Something about the beauty of a single blossom spoke to him. He had learned a little bit about *hanakotoba*, the language of flowers. Next year, he vowed, he would plant a garden with a wonderful message. He could hardly wait.

He found Hanako kneeling by the light of the fire, weaving strands of rope into a type of net. The woman was always busy doing something. She wouldn't know how to rest. But at least she wasn't as weary as when he had first met her. She looked healthier, more alive. She could sit down each night to a nutritious meal. And she didn't have the burden of heavy work. She would never know that kind of hardship ever again, he vowed.

"What are you making?" he asked.

She smiled up at him. "It's something to help you get through the snow. I'll have one of these done in a few minutes, and then I'll show you."

She worked quickly, her hands deftly tying knots in the ropes. Suddenly they stopped, and she looked up at him.

"Would you like me to get you some tea?"

Hiro laughed. "I am perfectly capable of getting my own tea, thank you. But right now I want to watch you. I want to see how this rope of yours is going to help me walk through the snow."

She grinned impishly at him. "Surely you have read about these in one of your many books!"

"Perhaps I have. But I must have forgotten. Or maybe you don't have enough of it finished so I can tell what you are making."

She made a face at him but continued her weaving. She

had already bent two narrow bamboo stalks into circles and tied the ends together with leather string. These were soaking in a tub of water. After she was done with the weaving, she took the circles out of the water and fastened one net inside each and attached more strands. They looked like large spider webs.

She held them out to him. "All finished." she exclaimed.

Hiro took one and inspected it. "I've never seen anything like this," he admitted. "What is it?"

"These are *kanjiki*—snowshoes," she explained. "When the snow gets deeper, it's difficult to walk through it. These will help you to walk on top of it."

Hiro frowned at the simple devices. "Are you sure these would hold a man of my height and weight on top of the snow?"

"Well, you would sink a little, of course, but not as deeply as you would without them. I'm going to make a pair for myself, and we'll use them when we do our chores tomorrow."

"Tomorrow?"

"Yes, we're going to get lots of snow tonight. Tomorrow when the sun comes up, it will be deep, so we'll need these to get to the barn."

"How do you know that?"

"I read the sky."

"How—"

"My father taught me," she told him simply.

Hiro closed his mouth. There were some things one could not learn through books.

****

The next night, Hiro read with light from a lantern. Hanako had gone to bed early, but he wanted to absorb all the news from Tokyo he could find. A recently arrived ex-samurai had brought an issue of a new publication from Yokohama called the *Daily News* and had given it to Hiro. The newcomer had told Hiro that a new issue of this publication came out every day, filled with domestic as well as foreign news. This was a new development. In the past, large newspapers like this were owned by foreigners and reflected European concerns. He read, fascinated by the news of the new government. It seemed Emperor Meiji was determined to make Japan an international power and embraced the knowledge and skills of the Western nations. Hiro nodded in approval.

Turning the page, Hiro's eyes suddenly zeroed in on the one name that made his blood run cold. *Hideyori Kato*. He sat up and pulled the paper close. Was the man on his way north? Would the former *daimyo* and his followers pose the next threat to this village?

Hiro quickly scanned the article. Apparently Kato-san had tried to form an alliance with other former *daimyo*, working toward the goal of overthrowing the Meiji government and restoring the former feudal system. But the others had soon seen the futility of his cause and abandoned him. Now, the Imperial Palace had received word of his plans and was looking for him, intending to charge him with treason. But he had disappeared.

Kato-san was now an outlaw, a refugee. Where had he gone? Was he alone, or was he leading a dangerous band of *ronin*? Was he the person the local *ronin* had been awaiting? He was an evil man. Until there was no doubt that he was eliminated, the militia had to keep going for the protection of the villagers.

The village now counted six former samurai among their residents, but they were spread out. Watanabe-san now lived west of the village on land the Nakamuras had provided, learning the farming trade with the brothers. The new samurai, Yoshimori-san, lived with a farmer north of the village. Fukazawa and Kobayashi stayed in the village. The villagers embraced all the newcomers heartily, bringing them gifts of food and other tokens of their appreciation.

With nightfall coming earlier in the winter, evening fighting drills stopped. Hiro convinced the men to stay fit by exercising.

"You must work to keep your reflexes and your muscles strong," he insisted. He proposed a compromise. Instead of the outdoor drills, he invited the men to one of the large open rooms inside his home to practice the art of *kendo*. Using long wooden sticks, he taught the basic sword techniques. Most of them would come once or twice a week, but some, like the Nakamura brothers, came more often. Hiro was impressed at the dedication of these brothers. Even the youngest, Yoshiro, worked with a fierce determination.

Since travel was often difficult in the harsh winter weather, Watanabe, Yoshimori, and the two soldiers in the village held their own sessions at their locations. People were encouraged to go to one of them whenever they could.

Families were reminded to keep their flares in a convenient place so they could be used at the first sight of any rogue soldiers. The Nakamura family provided extra flares for families living farther away from the village.

Hiro just prayed any warning would come soon enough.

****

When he wasn't teaching villagers to fight or working on the farm, Hiro studied. Agriculture was a fascinating science. It was so amazing, how something as tiny as a seed could grow into a plant, providing food and nourishment for people and animals. On a visit to Sapporo, he had found an interesting book on flowers. He told Hanako about an idea for growing some of the plants he read about.

"Why would you want to do that?" Hanako asked,

looking up from her sewing. Her distraction caused her to prick her finger, and a red stain grew on the white fabric. She sighed. The Widow Nakamura had just shown her how to make these pretty stitches, and she was eager to decorate her new home with things she had made herself. If the stain didn't wash off, she would have to start her project over.

Hiro, reading by the light of another lamp, waved a hand at the book he read.

"It says here the soil in this part of the island is good for growing flowers. I'd like to expand the flower garden and try out several different kinds."

"Flowers are pretty, but you can't eat them."

"Some flowers can be eaten. But I want to try some of these techniques. There is an article here about rotating crops. Certain kinds of plants actually put minerals back in the soil, so the earth doesn't get worn out from having the same plants grown year after year. And it says here that certain flowers can help your vegetables by keeping pests away. I'd like to try that out here." He looked up and gazed directly into her eyes. "If it's all right with you."

She opened her mouth to remind him the land was legally his now, but found she was intrigued by his choice of words. He was still giving her the right to object if she had misgivings about his plan. The thought filled her with happiness.

She nodded her assent. "It sounds reasonable to try out this procedure on a small scale. Tell me more about it."

Listening to her husband's animated voice, she marveled at the difference a year had made. Last winter, she had been huddled alone in her tiny hut, struggling to keep warm. Now, her immediate concerns were getting her stitches even, and wondering how to keep her husband from digging up her entire vegetable farm to plant flowers.

Six months ago, she had been afraid of the changes marriage would bring. Now she wondered why she had ever hesitated.

Chapter Fifteen

Spring finally arrived, and the farm bustled with activity. This year, many more varieties of vegetables were sown, and as Hiro suggested, several plots were dedicated to flowers. Near the house, Hiro had planted a few rose bushes. By mutual accord, Hanako tended the bushes on one side, and Hiro used his book-based knowledge to tend to the plants on the other side. It became a contest to see which plants would produce the biggest and healthiest flowers.

He carefully pruned the rose bush, unsuccessfully avoiding the sharp thorns. The new journal had recommended that he trim the plant from the bottom up. His hands and arms bled, but he was determined his bushes would surpass his wife's. It was research over experience. Surely the experts would know more than even his wife knew.

The pruned branches held some lovely blossoms, and he placed them into a bowl of water. It would be a shame to let the flowers die with the discarded stems. Perhaps Hanako would enjoy them.

Another sharp point pierced his skin. He had to stop

daydreaming while working on these vicious plants! The drops of blood fell on some of the white blossoms in the bowl, coloring them with a ribbon of red. *What a beautiful pattern*, he thought. Recently, he'd read an article about breeding flowers so the colors would be combined. Perhaps that would be a project for the future.

He couldn't wait to talk to Hanako tonight. A traveling merchant had seen the flower beds from the road that afternoon and had stopped to ask Hiro to sell him several bunches of an assortment of flowers to resell at the market. He had never thought about profiting from the plants; they had simply been a source of pleasure to him. The flowerbeds had grown as he discovered more and more varieties of beautiful fragrant blossoms, until the house was surrounded by a profusion of color and greenery. He had never before felt the peace he found walking through his garden. But the price offered had been so substantial, Hiro had sold the flowers to him. The merchant had then promised to return the following week for more.

Hiro bristled with excitement, wanting to share the good news with Hanako. Brimming with energy, he began preparations for the evening meal, wanting to talk with her as soon as she came in. Shadows appeared and lengthened, and worry replaced the excitement. Had she had encountered some difficulty in the field? He decided to look for her.

Fortunately, the crops Hanako cultivated were the short variety. It shouldn't be hard to locate her. And since her farm was relatively small, he didn't have far to go. But looking out over the fields of cucumbers, radishes, and beans, he couldn't make out her familiar form. His worry increased as he ran through each section, calling her name. Finally, at the end of a row of bean plants, he saw a blue heap among the green leaves. She had donned a new blue *yukata* that morning, complaining the older one she usually wore in the fields needed mending. Hiro hurried through the patch, his heart lodging more firmly in his throat with each step. Carefully, he lifted her head and shoulders as he pleaded with her to open her eyes. Her lids fluttered open then softly closed as she moaned.

He thanked the gods she was still breathing as he lifted her gently and hurried back to their home. His powerful legs moved with all the speed he could muster, but they weren't fast enough to suit him. He screamed to Ginjiro for help and was relieved to see his friend appear in the doorway of his own hut.

Ginjiro assessed the situation quickly and ran to the house where he rolled out the *futon*. Hiro settled her down gently, and bathed her face with some cool water. Finally, her brown eyes opened, and she stared at him with the fuzziness of confusion. Frantic with worry, he forced her to sip some of the water.

Somehow in his distress, he thought to ask Ginjiro to run to the Widow Nakamura's home. Hopefully, she would know what to do for her.

Reiko arrived quickly and asked to speak to Hanako privately. Although Hiro didn't want to let Hanako out of his sight, he grudgingly left the room. He paced, nearly wearing a path in the *tatami* floor. He wanted answers, and they were excruciatingly slow in coming. Hiro was about to stomp in frustration when Reiko finally came out. He met her with a barrage of questions, but she stared at him intently, effectively silencing him. She then uttered the few words that made Hiro's world spin.

"Your wife is with child."

****

Hanako swept her already clean floor for the third time that day. She wiped her spotless table and straightened the books on Hiro's shelf. After she had fainted in the field, Hiro had hired several local boys to assist in the fields. She'd wanted to supervise, but he would only allow her to do so in the cool mornings and late in the afternoons. A chair had been set out for her at the edge of whatever field was being worked. She'd felt ridiculous sitting there doing nothing. Now and then, she would sneak out of her chair to do some work herself, but always Hiro would come over from his flower beds to urge her back to her seat or to take her back to the hut for a rest.

She had to admit the mid-afternoon naps were nice. Never had she imagined that she would be able to lie down in the middle of the day. But as her body changed, her energy waned quickly, and she argued less when Hiro brought her back to the house.

Today, rather than nap in the house, she decided to go outdoors and relax by the stream. Fishing net in hand, she sat on the bank. Hiro had already checked on her twice, making sure she sat in the shade and assuring himself that she sat securely on a flat rock on the creek side. The water tumbled over a shallow area, and Hanako had only to reach out her net and scoop the carp as they swam past. But the creek was relatively quiet today, and Hanako had to wait. A soft footfall behind her diverted her attention. Ginjiro stood behind her, a respectful distance away.

"Has my husband sent you as my keeper?"

"Tanaka-san worries about you and the child."

"I've fished here over half of my life. Nothing will happen to me."

Ginjiro said nothing for a moment. Hanako squirmed under his scrutiny. "Must you stay here? I know what I'm doing!"

He simply smiled. "Yes, you do. As do I."

"You're doing nothing, except to annoy me and frighten away the fish!"

He shook his head. "No, my lady. I am providing peace

of mind for a friend."

"Peace of mind?"

"Yes. Tanaka-san knows the possibility of danger is small, but he knows also the unexpected can happen. If I am nearby, he will not worry that the effect of the unexpected will be great." He hesitated before adding, "Please help him to cope. If he could help you carry this child, he would gladly do it. But the gods have decreed only a woman can do this. All he can do is to make sure you are safe."

Hanako digested this point of view as she continued to wait for the fish to cross her vantage point. The afternoon's bounty was small, and she wasn't entirely sure whether it was because the fish were absent, or because she was too preoccupied to notice when they went by.

The next day, Ginjiro continued to act as a silent sentry whenever she ventured from the house. She spent hours grooming the horse, feeding the chickens, and doing other light chores, always aware of his presence. But now, having a new understanding of Hiro's reasoning, she came to accept it.

Hiro had summoned a prominent physician from Sapporo to come and examine her, demanding that she have only the best care. She had an extra-soft futon on which to rest and a great assortment of the freshest food to eat. She was used to eating her own homegrown vegetables and fish caught from the nearby stream, but now she sampled delicacies brought in from across the island, shellfish and ocean fish full of protein and nutrients to insure a healthy son.

Hiro had suggested they hire someone to come and cook for them, but Hanako had adamantly opposed the idea. "I need something to do besides simply growing larger and larger with our child," she'd declared. "You haven't complained about my cooking before. If you want me to eat this special food, I will do so, but you must let me prepare it."

But even cooking a large meal each evening didn't provide enough to keep her busy all day. Having worked so hard all her life, she was restless and bored with the inactivity. She wondered if her own mother had continued to work in the fields right up to the moment of childbirth, like many other women in the area. How she wished she had a mother to confide in, or even an aunt or grandmother!

She had complained about her boredom to Reiko during her last visit. The kindly neighbor had simply nodded sympathetically but offered no words of encouragement or advice. Hanako wondered if Reiko thought her ungrateful or eccentric. Most women would probably not complain of having too much time. She needed to learn patience.

The next day, Reiko returned with a bundle tied in a colorful silk scarf. Opening it, she produced two sets of knitting needles and several balls of yarn. "When I was with child, I found comfort in knitting. It kept my hands and mind busy while allowing the rest of my body to rest. If you like, I will show you how to make a small blanket for your child."

Hanako was overjoyed at the prospect of learning to knit something for the baby. Growing up, she had been envious of other girls who wore scarves and sweaters knit by their mothers or grandmothers. Having neither, she had endured the harsh winters without the warmth of those articles. Her child would always be warm, she vowed. She set about learning the skill with determination.

Reiko was a patient teacher, gently guiding Hanako's hands, taking out rows of uneven and missed stitches. All the while, she kept up a flow of conversation, drawing out all of Hanako's questions and fears, offering reassurance and advice. Hiro's reaction to her pregnancy was a topic they discussed more than once.

"I don't understand why he refuses to let me go to the north field. The cabbages are probably wilting from the sun!"

"You have other workers who are caring for those crops."

"But the work will go faster if I join them."

"If the plants can wilt from too much sunshine, so can

you. Didn't your husband find you lying in the field after you had worked too hard?"

She was forced to admit that her fainting incident had occurred after a long day in the sunshine. "I could go only in the morning."

Reiko laid a hand on hers and waited for Hanako to look into her eyes. "Child, be thankful your husband has your health and comfort uppermost in his mind. I have seen women lose their children because they weren't able to rest and take nourishment when they needed it most. Let him take care of you while you keep your child safe in your womb."

Ashamed of her ungratefulness, Hanako nodded and returned to her knitting.

Reiko returned often, bringing more yarn and maternal comfort. Hanako looked forward to each visit. Once the blanket was finished, Reiko taught Hanako some fancier stitches. At first the needles seemed to have a mind of their own, but with practice the rows were almost as even as Reiko's. If the child was a girl, she would have some pretty clothes. She thought of her own clothing as a child—they had been castoffs given to her by sympathetic townspeople. Until she had married Hiro, she had never worn anything new, or what could be called pretty. This child would indeed be fortunate.

As a result of Reiko's visits, the months of Hanako's pregnancy flowed much faster. The baby now had clothing and lovely new bedding, and, thanks to another successful harvest, would eat good, nutritious meals.

Chapter Sixteen

Hiro was tending the plants closest to his home one morning when Reiko arrived. She greeted him politely, but instead of going inside, she watched him work.

"Is there something I can do for you, Nakamura-san?" he asked

"Would you allow me to bring some of these beautiful blossoms inside? I believe they would add loveliness to the inside of your home as well as the outside."

Memories of Hiro's boyhood home flooded him. His mother, Michiko Tanaka, had added elegance to each room of her home with her beautiful floral arrangements. He remembered how he had loved watching his mother spend time on each arrangement, placing each stem in a specific position in relationship to the rest. She was a master at *ikebana,* the art of flower arranging.

"Nakamura-san, I would welcome some fine floral arrangements. I am not certain my wife ever learned the art of *ikebana.*"

"I thought not. The poor girl has not had the benefit of

having a woman guide her. Nor has she had the luxury of time for learning the arts of a gentlewoman. I would be happy to instruct her—if she so wishes."

Hiro bowed low to the wise woman. "You have my deepest gratitude for being here for her now. When she sees what you do with the flowers, I believe she will wish to learn from you, as she has enjoyed your instruction in knitting and embroidery. You are welcome to take whatever you wish from the garden."

****

Reiko watched her pupil's hands as they arranged the roses in the clay pot. It was a shame such young hands looked as rough as they did. The hard work Hanako had been forced to endure added ten years to her skin. So often she had ridden by, watching this young woman toil in the fields alone, providing the only support for her alcoholic father and lazy husband. Even Reiko's servants were not expected to work so hard. It was only right that Hanako, as the owner of these fields, could finally pursue more lady-like activities, sheltered from the cruel sun.

"Hanako-san," she began, "you must have cut yourself on the thorns. I have some cream that will help soothe those cuts, and it will make your skin soft. I have used it for many years when my hands felt rough and dry."

Hanako glanced up, a puzzled expression on her face. Reiko held her breath as the younger woman studied her own hands, and then Reiko's. Working on the farm, Hanako was probably accustomed to having cuts on her hands. Hopefully she hadn't been insulted by the suggestion of using hand cream.

"Nakamura-san, I would be honored if you would show me how to care for my hands. I have never known about this cream. Do you use it on your face, too?"

Reiko smiled. The girl was very perceptive. "I will bring some of my special lotions tomorrow. There are some things you can prepare from the plants in your fields, but others are purchased in the city. I'm sure your husband can arrange to get them."

****

Over the next several months, Hanako and Hiro shared the joy of the pregnancy together. Hiro continued his vigilant efforts to keep Hanako from working too hard. The gardens flourished and again brought in a healthy profit. Hanako was forced to acknowledge Hiro's flower "hobby" brought in nearly as much as her vegetables.

Nothing excited Hiro more than to feel his son move within Hanako's belly. In the evenings, he massaged her swollen feet and aching back. He made her tea and bought special sweets and gifts to cheer her when she despaired at her increasing size. And at night, he cradled her in his arms as if to protect her and the child they had created. Hanako had never felt more cherished.

The New Year brought hope and optimism for the future. There had been no reports about the *ronin* for months. It was the ninth year of the emperor Meiji's reign, the year the Western world called 1876.

The entire house shone. Walls had been washed, floors swept, and every corner thoroughly cleaned. Of course, Hanako had not been allowed to do any of the heavy cleaning herself. She had directed the activities, performed by women brought in from the village who were grateful for the work. Bowls of hot rice were mixed with vinegar for sushi, and special prayers were said for the spirits of deceased relatives. Decorative lanterns hung from the ceiling, and everyone prepared to visit the temple.

She and Hiro walked through the streets, enjoying the

sights and greeting the other villagers. Progress was relatively slow, as Hanako was now growing larger, and walking was more of a chore than she had ever remembered. As they made their way through the streets, they were recognized and greeted happily. Hiro continued to be held in esteem as a local leader, even though he refused to hold an official office.

Several young boys danced around with strings of firecrackers. They threw the noisemakers about, shouting greetings as they went. The boys' antics soon turned into a contest to see who could throw his firecrackers higher, but one errant missile landed on the dried grass of a roof. The grass immediately burst into flames.

A shout of alarm spread through the crowd.

Merrymakers abandoned their celebration to spring into action. Hiro pushed Hanako to a bench, ordering her to stay away from the danger. His deep, resonant voice, developed through years of military training, could be heard cutting through the chaos as he organized the volunteers into a line, passing buckets of water from a well to the blaze. Hanako was torn between jumping into the fray and abiding by her husband's wishes to protect the baby.

Thankfully, the fire was contained quickly, though there was much damage to the structure. Everyone breathed a sigh of relief, when a small, weakened voice was heard coming from the blackened structure. A woman screamed from the back of the crowd.

"Mother! My mother is inside!"

Hiro, standing near the doorway, turned and dashed back into the building. Heavy smoke and the darkness of the night made it difficult for him to navigate through the rooms, but he continued to plunge through. He called out to the woman, begging her to help him find her. Following the sound of her voice, he found her huddled in a corner. A beam had fallen on her leg, trapping her on her *ofuton*.

Gathering all his strength, he raised the beam and moved

it aside. Then he lifted her and turned to carry her to safety. He had to rely on his memory to find his way back through the blinding smoke. His exertion from moving the beam and carrying the woman had his lungs burning from the smoke. He quickened his steps, making a few wrong turns before finally locating the doorway.

He had nearly reached the threshold when he heard the deadly sound of cracking wood. Frantically, he sprinted toward the opening and thought he had succeeded, when a beam fell and hit him solidly across the shoulders. The impact had him falling forward with the woman sprawled in front of him. Through the smoke, he saw someone else taking her from him before his world went black.

****

Hanako bathed her husband's face with cool water and sat back on the cushion next to his *ofuton*. It had been three days since the fire, and he had yet to open his eyes.

The physician had come each day, treating his wounds and giving her instructions for his care. His grave expression told Hanako the extent of Hiro's injuries was great, and she feared her happiness with him was at an end. When she wasn't sitting by his side, she would light incense and offer prayers, earnestly petitioning the gods for his recovery.

Ginjiro spent part of each evening with Hiro. After spending the day tending the animals, he would come and encourage Hanako to rest and eat while he sat with his friend. Reiko came during the day and served the food people brought. Her sons often came with her and took care of chores around the farm. Neighbors and people from the village came as well, bearing food and wishes for Hiro's recovery.

The daughter of the woman Hiro had saved came as well. "My mother was weary of the celebrations and had just gone home to rest," she told Hanako. "If your husband had not risked his life, she would have suffered much more than a broken leg."

Although she appreciated all the support, Hanako despaired of ever looking into her husband's eyes again. Surrounded by the succulent dishes brought by the village women, she found it difficult to eat. Household duties were ignored, and the flower arrangements she had so painstakingly created wilted. Reiko finally convinced her to take care of herself, to consider the child she carried.

"You are doing all you can for your husband. When he awakens, he will want to see a cheerful home, preparing for a healthy baby. Surely you do not wish to endanger your child by not feeding him."

Hanako laid a hand on her rounded belly. Through the turmoil, she had forgotten about the plans she and Hiro had made to prepare for the baby. *Would Hiro ever hold their child?* She shook the thought away. She had to remain optimistic.

"Nakamura-san, you are so wise. I must think of our child. He will arrive in a few more weeks, and will need some more clothing."

"I will help you. But first you must eat."

A week later, Hanako sat near the window, counting stitches on the tiny sweater Reiko had showed her how to make. Finding an error, she grumbled in frustration and tore out the offending stitches.

"What has upset my little flower?"

The voice was raspy and soft in volume, but at the first syllable, the knitting fell to the floor. Hanako threw herself into her husband's arms and sobbed. "You have returned to me!" she cried.

A gentle hand ran up and down her spine. "I did not realize I had left," he said. "I was dreaming of you and our child. I saw you with him in the field, teaching him about the plants you grow. You were so happy. And then you found some of your plants had not grown as they should. No matter what you did, the plants continued to wilt and die. I tried to call out to you, to help you, but my voice would not come. I tried again and again and realized my throat was dry, and I needed a drink. And that is when I awakened to find you cursing at your yarn."

She sat up, wiping her tears. "I was not cursing at the yarn."

"Perhaps not, but you were definitely letting the yarn know what you thought of it," he teased.

****

Reiko, coming in with a tea tray, found husband and wife talking, wrapped in each other's arms. She saw the look in their eyes and remembered a time when she, too, experienced that magic. Silently, she turned around and left to have tea alone in another room.

Ginjiro nodded to her as he came in from the field.

"How is he?" he inquired.

"He's awake now."

His eyes lit up. "That's wonderful! I must see him." He turned toward the bedroom but stopped when a hand caught his elbow.

"Yamada-san, I think you might want to delay your greeting." Reiko met his inquiring gaze with a serene smile. "He and his wife are getting reacquainted. They need some time alone. Perhaps you would like to have tea with me here in this room until they are finished?"

Ginjiro looked down at the tiny hand still cupping his elbow, then up to the still unlined face of its owner. "I would like that very much."

Chapter Seventeen

It was a cold, wintry night when little Yasahiro Tanaka made his entrance into the world. His ecstatic parents presented him in the temple, where the priests proclaimed the child had indeed chosen a fortunate day to arrive. He would be strong, brave, and trustworthy.

The family spent the snowy days getting acquainted. Hiro went outside to tend to the livestock, and sometimes visitors braved the weather to bring gifts for the village's newest citizen, but most of the time the family stayed cocooned in their home.

Hanako wished the world would stand still and they could stay like this. She had nothing to do but tend her child and husband. But time stops for no one, and the days grew longer, bringing the promise of spring.

One day, soon after the snows melted, an elderly couple came to visit. It was early afternoon, and Hiro had gone out to the field. The baby slept, and Hanako worked on yet another tiny sweater. The knock at the door took her by surprise. She didn't know the couple, but the woman looked vaguely familiar. Her fears faded when she noticed Ginjiro, the ever vigilant guard, watching from his own home.

The man bowed and introduced himself.

"Good afternoon, Tanaka-san," he began. "I am Takahashi. I have come from Sapporo, and I represent the northern branch of the Nanbu clan. We have received word that you have married, and we wish to offer our congratulations."

"You represent my mother's family?" Hanako's eyes widened. "I didn't know any of her relatives—other than a nice lady who told me to call her *Obasan*. I went to visit her with my father, but her husband threw us out when we asked for help."

The man's face turned red, and his wife turned her face away. Hanako took a closer look at woman's cowering posture and remembered.

"You're the lady! It was your house we visited. I remember we walked for days to get there. You were so kind, and gave me a nice cool drink. I loved your beautiful home—it was so peaceful. I kept that memory for years."

"Perhaps we should return the kindness by inviting her into our home." Hiro suddenly appeared behind them. He bowed and introduced himself to the visitors. "Forgive me for not being here when you arrived."

The four went into the house, and Hanako prepared refreshments. Hiro and Takahashi-san sat at the table, and Hanako poured tea for the men then took the woman to an adjoining room. As soon as Hanako slid the door closed, the lady bowed low and spoke in a trembling voice.

"I am so sorry to come to you like this, but my husband insisted. He read about your marriage in the newspaper and had to come and see for himself if you were the same girl who came to visit us so long ago. He was afraid you would influence your husband to retaliate against us for not taking you in when you were struggling so. He insisted we come and make amends."

Hanako's jaw dropped. "Why would he think I would want to retaliate?" she asked when she found her voice.

"Since the samurai are no longer fighting for *daimyos*, many are taking up individual causes. And we were afraid your husband, being a former samurai, would want to punish us for slighting you."

"But that was years ago! And my father owed debts to your husband as well as many other people. He wasn't the only one who refused to help him."

"Perhaps not, but you were family. You were the only child of my cousin. We should have looked out for you at least, for my cousin's sake. Perhaps we could have offered to adopt you."

Hanako thought about the lovely home and wondered how different her life would have been if she had lived there. She would never have gone hungry, and would have had nice clothes to wear. But would she have been happy? Remembering her uncle's temper, she doubted it.

She reached over and squeezed her aunt's hand. "I would have loved living in your home. But I had some good years with my father, and I would have worried about him. He needed me to take care of him."

The woman sighed. "I thought about you often. I wondered what had happened to you. Two years ago, we heard about the raid in this area, and I sent a servant to inquire about you. He told me your fields had been burned and there were many deaths. He couldn't find you." She grasped Hanako's hand tightly. "I am so glad you are safe, and have a good husband to provide for you. We will not ask anything of you, except your forgiveness."

"There is nothing to forgive. I am glad to claim you as my *obasan*."

****

The spring planting began, and soon Hanako, under Hiro's watchful eye, ventured out to the fields to oversee the day workers who would do most of the manual labor. Hanako missed the feel of earth on her hands and the sun on her face, but she appreciated her husband's concern. Besides, she loved having the opportunity to spend time with her son. Strapped to her back, the baby accompanied her to the field, both of them protected by her wide parasol. After inspecting the morning's work, she and the baby would return to the house, and Hanako kept herself busy with housework or knitting while the baby slept.

Evenings were her favorite time. Hiro would return from the field, and eat his dinner. As he did on his first evening, he insisted Hanako sit with him as he ate. They would discuss the day's progress. He still valued her opinion and deferred to her when it came to major decisions, including the hiring of laborers, crops to be planted, and livestock to be purchased. Hanako appreciated having a role in running the farm, even though she wasn't actively working it.

After Hiro finished his meal, it was playtime with little Yasa. Hanako ate while she watched them interact. Her heart warmed as she watched her tall, muscular husband hold the tiny infant. He would talk to his son about the people he had met, the things he wanted for Yasa, and the dangers he might face. And then the games would begin—the tickles, the teasing.

Each time he went into the village, Hiro would return with a new toy or article of clothing for the baby. Many of the gifts were given to him by grateful locals—tiny robes and blankets hand-sewn from the finest fabrics people owned, little toys handcrafted with care. Hanako was overwhelmed by the high esteem. Only a few years ago, these same people viewed her with pity and disdain.

Reiko continued to be a frequent visitor. Besides acting as an honorary grandmother, she became Hanako's teacher in the new endeavor of learning to read and write. The lessons were kept secret from Hiro. Hanako wasn't sure she could succeed, and she didn't know what Hiro's reaction would be. But she realized an entire world existed for those who could interpret the swirls and slashes that made up the written language. Even Sato-san had only a limited understanding of some of the characters, enough to recognize the labels on some of the packages at the market.

At first the lines all looked the same, but Reiko was a very patient teacher, introducing only a few characters at a time. Painting the characters correctly was much more difficult, and wielding the brush proved to be much more troublesome than using an axe or hoe. Finally, she was able to form a reputable imitation of the flowing strokes Reiko produced.

****

Reiko smiled as she walked out of the Tanaka home. It had been a good day; Hanako was making progress learning to read, and the baby was growing strong and healthy. She enjoyed her time with the young family. The love and laughter in the house reminded her of similar times with her own husband and sons.

A servant had brought her in a rickshaw, but she had sent him back to her farm, telling him she would walk home. It was a lovely sunny day, and a recent rainstorm had freshened the air. The young man had protested, but at his mistress's insistence, he had bowed and left.

About halfway home, Reiko began to regret her decision to walk. The distance was much farther than she remembered, and navigating the ruts in the road was difficult with her legs confined in the light summer kimono she wore. But she had always loved walking through her gardens and wanted to get more exercise.

She had gone only a few steps along the dusty road when

the hairs on her neck rose. A sixth sense told her someone walked behind her. A glance down at the road confirmed it—a second shadow following behind hers. Her first reaction was fear. Was it the *ronin*? But instinct told her this was not an evil presence. She turned to face her follower then schooled her features to hide her pleasure when she saw who it was.

"Is there something I can do for you, Yamada-san?" she asked.

Ginjiro stopped and bowed. "No, Nakamura-san. Forgive me if my presence alarmed you. I merely wished to make sure you arrived at your own home safely. If the *ronin* are in the area, it would be dangerous for you to be alone on this road."

She returned the bow. "I am grateful for your concern and protection, Ginjiro-san. Normally one of my sons accompanies me, but today they were all occupied in the fields. However, it is unseemly for you to walk behind me like a servant." She kept her eyes lowered, a sign of respect. "You are a samurai, and I am merely the widow of a farmer. I should walk behind you."

Ginjiro wanted to argue but held his tongue. He took a few steps toward Reiko's farm, but soon realized this wouldn't work. He stopped and turned.

"I can't watch you if you are behind me!"

The widow hid her smile. "Then perhaps we should walk together."

****

Hiro cringed at the wails coming from his tiny son. It was nearly crippling, this sudden wave of panic at the responsibilities of parenthood. He knew he could provide for the boy's physical needs. His son would never want for anything. But he was now responsible for shaping a life. He thought of the things he had learned from his own father. How had Yukio Tanaka taught his sons to become men? There was, of course, the *Bushido*—the Way of the Warrior. The eight virtues of the *Bushido* were the framework for his life, and he wanted to pass these on to his own son.

He watched as his wife brought the child to her breast. The baby settled in, content to take his nourishment from her. Hiro felt a temporary envy at Hanako. This was something only she could do. He knew the jealousy was unfounded; there would be other things he would be able to do for his son later on. But this first connection, this intimacy between mother and child was something he could only imagine.

Hanako separated little Yasa from her breast and brought him up to her shoulder, patting his back until the tiny burp came out. She switched him to her other side, settling him down on the *ofuton* and lying next to him. The change required her to lie facing away from Hiro, shielding his son from his sight. Hiro sighed and turned to leave.

"Hiro."

He turned back toward her.

"Yes?"

"When Yasa is done, would you mind taking him for a walk? I am very tired and would love to rest. He likes to watch the stars at night. Perhaps you could teach him a few things about them."

Hiro nodded solemnly, though his heart leaped with joy. "I could do that. Call me when he is finished."

****

Masao took his time getting back to the camp. For almost a year, he had followed Kato-san and had come north to this frozen land so far from civilization. He had been eager for the chance to prove himself as a samurai. But so far, the only flesh his sword had met was that of the farm animals he slaughtered for food.

Kato-san had promised glory and honor. He promised a

return of the old order, the renewal of the *Bushido*. What empty promises! Perhaps he should have joined the Imperial Guard when he'd had a chance.

Now, they were encamped near this tiny backwoods town, where Kato-san had decreed they would refuel and continue recruiting. If it weren't for the possibility of payment, he would leave the bothersome man here to shrivel up and die. The ferret-faced man was a mouse, totally helpless without his valet who had died during the harsh winter. The town was small, but the tavern served decent food. The people outside the village had nothing worth taking. A band of *ronin* had come a few years before and had burned or taken almost everything of value, and the farmers still struggled to get their fields producing again.

But despite their hardships, there was a positive energy among the townspeople. He heard that Tanaka-san, a former samurai from one of the more prominent Tokyo families, lived nearby. Several of Tanaka's former fellow samurai had also come to live here. They stood out among the residents—their proud, erect bearing proclaimed their station, even without the deferential treatment they received from the people. If it hadn't been for Emperor Meiji abolishing the samurai class, he, Masao Akira, would now be as important as they were.

What enticed these warriors to come to this out-of-the-way town? There is nothing here to fight for, no fierce warlord to defend. Are they passing the time here until their next opportunity?

Ahead of him, a man stumbled and fell. Masao recognized him as one of the older members of the group. Ito-san was not a soldier, but he had no place to go as his home and business had burned to the ground. With the little money he had left, he had bribed his way into the group, but his skills with weapons were practically nonexistent, and the would-be warriors teased him mercilessly. Masao watched to see what the others would do. As he expected, they kicked him, spat on him, and left him by the side of the road.

Masao's stomach roiled to see such needless violence. While he was eager to see combat, the callous way these men treated Ito-san went against many of the *Bushido* codes, especially benevolence and respect. While he didn't condone their actions, he knew he couldn't interfere. They were hungry, bored, and unhappy with their leader. If he were to step in, he would only add fuel to their discontent.

Ito-san moaned in pain, lifted his head to turn pleading eyes toward Masao, and then closed them for the last time.

Chapter Eighteen

Yoshiro Nakamura ran as fast as his eleven-year-old legs would carry him. His vision blurred from the tears running down his cheeks, but he kept going. He had a mission, and he could not fail. The safety of the entire region depended on his success.

He tried to block from his mind the picture of his eldest brother coughing up his life's blood as he urged Yoshi to go to the family home and sound the alarm. Help was needed, fast. There was no time for sad good-byes or tending of wounds. He had to alert the townspeople. The day they had all dreaded had arrived.

The path through the woods was overgrown, and anyone not familiar with the area would be unable to follow it. Finally, he reached the house and dashed to the wooden box next to the doorway. He carefully placed three flares in the ground, struck the flint, and lit them one by one. Each flare traveled upward, lighting the sky with streams of red light. This was the agreed signal for help needed at the Nakamura land. Hopefully assistance would arrive soon enough to save the rest of the family. Even now his other brothers were working on various sections of the farm, unaware of the tragedy.

Shinobu, the second eldest, arrived quickly.

"What happened? Did you set off the flares? You know those are only to be used for—"

Yoshiro's cry of anguish cut off Shinobu's tirade. The older brother stood in stunned silence then slowly, awkwardly opened his arms. Yoshi flew into them, needing the warmth, the verification of life.

Finally, Yoshi's sobs began to subside, and as the youngster choked out his message, Shinobu used his sleeve to wipe his younger brother's face, desperately holding back his own tears.

"The others will be here soon. You must stay at the house and protect Mother."

Yoshi sniffed and looked up. "But I want to help."

"I know you do. But what if some of them come here to the house? We can't leave her here alone. You have done really well at target practice. There is an extra gun behind the family *obutsudan*. Load it and be ready to use it, if necessary."

Reluctantly, the boy nodded. Hearing a commotion in the woods, they quickly stepped into the house until they saw their friends and neighbors arrive. Hiro and Ginjiro, coming from the closest farm, were the first. The brothers stepped outside to greet them, and Yoshi was asked to explain again what had happened.

Though it was clearly painful, the boy cooperated, bravely answering questions, his voice quivering only slightly as he described the ambush. Noburo had been killed by a barrage of arrows. The ambush had come from the east, a sparsely wooded area next to the field where he and Yoshi had been harvesting the crops. No, he hadn't seen how many there were. No, he hadn't heard any gunshots, only the swish of arrows as they had pierced his brother. No, they hadn't made demands or threats. One moment, he and Noburo had been checking the crops for ripeness, the next moment his brother had been on the ground, mortally wounded.

****

Reiko Nakamura stood by the doorway of her home, listening to her youngest son describe the death of her eldest. Her left hand gripped the doorway, supporting her, and her right hand clutched at her heart. Her face was wet with tears, her mind's eye seeing him as a little boy, so earnest, so loving.

Ten years ago, she'd thought she couldn't possibly endure any more pain than what she had felt at the death of her husband, her soul mate. But this—the death of her firstborn—was almost too much to bear. Noburu had taken his responsibility seriously, shouldering the weight of manhood at such an early age. Now, he was gone as well. The *ronin* had taken him from her. Perhaps, before the day ended, she would lose another son.

Her heart ached, knowing Noburo still lay in the field alone. Perhaps she should go—

"*Okaasan?*"

Her third son, Takaro, stood before her, avoiding her eyes. Knowing the teenager was uncomfortable seeing her cry, she hastened to dry her tears. "What is it, son?"

"Tanaka-san and his friend have gone to search out the *ronin* camp. Shinobu and I—" His voice wavered, and he swallowed, visibly summoning the strength to continue. "We will go to the field and take care of *onisan*—our older brother. We do not want you to go there."

Reiko wanted to stop him from going but could only nod her acceptance. "Thank you, Taka-chan. When you return, I know you and Shinobu will need to join the other men. I will prepare food for you and the others, and then I will take care of Noburo's body."

"But, Mother—"

"I will help her."

Both turned toward the newcomer. Hanako stood a respectful distance from them, Baby Yasa tied to her back. She bowed to Reiko. "It would be my honor to assist you, Nakamura-san."

****

Hiro felt his stomach clench at the sight of his wife entering the Nakamura home. She knew the flares meant the *ronin* were here. Why had she subjected herself and their baby to such danger? She could have come in contact with the *ronin* cutting through the woods. He forced himself to breathe normally. At least now she would not be alone. The Nakamura brothers had agreed to wait here and inform the rest of the locals while he and Ginjiro looked for the *ronin* camp. He nodded his readiness to Ginjiro, and they slipped into the woods.

****

Hideyori paced, tracing a path around the dying fire. He was alone, since all the men had left him to hunt earlier that afternoon. As the sun began to sink behind the trees, he grew more and more agitated. The men had been gone for hours, and he was hungry. *Whatever happened to strong, reliable samurai who valiantly fought simply for the honor of dying for one's warlord? These men are pond scum, not fit to wash my sandals.* He took a deep breath, trying to calm his rage, but the stench of the camp made him regret the action.

There had to be a better way. He had offered every incentive he could think of to entice stronger, more intelligent warriors. But he was stuck with a rag-tag group of vermin who were here because they had nowhere else to go.

He had been a good leader, he thought. Strong men had

quaked before him. At one time his lands had spread far and wide, and his wealth had been unlimited. His courtesans, kept in each village of his lands, had dressed in only the finest silks. It was a shame none of them had managed to give him an heir, but that couldn't be helped.

The sun sank behind the trees, taking with it the warmth of the day, and he paced around the dying fire, pausing to warm his hands. Hopefully, the men would return soon and revive this fire by whatever means they used. He knew wood was needed but had no tools to cut firewood, nor any idea of how to use them. Cutting wood was work for the underlings he hired, not for a nobleman like himself.

Perhaps they would come with some decent food, or perhaps a woman who could cook. He hadn't had a decent meal since he had been forced to leave his castle. These foul creatures certainly didn't know how to create anything resembling the meals he'd grown used to as a *daimyo*. Perhaps his next move would be to take over one of the better homes in the area.

The voice of approaching men's voices shook him from his reverie, and he hid behind a tree until he knew who was coming. As the crowd drew nearer, he caught the unmistakable slur of intoxication, the shuffling of unsteady footsteps. His mouth firmed into a scowl. It was bad enough they were incompetent, but their drinking habits made them even more useless.

He stepped out from his hiding place, ready to confront the motley group. They were hampered by their inability to navigate the wooded terrain. It was certainly easy to follow their progress, as they carried torches and belted out a popular drinking song.

Finally, the ragtag bunch made it back to the clearing. They staggered toward the fire, cursing at the lack of warmth from the dying embers. A few of the men knelt at the fire pit, coaxing a flame from the hot logs. Other than an occasional glance, the men ignored him.

Masao Akira, his second in command, entered the clearing. Unlike the others, Akira-san showed none of the effects of alcohol.

"Where have you been?" Hideyori demanded.

Masao threw a dead rabbit, narrowly missing Hideyori's head.

"We were taking target practice." He grabbed some brush, threw it on the fire, and settled himself on a stump.

"One rabbit? Where is the rest of your catch? We have not eaten all day. Couldn't you and your men could have caught enough for a decent meal?"

Masao ignored him, stoking the fire and warming his hands. Finally, when Hideyori thought he could bear it no longer, the soldier spoke.

"We didn't bring anything else to eat because we didn't see any animals worth hunting. Katsuo shot a farmer. I didn't think you wanted him for dinner."

"Farmers have livestock! If you were shooting, why didn't you shoot one of his cows or a chicken? Was your aim that lousy?"

Hideyori regretted his last question when Masao leveled a glare and reached for his bow. "I would be happy to demonstrate my shooting skill, if you wish."

The once-powerful *daimyo* clamped his mouth closed. He put a hand to his grumbling stomach and turned away.

Chapter Nineteen

The sun descended, affording them less light, but Hiro and Ginjiro pressed on. Following the bank of the stream, they kept their footfalls silent. They had decided the *ronin* must have camped by the stream in order to take advantage of the water and the fish.

Their outright execution of Noburo baffled the two samurai. The young man had been unarmed, and other than training with the militia groups, had never been a threat to anyone. How could men who had taken the oath of the *Bushido* have sunk so low? Even though their place in society might no longer exist, their ideals should have been ingrained.

Hiro noted the smell first. The dank, rancid odor of unwashed men. His lip curled in disgust. It was one thing to go unbathed when fighting prevented it, but here in the peaceful woods near a clear stream, there was no excuse. The Shinto priests who had guided him in his youth had always stressed the importance of cleanliness, both physical and spiritual. If these men had ever been samurai, their filthy habits as well as their despicable actions proved their unworthiness.

He pointed ahead to signal their nearness, and Ginjiro nodded in understanding. They slowed their pace even more, careful to prevent detection.

They needn't have bothered. Most of the men gathered around the fire in the clearing were in no condition to fight. A few snored loudly, and others sprawled in various stages of intoxication. Only one man stood. Dressed in a frayed brocade robe, he paced around the fire and berated the men. Another soldier, though he sat with the others, cast a bored, though clear-eyed gaze at the speaker.

Hiro immediately recognized the speaker as Hideyori Kato. He motioned for Ginjiro to circle around to the sober soldier then waited for his friend to get in position. The anger he'd held simmering inside for years came to a boil as Hiro stepped into the clearing. From the corner of his vision, he noticed the soldier sit up, but the man quickly backed down when Ginjiro's sword flashed in front of his face and stopped at his neck.

"It appears you should look elsewhere for 'strong, honorable men,' Kato-san, if this is the response you got from your newspaper ad."

The older man stopped in his tracks. He turned to face Hiro, and his eyes widened in recognition. "Tanaka-san?"

"Why have you moved your operations here to the north, Hideyori? What happened to all your holdings on Honshu?"

Hideyori scowled. "The Emperor seized my lands. His Imperial Guard took over my castle, my lands, even my army! Those worthless soldiers wouldn't even fight for me!"

Hiro laughed. "Why would they fight for a dishonorable man against the emperor?"

"You dare to speak to me that way? I could have you beheaded."

"You would have to do it yourself." Hiro gestured toward the inebriated soldiers. Those who were still awake stared uncomprehendingly at them. "Your minions are in no condition to take orders. Why would you think about recruiting trash like them? These are the very men you announced you would eliminate!"

Hiro noticed a few of the soldiers had roused themselves at his insults. But before they could seize their weapons, another man leaped into the clearing and kicked the swords out of their reach. Watanabe stood in front of the men, his sword raised and ready to cut down anyone who dared to rise. Could Kato-san be convinced to surrender?

Hideyori drew himself to his full height. "The men I recruit are none of your concern. I am the *Daimyo*—"

"The *daimyo* class has been abolished. You have no power."

"I have more power than you! The samurai class also has been abolished." He cast a cunning grin at Hiro. "You should come and work for me. I would pay you very well."

"Your money is worthless to me. I would not carry a sword for anyone as unscrupulous as you."

"Then you will die. There are plenty who would fight for me."

"Worthless vermin who would shoot an innocent man for target practice? The man they killed had more honor than this entire group together." Hiro stepped closer. "A mother, a wife, two children, and three brothers are mourning because of that senseless murder. That is not the teaching of the *Bushido*—the Way of the Warrior."

Hideyori reached toward the body of one of his unconscious soldiers and drew the man's long sword. "You dishonor me," he cried, "and now you must die."

Hiro was stunned. Kato-san was almost twice his age and had never done his own fighting. This challenge was suicidal. The elder man rushed forward, prompting Hiro to unsheath his own sword, though he used it only to deflect the blows aimed at him.

Over and over, Hideyori swung the heavy sword. It was like sparring with a beginner, Hiro thought. His opponent's technique was clumsy and ineffective, and the weight of the weapon quickly tired him. The thrusts slowed, the arcs became erratic, but still he fought on. Sweat poured down his face, and he blinked, trying to see.

Hiro was vaguely aware of the circle of men who surrounded them. Had the drunken soldiers roused themselves enough to fight? Where was Ginjiro? He didn't hear any other swords connecting but didn't dare interrupt his concentration to look around. A break in his attention could be fatal.

The elder man clumsily swung the weapon around his head. He tried to stay on the offensive, but his long robe dragged in the dirt, tripping him up, and his eyes shone with desperation. Hiro had several opportunities to cut him down but couldn't bring himself to do so. He simply fended off the older man's ineffectual swipes of the sword.

The smell of burning fabric alerted Hiro. The long hem of Hideyori's robe had dragged over the fire and the flames worked their way up the garment.

"Kato-san, your clothes are on fire!" Hiro would have pulled him away from the flames, but couldn't put down his sword while the older man continued to swing his weapon.

"I don't believe you. You're just trying to trying to distract me." Hideyori fought on, his flaming coat trailing behind him. His frantic movements only fanned the fire, and by the time he understood the danger, the flames had engulfed him. He dropped his sword and screamed.

"Masao! Help me!"

With his free hand, Hiro grabbed Kato by the arm and dragged the smaller man to the ground. He pulled off the heavy robe and rolled the burning man in the dirt, extinguishing the flames. When he knelt to check for injuries, Kato pushed him away and struggled to sit up. In the firelight, the man's face and arms glowed bright red from his burns. His long hair was singed, and he struggled to speak.

"You may think you have defeated me, Tanaka-san, but my men will avenge me," he gasped as he reached for his sword.

"If anyone harms Hiro, you will all die." Ginjiro spoke for the first time, startling the older man.

Hideyori cast a quick glance around, and his eyes opened wide. The soldiers who were awake enough to understand what was happening huddled together in fear. Glancing around, Hiro was nearly as surprised as Hideyori.

Gun barrels pointed at them from behind every tree. Apparently, the men of the village had followed them into the woods.

"You are surrounded, Kato-san," Ginjiro taunted. "And you are seriously outnumbered. What will you do now?"

"You will never take me," the older man declared. "I will die with dignity." Then, before anyone could stop him, the former *daimyo* plunged the blade into his abdomen.

Hiro rushed to Hideyori's side, but the sword had done its damage. Hideyori Kato would no longer bring fear and suffering to their village.

Around them, several of the gun barrels lowered. A few of the villagers, led by Fukazawa and Kobayashi, entered the clearing and quickly disarmed Kato's men.

Sato-san came forward. "We grew concerned for you, Tanaka-san," he said, "but we weren't sure what to do. It was your wife who came up with this plan."

"My wife? She is here?"

"Yes. I couldn't stay away." Hanako stepped out from behind one of the trees, holding a rifle in each hand.

Hiro recognized the old, dusty guns found in the Nakamura's shed. "You figured out how to load these?"

"Load them? With what?"

Hiro groaned. He cast a quick look to be sure all the *ronin* were still guarded by men with swords then bent to whisper to his wife. "You came with empty guns?"

She colored. "I hoped the sight of all the guns would be enough to make them think you had an advantage."

Hiro's mouth twitched. His wife never ceased to surprise him. He reached out and caressed her cheek. "You little fool. You could have been hurt." Looking over her shoulder, he noticed she didn't wear her baby-pack. "Where is Yasa?" he asked.

"He is at the Nakamura home. Reiko and Yoshi promised to guard him well."

At least she hadn't brought the baby into the camp.

Chapter Twenty

Friends and neighbors gathered around the Nakamura family, facing the funeral pyre. Thanks to the incredibly short confrontation, Noburo Nakamura was the village's only casualty from the conflict with the *ronin*.

Reiko knelt on her mat next to Noburo's widow, stoically facing the casket. Her sons surrounded her. Shinobu, now head of the household, sat on her right. His shoulders drooped, as the burden of his responsibility seemed to settle heavily on them. Yoshi sat behind Shinobu, struggling valiantly to keep the tears from falling. Taka, seated behind his mother, stared vacantly ahead, his expression cold. Two priests stood on the other side of the body, chanting prayers. Ginjiro stood nearby.

Standing with the other guests, Hanako watched the proceedings and added her own prayer for Reiko. The dead man was Reiko's child, had once been carried in her body, held in her arms, fed with her milk. Hanako's heart constricted at the thought of anything happening to little Yasa, who now snoozed contently in his pack. It was not the natural order of things to bury a child.

The pyre was lit, and the blaze soon engulfed the wooden box in which Noburo's remains lay. The priests continued to chant, their droning voices adding to the surrealism of the day. Noburo's death had brought about the final confrontation with the *ronin*; because of the confrontation, the threat of danger was finally over. Now, the villagers were here to mourn with the Nakamura family.

The blaze roared and then died down. One by one, the guests came up to the pyre, bowed respectfully, and then left. The family would stay to place Noburo's bones into an urn, which would eventually rest in the family plot, next to the remains of his father.

****

Since the Nakamura home was the farthest from the village, most people passed the Tanaka land on their way back to their own homes. Everyone wanted to thank Tanaka-san personally for his role in saving their lives and their homes. Hiro was uncomfortable with the praise, but graciously acknowledged each admirer, insisting that it was their own bravery, as well as assistance from his friends, that caused the victory.

As people left the Tanaka home, their mood was lighter and voices became louder. Their mourning was done and there was sure to be a celebration in the village tonight.

Hanako moved to the rear of the house. Little Yasa had become fussy, and it was time for him to sleep. She gently placed him on his *ofuton*, stroking his downy head as he settled into slumber. If the gods were willing, Yasa would grow into a fine, strong man like his father. He would not be a samurai, for that way of life was gone. But with a father like Hiro, he would learn the values of the *Bushido*, "the Way of the Warrior". He would be a noble, disciplined man.

She continued to kneel there beside her son, softly humming a lullaby tucked into the deepest recesses of her memory. Had her mother knelt beside her like this, humming softly, praying for her future happiness?

The light outside the windows began to fade. It was past time for her to prepare the evening meal. She gave Yasa's chubby cheek one final caress, stood, and slid the door closed before going to the kitchen.

She found Hiro there, making tea. Aware of her presence, he looked up. "Yasa-chan is asleep?"

"Yes. He's had a full day. He's always happy to see other people. I was afraid he would disrupt the funeral this morning, but he was content."

He poured a cup of the fragrant brew and passed it to her. "He is an intelligent young man. He sees no one else speaks, so he remains silent, too."

Hanako dipped her head toward her cup, hiding her smile. *How like a man, to see the child's silence as a measure of his intelligence, rather than a show of contentment.* Nevertheless, it was pleasing to see Hiro so proud of his son. She prayed father and son would continue to have a strong relationship.

"Do you want to go into the village tonight?" she asked.

He cast a curious look at her. "Why?"

"It looks like a celebration has begun."

They both looked toward the open window at the fireworks lighting the sky. "I can cook something quickly if you want to join your friends."

He turned to her, his look melting her. "Everything I want to celebrate and everyone I need to celebrate with are here in this house."

Dinner preparations were forgotten as a different hunger was fed.

****

Reiko stood at the doorway of her home, watching the fireworks light up the night sky. Noburo had always loved fireworks, she remembered. He would have enjoyed the celebration. The memories brought a bittersweet smile to her face, even as the pain of losing him squeezed her heart. How she would miss him. It had been torture, placing his bones in the urn that now rested in his home. She didn't begrudge them to Noburo's wife, but wished she could have kept a part of her son with her.

A movement to her left had her turning sharply. All the relatives who had not gone to the celebration were in their own homes. "Who comes here?" she called out.

Ginjiro stepped out from behind a tree and bowed deeply. "Forgive me, Nakamura-san," he began. "I did not mean to alarm you."

Reiko's heart lifted. "Are you hungry?" she asked. "There is much food remaining from today's funeral service. The village women were very generous with their gifts."

In the city, gifts of money were traditionally given to the bereaved. But people in remote villages such as this showed their support by giving what they had. And for the esteemed Nakamura family, the gifts had been plentiful.

"It was not my intention to take anything from you," Ginjiro said. "I merely wished to make sure you were—safe."

"Of course," Reiko assured him. "But I have much more food here than my sons and I can eat, and I would like to offer some to you, as thanks for your service to the village." She paused, looking down as she added, "And your presence here is a great comfort to me."

The man's stature increased at the compliment. "I would be honored to take a meal in your home."

Chapter Twenty-one

Spring, 1877

Hiro had spent a long day at the market. Hanako had given him a long list of supplies needed for the farm and the house, and he had things he wanted to get for his own flower garden. After researching all winter, he had several new ideas he wanted to try. He had sent for special seeds, hoping to find varieties of blossoms that would grow at various times, even though the growing season in Hokkaido was relatively short. Hanako had been supportive of his plans for expanding the flower business of the farm. Never had he been so excited about a new endeavor.

He urged the horse to a faster gait as he neared his home. Hopefully the baby was still awake. Nothing in his life had ever given him such joy as looking into his son's eyes. This tiny being held a big piece of his heart, and he knew he would do anything for this child and the mother who had borne him.

Coming closer to his home, he gazed with pride at the neat rows of vegetable plants and the seedlings in the flower gardens. On the other side of the house, several cows grazed in neatly fenced-in pastures. Smoke rose from the chimney, assuring him the people inside were warm and snug against the chilly night air. It had been almost three years since he first came down this road to Hanako's home. What a difference those years had made in both their lives! His family and his new vocation gave him the peace he had sought all his life.

He stowed his purchases in the storage hut then stepped to the threshold of the house. Before he entered he could hear his wife's melodic voice. She sang an old tune, one he remembered his mother singing to him and his younger brothers. His childhood had been a happy one, though he couldn't remember his father being present much of the time. Yukio's life had been dedicated to his daimyo, and it was only when Hiro had joined the ranks of the samurai that father and son had made any close bonds. Hiro swore that would not happen between him and his own son.

The fire burned brightly and the aroma of a delicious meal greeted him. Hanako turned briefly from the stove, smiling a welcome before turning her attention back to their dinner.

Hiro went through to the bedroom and changed out of his traveling clothes. A hot soaking bath was just what he needed. He remembered the first time Hanako had walked through the house. She had never seen a room devoted specifically for bathing and had bristled at the expense for such a thing. But after the first time she scrubbed herself clean in the privacy of her home, rinsed herself with water much warmer than any stream, and then soaked her tired muscles in the hot, steamy bath, she never complained about the luxury again.

Feeling energized after the hot bath, he dressed in a light *yukata* and went in search of his family. Hanako had set the table while the baby sat on a soft furry blanket, playing with a stuffed kitten Reiko had made for him. Hiro knelt to the floor to get a better view of this miracle who was his flesh and blood.

Yasa-chan dropped his toy and stared up at Hiro's face. His son's tiny hand reached up to touch his grizzled cheek. Hiro was again struck with awe and wonder. Each time he looked in his son's eyes, he saw those of his wife. But Hanako claimed when Yasa cried, he resembled his stubborn father.

Hiro picked up the discarded toy and tickled Yasa's tummy. The baby responded with a delighted giggle, kicking his feet with glee. He moved the furry toy to tickle the little neck, the arms, and toes, each time eliciting a playful response. Father and son continued to entertain each other until Hanako proclaimed dinner ready. Not wanting to end his time with Yasa, Hiro picked up the baby and brought him to the table. Yasa sat quietly on his father's lap, watching intently as Hiro used his chopsticks to pick up the savory bits of meat and vegetables. Hiro couldn't resist feeding a few of the soft grains of rice to his son.

Soon, the tiny eyelids began to droop, and the little body on Hiro's lap sagged. Hanako gently picked up the tired baby and laid him down on his little *ofuton*. Hiro missed the warmth the tiny body had emitted.

Hiro had just finished his last bite when he heard a knock. Hanako hurried to the doorway and returned with a young man dressed in the uniform of the Imperial Guard. The stranger bowed low and addressed Hiro with respect.

"Tanaka-san, I bring a message from the capital." He held out a document tied with an elegant gold ribbon

Hiro frowned. "A message? From whom?"

"I come from the emperor himself."

"The emperor? How did he find me? And why?"

"He has been searching for you for almost a year. He heard you had been in Hakodate, meeting with the Minister of Finance."

Hiro remembered the circumstances that had taken him

to Hakodate. The memory of his experience with the former government official had left a sour taste in his mouth. "But why does the emperor want to see me?"

"I was not told the contents of his message. I know he sends it on behalf of your family. My task was to deliver it to you."

The announcement brought a sense of unease. His family would not have appealed to the emperor for help unless there had been an emergency. He reached for the document and tore off the seal. The messenger backed up and waited quietly. Hiro scanned the short missive. His shoulders sagged with dejection. His perfect world had come to an end. Groaning with frustration, he rose and went outside to clear his mind.

****

Hanako wondered if she should follow her husband. Whatever the message was, it had upset him. Inwardly, she cursed the messenger who had brought such pain to him. Her husband had been so happy when he came home from his errands in the village, and now he looked as if his world had crumbled. She had spent the entire day preparing for his return. The walls and floors had been washed, the most beautiful and fragrant flowers from the garden had been artfully arranged throughout the house, a special meal had been painstakingly prepared—and she had a special surprise for him.

But the unveiling of her surprise had been delayed by unwelcome news from his family. She had watched his face grow pale as he had read the message. Perhaps something terrible had happened to someone in his family. She wished she knew more about his people, but whenever she had asked, he had answered vaguely and changed the subject.

She had never seen her husband so agitated. How she wanted to comfort him! He had been so patient and loving all through her pregnancy. But she had learned he was a private person. He had not told her much about his past, and he did not offer much insight into his own thoughts.

Turning to the messenger, she offered him tea and supper, which he gratefully accepted.

"Will you be here long?" Hanako asked.

"I have been instructed to wait for a response from Tanaka-san before I return."

"You will have a long journey back to Tokyo. I will prepare a room for you. Please have some more tea."

The young soldier, happy to find a comfortable place to rest, eagerly settled in to eat. Hanako waited for him to finish his meal then led him to an extra room at the back of the house.

Finally, it was her turn to eat. She was glad she had made extra food, since the messenger had been quite hungry. The aroma of the grilled chicken and vegetables had piqued her appetite, and she had grown hungry waiting for Hiro to finish eating, but the arrival of their male guest had delayed her meal.

The message lay where Hiro had left it. She took her bowl to the table and knelt on her cushion. She ate her entire meal staring at the scroll, deciding whether to open it or wait for Hiro to return and explain. The scroll seemed to stare at her in return, calling to her. A year ago she would not have considered reading it, as the painted characters would have made no sense to her. But she and Reiko had been working on both reading and writing. She had planned to surprise Hiro tonight by reading a short poem she'd written for him. This document was much longer. Would she recognize enough characters to make sense out of the markings on the page?

Finishing her meal, she took her dishes to the washbowl. Hiro had been gone for quite some time—she had no idea when he would return. Perhaps she could be of comfort to him if she knew why he was upset. Carefully drying her hands, she knelt again at the table and unrolled the rich, thick paper, then concentrated on the figures before her.

The paper contained many characters she didn't understand, but she recognized a few — "mother" and "family" stood out. She recognized the symbols for Tokyo, the capital city. She frowned. So many symbols! She had been a fool to think she had learned enough in the months Reiko had tutored her. No wonder priests dedicated themselves to years of study.

She concentrated and reminded herself what Reiko had said: many characters were combinations of smaller ones. If she could only recognize the parts — here, a symbol for "death", and over there, the symbol for "person." Had someone in Hiro's family died? The handwriting was bold and striking; so unlike the flowing lines Reiko produced with her brush. Perhaps there were some other words she could recognize. There, at the end, a symbol she remembered from last week's lesson. The character was *kaeru* — "to return home."

Had Hiro been commanded to return to Tokyo?

If so, he would have to leave. It would be his duty, and she could do nothing to stop him. There would be no room for her in his world. She would be out of place and rejected, more of a detriment to him than a help. Her perfect world would come to an end.

She re-rolled the document and cleared away the remains of their interrupted dinner. It would serve no purpose to dwell on it. If he left, she would go on. She had always managed to survive, no matter the obstacle. She would do so again. She took a small comfort in knowing Hiro, too, had seemed upset by the contents of the message. But he must be loyal to his family as well as the emperor.

At least she had their son. She prayed Hiro would not take Yasa from her. Life without either of them was inconceivable. But the memory of father and son playing on the tatami mat just moments ago confirmed the close bond they had already formed. Perhaps Hiro would insist Yasa be educated in the finest schools and train for a respectable profession. If he did not allow her to come with him, how worthless her life would be! Her hands trembled at the possibility, and a fragile cup slipped out of her hand. It fell awkwardly onto the edge of the wooden washbowl and shattered.

It was, to Hanako, symbolic of her life with Hiro. The shattered pieces of the beautiful cup represented the joy she had experienced in the brief time she had known him. Her first impulse was to gather the shards and try to put them back together, but the first piece she touched tore through her skin. Hardly aware of the pain, she watched as her crimson blood mixed with the clear water, swirling around in a circular pattern before fading into pale pink. Time lost all meaning as she watched, entranced. The candle beside her burned itself out. Still, she knelt, her injured hand immersed in the liquid.

Hanako knelt on a plush cushion in a sumptuous *tatami* room, dressed in the finest silk. Attendants fixed her hair in an elaborate knot, dressing the coiffure with jeweled combs. She held out her hand as another attendant smoothed exotic creams on it. Across the room, a nursemaid played with the baby. She was cocooned in wealth and security.

What an honor to be the wife of a noted samurai, now a respected general in the Imperial Army. How lovely to reside in an elegant mansion, with servants bustling about, ready to see to her every whim. Wives of such important men did not need to worry about successful harvests or rising costs. Their only concern was to keep themselves beautiful.

She felt, rather than heard, him enter the room behind her and call her name. Curiously, the attendants melted away, and the luxurious surroundings faded into darkness. *What happened to the light?* She saw his shadow creep across the room and tried to call out to him, but no sound came. A flame leapt to life beside her as he lit one lantern and then another, and she recognized the specter as her husband. She looked down at the hand that had been extended toward the maid and found the lotion covering her hand had turned red. She lifted her hand to look more closely and stared at the jagged cut crossing her fingers. What had happened?

Hiro's hands held hers, and he murmured something. She felt him lift her, settle her on his lap, and wipe her injured hand. He checked it for stray pieces of broken china and wrapped it in a soft cloth. His strong arms surrounded her, holding her close. How amazing to feel such security, to give up all worries and concerns, and let someone else deal with them.

Vaguely, she heard the sounds of a fussing baby. Should she do something? Her arms felt heavy, her eyelids lowered, and the world faded away.

Chapter Twenty-two

Hiro gazed up at the palatial structure where his mother lived. It was a far cry from the building he had come to consider his home. All the trappings of wealth and nobility were proudly displayed here. Briefly he tried to imagine Hanako in these surroundings, but the picture didn't gel. Her way of life came from a love and respect for the tiny parcel of land she was proud to call her own. *If she could love me nearly as much as she loves her farm, I would be a wealthy man.*

The brief message from the Emperor had told him his brother Taro had been killed in the line of duty. Hiro was now the head of the Tanaka family, and was expected to take his place in the Emperor's service. He'd begged Hanako to come with him, but she'd refused. Her place was on her farm, she'd said. While she understood his duty to his family and the Emperor, she could not follow him to Tokyo.

They'd finally compromised—Hiro would go, and Hanako would stay and finish out the growing season on the farm. After the harvest, they would discuss the matter again. If Ginjiro and the Nakamuras hadn't promised to look out for

Hanko and the baby, he would never have left without her.

It had taken him two weeks to return to the home of his birth. When he had left for the far north, he had been a bitter ex-soldier, seeking a plan for his life, looking for the elusive element that would give meaning to his existence. Now, he felt, he had found what he needed, but by returning here to take care of his birth family's needs, he may have lost the family of his heart.

Taking a deep breath, he entered the gilded gate. A tiny, gnarled man scurried forward to greet him as he removed his sandals at the doorway. "Welcome home, Master. Your mother is in the garden."

Hiro nodded at the servant and strode through the ornately furnished house to the exquisitely landscaped garden beyond. All his life he had taken this grandeur as his due. Though he had seen poverty and hardship during his travels as a samurai warrior, he had always had this palace to return to. Living with Hanako had taught him more about the important things in life. Returning to this, his childhood home, he was a bit ashamed of the extravagance, knowing so many of the people he had befriended could live for an entire year on the price of one painting.

His mother sat on a bench near the center of the gardens. At fifty-three, Michiko Tanaka had aged gracefully. The daughter of a successful merchant, she had been raised in comfort and tradition, but she had a spark of fire and a sense of humor that kept her young. Seeing her son, she rose eagerly to greet him.

"How wonderful to see you again, Hiro. I am pleased you have completed your travels unharmed."

Hiro bowed in respect. "I am pleased you are well, *Okaasan*."

The corners of her eyes crinkled, and her lips curved upward. "And now that we have dispensed with the formalities, come closer so I can hug you."

He laughed aloud. He should have remembered his mother's disdain for many of the conventions of polite society. Her willingness to voice her true opinions had caused his father to cringe with embarrassment on more than one occasion. She made her own rules, and one tradition she had never followed was keeping distance between herself and her adult children, physically or emotionally. He crossed the remaining steps to her and hugged her tightly. She seemed more frail than he remembered—or was he comparing her to the rugged woman he had left behind?

"You have grown even larger and stronger, my son," Michiko noted as she led him back to her bench. "Obviously you have found a way to keep fit. Have you come into the employment of an errant warlord?"

"No, *Okaasan*," he assured her. "I have been learning the ways of a farmer."

"Really?" She looked up at him. "We heard you were in Hakodate. Have you apprenticed to an estate near that city?"

"Not really. I am doing the actual labor on a tiny farm near Furano."

"A common laborer? Why? Have your travels left you destitute? Surely you could have sent for some money or—"

"No, no, I'm fine. I met a farmer who needed my help, and became interested in the work there. I am learning about agriculture, as well as the care and feeding of animals, and a little carpentry besides."

"I see. And this farmer, does he treat you well?"

Hiro thought of the contentment he felt working side by side with Hanako, the pride he felt in helping to work the land, and the joy she brought him each night. But he was not ready to talk about this yet. His life with her was so precious; he wanted to keep it close to his heart. And his choice to bind himself to a poor subsistence farmer would not be something his mother would easily understand. He would need time to approach the subject with her. For now he settled on vagueness. "Yes, *Okaasan*, I am well treated. Shimizu-san is a good farmer and teacher. I have learned much about agriculture and the care of animals." Calling his wife by her former name seemed odd, but it kept her identity hidden for now.

"Please tell me about this person. How did you meet?"

Mother and son spent the next hour in the garden. The painful subject of Taro's death was avoided for now, and the time was spent happily reminiscing and catching up on other family matters. They talked until a servant announced dinner was served. He assisted Michiko to her feet and accompanied her inside to the elegant lacquered table, spread with the finest delicacies in the land. He mentally compared the meals before him to the simple but tasty dishes Hanako prepared each evening after working in the fields all day. Surely none of the ladies in his former life would be able to do either fieldwork or cooking without major complaints and a lot of whining.

He nodded in greeting to his youngest brother, who bowed low in respect before sitting down. At twelve years of age, Toshiro was brimming with questions about his older brother's exploits as a samurai, knowing only about the glorious and none of the ugly side of fighting. "Why isn't anyone at war?" he whined. "What good is a samurai without a battle to fight?"

Hiro smiled inwardly. Only a few years ago he had been a warrior without a cause, a lost soldier. Gently, he answered his brother's questions, but deflected any suggestions about his future. He wanted to return to Hanako and Yasa-chan immediately, but he had to take care of his mother and brothers. He would also have to take care of his military responsibilities. How could he do both?

Would Hanako ever agree to come and live here, in the city? He tried to imagine his sturdy wife, her lovely tan covered with white makeup, her shining ebony hair covered by an ornately styled wig held in place with bejeweled combs, her feminine figure trapped in yards of embroidered silk. Could she adjust, or would his beautiful flower wither and die in this artificial setting? She shone in her natural element among her fields of growing plants in the bright sunshine. How could he take her away from that?

****

Michiko Tanaka knelt on a cushion near the table, watching her sons interact. While Hiro listened to his brothers' stories and answered each question politely, she could see his mind was elsewhere. His physical being was at home here, but his heart had not returned with him. He had not been forthcoming about his life in Hokkaido. She only knew he was content to stay there. It was no surprise to find he had embraced a more peaceful profession. Hiro had always been more studious than his brothers, but his sense of duty had forced him to follow his father's footsteps and carry the swords of the samurai.

He wears the mantle of authority well, she thought. *His father would be proud of him.* Yukio Tanaka had been a samurai of the first rank, answering only to the emperor. He had expected his four sons would follow in his footsteps and had overseen every step of their martial training. Taro, the eldest, had been a natural warrior, like his father. Young Hiro had been eager to please his father and had excelled in the grueling exercises. But he had always had a gentle side. He had always treated his younger siblings with compassion and had often brought home stray animals. After the death of his closest friend, Hiro's zest for life had fled, and she had been concerned for his mental well-being when he had left.

Because Taro had died, Hiro had returned out of a sense of duty, ready to assume his place in society. As a mother, she was happy to have him home. But seeing his half-hearted smiles, she wondered if perhaps the old ways were not always right. He had found happiness as a farmer. He hadn't embraced one of the usual trades for a high-ranking samurai, but it was a respectable vocation. He seemed much more content than when he had left. *Who was this simple farmer who had taught her son a different path, one that embraced life, rather than taking it? Was this man more than a mentor? Had Hiro missed Yukio so much he had sought out a father figure?*

Her opportunity for discussion did not come for several days. Relatives and neighbors had heard of Hiro's return and had come to visit. His reputation as a fierce warrior defending an entire town against the band of renegades had made him a celebrity, and he had been summoned for an audience with the emperor. While he prepared for this honor, Michiko stole a few moments alone with her son.

"Hiro, you are so handsome wearing your father's ceremonial kimono. You wear the family crest well. Surely, Yukio's spirit is smiling as you bring honor to the family name."

Hiro glanced down at his clothing. Though he appeared every inch the gentleman, she noticed he looked uncomfortable wearing the fine silk kimono and gold brocade *obi*. It was as if he wished he were in another place. *What soldier would prefer to avoid a meeting with the emperor? Something must have happened to change his priorities.*

"Hiro-chan, are you all right?"

He looked up at her with a crooked smile. "I'm fine, *Okaasan*. Just lost in thought."

"And these thoughts, are they of your life in Hokkaido?"

He hesitated. "Yes."

"You found contentment there, did you not?"

"Yes, I was very content. I enjoyed working outdoors, seeing things grow."

"And you wish to return there, don't you?"

Another hesitation. "Yes. But—but I know that it was not the life *Otousan* wished for me."

"Your father is not here now. It was his expectation that you, like he and his father and many more before them, would be a samurai. But the time for those warriors is past. Since the *shogun* no longer rule, the men of the samurai class must find other vocations. You must find another purpose for your life."

He seemed surprised at his mother's words. "But as the eldest son, it is now my responsibility to care for you. Many of the samurai remain here, in the city, and they have occupations with more prestige. If you were to come to my home in Hokkaido, you would not have the luxuries and social life you have here. I would see to it that you were comfortable, but a common farmer lives much more simply than a merchant or politician."

Michiko raised a brow. "I did not realize I was infirm enough to require constant care."

Hiro groaned. "You are far from infirm, *Okaasan*. And I know *Otousan* left you with enough resources to live comfortably for a long time. But unless you remarry, I am the head of this household, and I need to make sure that you remain safe and well provided for."

Michiko grimaced inwardly at the thought of remarrying. Though her life with Yukio had been pleasant, she had come to enjoy the freedom afforded her as a widow. If she ever married again, it would be on her terms, and her husband would have to be content with a very independent wife. No one, including her strong, traditional sons, would ever rule her.

"I am not afraid to live simply, but I would prefer to remain here in the city. I am not so tied to tradition that I expect you to have sole responsibility for my care. I still have two other healthy sons, one of them a successful businessman here. If you choose to go back to your farm in the country, I would miss you, as I always do when you are away, but I want you to find the life that brings you happiness." She knelt on an embroidered cushion. "You are not expected at court for some time. Tell me about this new life of yours."

Hiro pursed his lips and frowned. Instead of sitting with her, he paced back and forth. Then, instead of answering her, he asked a question of his own.

"*Okaasan*, did *Otousan* bring you happiness?"

Michiko started in surprise. "I was content. Why do you ask?"

"I need to know. Were you happy to be married to a samurai, or was it difficult to be married to a man whose career was built on violence?"

"The violence was not welcome, but your father tried hard to shelter us from it. I was proud to be wed to your father. My father was happy he was able to arrange such an advantageous union."

"Did *Otousan* treat you well?"

"He treated me with respect. And I never wanted for anything."

He looked as if he wanted to ask another question, but apparently he decided against it. "I am glad *Otousan* was good to you," he said as he adjusted his jacket.

Michiko got up to follow her son from the room. *Why is he asking questions about my life with Yukio?* The answer hit her with a force so powerful she stopped in her tracks. "Hiro, you have met a woman!"

Hiro froze in mid-step. She scurried around him to look up at his face as she grabbed his sleeve. "Is it true? Have you met someone you wish to marry? When can I meet her? Is she from a good family?"

Her son was silent for so long she feared he would not answer. Finally, he sighed. "I need to leave now. We will talk when I return."

****

Hanako awakened to her baby's cry. Little Yasahiro was

hungry again. Bone weary from the day's work, she reached over to the little *ofuton* placed next to hers, picked up the baby, and opened her yukata. As her son drank greedily, she lay back and closed her eyes. She had accomplished much that day and had come home ready to share the day's news with her husband before she remembered he wasn't there. Her elation had turned to despair. She understood the need for Hiro to return to his parents' home, but she and Yasa needed him, too. He had become so much more than her husband. He was her friend, her confidante, her soul mate. He had become...her life.

Hot drops seeped from beneath her eyelids. She breathed deeply, willing herself not to sob. It would not do to disturb the little one. Yasa-chan seemed to sense her moods, and wailed his displeasure whenever Hanako was unhappy. He was so like his father. What a precious gift she had in him. No matter what happened, whether Hiro returned or not, she had this living reminder of her time with him. Growing up, she had heard stories about the gallant samurai, about their bravery as well as their code of ethics. She had never expected to meet a real-life samurai, let alone marry him and have a son with him.

Yasa stirred, and she carefully rolled to her other side so he could drink from her other breast. She gently cradled Yasa's downy head, covered with jet-black hair. He would know about his father, she decided. He would be able to defend himself with dignity, but would learn to love the fields and the animals his father had grown to appreciate. Briefly, she wondered how she would manage this alone.

It would be difficult to run the farm alone, as well. At least Sato-san and the other merchants would not pose a problem for her. Before he left, Hiro had gone into the village and informed all the merchants that he had been called to Tokyo, and that his wife was authorized to act as his manager. Any supplies she needed for upkeep on the farm were to be given to her immediately. If she did not bring enough money with her, he would settle the debt upon his return. The merchants were more than willing to agree to his request.

The baby detached himself from her, signaling the end of his nighttime feeding. She rearranged her *yukata* and got up to walk with him until he went back to sleep. It had been an unusually hot day, but the cool night breeze called to her and she stepped outside

The moon cast an eerie glow over the yards. The new chicken hut stood like a silent sentry post. She made her way to it, noticing the chickens were being unusually noisy tonight. She wondered if she had left the doorway open again. The new rooster had a habit of making a nuisance of himself. She must not allow herself to be so distracted.

Halfway to the coop, she noticed a dark ball of fur floating back and forth, back and forth. Glowing orbs shone from the front of the furry mass, and sharp fangs jutted out from enormous, salivating lips. The creature had not yet seen her, and she silently appealed to the gods for Yasa-chan to remain quiet as she backed up, retracing her steps to the house. She laid her now sleeping son back onto his *ofuton* and reached for the sword Hiro had left for her.

"Please help me to remember all that Hiro taught me," she begged the gods.

By the time she returned to the doorway, the wild dog had recognized the scent of people and had abandoned its mission at the chicken hut in favor of a bigger prey. Noiselessly, it crept across the grass toward the house, staring at Hanako. She was grateful Hiro had insisted on leaving one of his swords with her. He had installed hooks above the doorway so it would be out of the way, but accessible. She hoped his lessons during the drills would not be forgotten. She would have only one chance to protect her son.

Just outside the hut, her foot brushed against the box of flares. There had been no incidents of *ronin* attacks since Hiro's confrontation with Hideyori Kato and his men the previous fall. After sitting idle during the cold winter, would they light to summon the people nearby? Would her neighbors come? She told herself she had nothing to lose, and using one hand to keep the sword aloft, used her other hand to set a flare in the ground and light it with the candle from her lantern. The first flare lit, but the flame died out before launching. Her heart sank.

Grabbing another flare, she glanced at the dog to see if he had come any closer. He sat still, eyeing her. *Did he plan to attack?* She prayed as she lit the second flare and rejoiced when it shot high into the air, lighting the night sky.

The animal was startled at the sudden bright light and noise. Hanako harbored a small hope that the noise would be enough to scare him away, but instead he crouched, as if deciding whether or not to advance.

Encouraged by her effort, Hanako lit another flare, hoping to keep him at bay. Inside the house, little Yasa started to wail, but she didn't dare stop to go to him. The commotion was enough to keep the animal from advancing, but it wasn't enough to make him leave. She set out the remaining flares in the box and lit them, one by one, encouraged when the dog stepped back a little.

The last flare went up with a sputter. If the dog didn't leave she would have to fight for her life and for her son. Gripping the sword tightly with both hands, she held it out in front of her and stepped out of the doorway. The animal growled deep in his throat, his razor-sharp teeth bared. He seemed totally unthreatened by the weapon in her hands. He stood, poised for attack, his eyes narrowed in concentration.

A chorus of male voices made the animal's head turn sharply. She sighed in relief as she beheld several of her neighbors, led by Sato-san himself, carrying ancient swords and pitchforks, anything that could act as a weapon. Sato-san raised his sword and let out a war cry that had the unfortunate creature backing up. Encouraged by the animal's retreat, the group advanced, shouting and making such a commotion that the once fearsome creature turned and ran.

Hanako's legs wilted beneath her, and she sank to the ground. *The alarm system worked!* She lay in a heap, sobbing, while her rescuers huddled around her, unsure of how to proceed now that their mission had been accomplished. While Hiro had trained them well to deal with danger, they had absolutely no idea what to do with an emotionally spent woman.

Her baby's cries finally broke through Hanako's frantic thoughts, and she raised herself up to go to him. Wiping her eyes, she realized that the men who had come to help her still surrounded her with looks of shy concern on their faces. The expressions eased as she stood.

She stifled her sobs and bowed low to thank her rescuers, hoping her voice was steadier than her nerves. "My son and I are deeply indebted to you for saving us from the wild dog," she began. "I am embarrassed I have no refreshment to offer you after your hard work."

Sato-san, having designated himself the leader of the group, returned the bow. He still breathed heavily from the unaccustomed exertion and adrenaline rush from the danger. "Please do not trouble yourself, Tanaka-san. We are relieved the danger is past, and you and your son are safe. We will return to our homes now."

Hanako watched the group leave then turned to care for the baby, who had calmed down, having sensed all was well. He lay gurgling on his mat, happily raising his arms for his mother to pick him up.

The baby snuggled against her shoulder as Hanako walked back and forth across the floor. Slowly, the child's eyes closed, and as he drifted again into a peaceful slumber, Hanako came to a difficult decision. She had been a fool to refuse to accompany Hiro to Tokyo.

Yasahiro deserved to have the rights and privileges his samurai father could give him. As a young heir, he should have the protection of the city gates and the education available to him there. Hiro had become the man he was because of his family. It was what she wanted for little Yasa. If Hiro's family would not accept her, surely they would accept Hiro's son. Giving up her child would be akin to tearing her heart out, but she must do what was best for him. Laying the sleeping child back on his mat, she formulated her plan. As soon as the harvest was in, she would leave the farm in Ginjiro's care and go to Tokyo.

****

"Tanaka-san, it is good to see you again."

Hiro, his face nearly touching the *tatami* as he knelt and bowed, grimaced inwardly, but kept his head low as protocol demanded. It would not do to contradict the Captain of the Imperial Guard, whom he had never met.

The Captain continued, "You do not remember me, of course, but I heard much about you as I fought with your father. He often spoke of his pride in having four sons. On one or two occasions, as we returned to Tokyo, I saw your family when your father invited us to your home. Your older brother was destined to be a warrior like him, and your younger brother was an outgoing child, but when Tanaka-san spoke of you, his eyes would shine as he bragged of your quiet intelligence, your sense of honor. He knew you were destined for greatness." He looked down into Hiro's face, which had turned upward at the captain's words. "It was as if he were in awe of you."

Stunned at the unexpected praise, Hiro remained on his knees, his mind reeling at the revelation. He had always wondered what his father had thought of him, the second son. He knew that he was not the fierce warrior his *onisan* had been, but he had always worked hard, trying to prove himself to his larger-than-life father. And he had always been afraid that he had fallen short, that his desire for peace was a fault. Remembering his manners, he brought his head back down.

"I think perhaps your brother was a bit jealous of you."

Taro, jealous of me? Hiro couldn't believe his ears.

"He used to tell me how proud your father was of your intelligence, your quick wit. Taro was a fierce warrior, but he lacked your insight, your compassion, and your diplomacy. And he always kept track of you, especially while you were in Kato-san's employ. We had heard rumors about Kato's deviousness, but had no proof.

"It is because of your brother's concerns that the Emperor demanded an investigation when you disappeared. Kato had originally pledged his allegiance to the emperor, so he was allowed to keep some of his land holdings and a few servants. But while he publicly supported the Emperor, in private he plotted an insurrection. When his duplicity was discovered, his lands were confiscated and he was sentenced to prison, but he escaped. He traveled north, recruiting wandering *ronin* as his soldiers. I understand you dealt with them in Hokkaido."

The captain explained, "Some traveling merchants came to Tokyo recently. They told us much about your leadership and how you trained a band of simple villagers into an army brave enough to face them. Their story was truly inspiring.

"The Emperor's investigation also uncovered Kato's deviousness in ordering the *seppuku* of some of his best warriors." At this, Hiro's head popped up again. He quickly lowered it again, mindful of the rules of etiquette.

"Yes, your friend Fukada-san and several others had been eliminated because their honesty and integrity had threatened Kato-san's plot to overthrow the Meiji government. Restitution has been made to their families from the holdings we seized from his estate."

Hiro couldn't contain his smile. Finally, justice for his

friend!

"You may face me, Tanaka-san. You have earned the right. You have grown into an honorable man. Your gift of diplomacy will be a great asset to the Emperor."

The captain turned and reached for the golden doors leading to the seat of the Chrysanthemum Throne. "Come with me."

****

Hiro knocked on the door of the little hut on the outskirts of the city. The size and condition of the dwelling reminded him of the tiny structure where Hanako had lived when he had first met her. A tiny woman, her face lined and her body bent from years of hard work, answered his knock. She glared at her unexpected visitor, and Hiro quickly bowed.

"I am Hiromasa Tanaka. I wish to speak with the family of my friend and comrade, Kunio Fukuda."

The woman's face brightened. "Tanaka-san, it is an honor to meet you in person. I'm Kunio's mother. I've heard much about you."

"I am honored to meet you," Hiro replied. He faltered, not knowing what else to say. But the woman spoke readily.

"My son was in awe of your skill and intelligence. From the time you both began training together, he strived every day to match your abilities. He believed his friendship with you made him a better samurai."

Hiro hung his head. The friendship had also caused the man's death. It had been Hiro's idea to seek employment with the treacherous Kato-san.

"It was because of you that he had the courage to face his demons."

Hiro looked up at her, questioning.

"My son had an illness when he was younger. He couldn't walk for many years, and in school he was teased for his awkward gait. Determination to become a samurai made him work hard to overcome his physical limitations. But a part of him always doubted his ability—until he met you. You were the one who made him feel worthy of his calling. You helped him believe in himself. When the end came, he faced it bravely because you were there. My family is deeply indebted to you."

For long moments, Hiro stood, speechless. *How could she feel gratitude?* "I am ashamed I was not there with him when the difficulties began," he told her.

Fukuda-san interrupted him with a slice of her hand. "That is nonsense," she declared. "You were following orders, fighting elsewhere as you should have been. We have heard about Kato-san's downfall. His lands were taken away, and he left in disgrace. He should have committed *seppuku*."

Hiro swallowed. "He did. He went north to recruit more soldiers." Briefly he explained what happened to the disgraced *daimyo*.

The woman nodded. "That is as it should be. He was foolish to oppose the emperor." She looked up as she realized they were still standing at the doorway.

"Will you have tea?"

Hiro bowed. "It would be an honor."

For the next hour, Hiro sat with her, hearing about his friend's childhood, learning about his wishes and dreams. Listening to the woman reminded him of Hanako. *Would she someday tell stories about Yasa?*

He had to get back to them.

Chapter Twenty-three

Hanako's feet dragged as she neared the end of the furrow. She didn't have to work in the field, but driving herself to exhaustion was the only way she could bear the sense of loss from Hiro's absence. The baby babbled merrily as he rode in his pack, blissfully unaware of the turmoil in his mother's heart. Thanks to his wealthy father, Yasahiro would never live in poverty. As soon as the harvest was in, Hanako and Yasa-chan would travel to Tokyo. She had no idea how she would locate Hiro, but she had to try.

Her husband had been gone nearly two months now. Yasahiro was already walking and starting to talk. He might have already forgotten the gentle giant who had held him so tenderly and played with him on the *tatami* floor.

She prodded the ox, urging him to go faster. Soon it would be time for the baby to eat. Yasa-chan could be very impatient when he was hungry. She had rice soaking in the pot. They would have it for dinner, along with some dried fish and vegetables. Most of the time, she had difficulty summoning enough appetite to eat at all. But she knew if she didn't keep up her own strength, she would not be able to properly care for the baby.

Yasa-chan was the one bright spot in her dreary life. If not for her son, the passionate unions with Hiro might have been a wondrous dream. Hanako prayed he would grow to have his father's compassion and bravery. Once he was ensconced in his father's wealthy family, he would learn the ways of the *Bushido*. Even if he never fought in battle, he would learn the noble code of ethics, as well as the mysteries of the written word.

She pulled on the reins to lead the animal to the next row. Again, doubts assailed her. *Will I be allowed to stay with Yasa-chan and care for him? Will Hiro even recognize Yasa as his son, or would he dismiss him as the product of a casual dalliance?* Before he had left, he had promised to return, but in the months of his absence, no word had arrived from the city. Perhaps his family had convinced him of the folly of his life in the country. Surrounded by the comforts of his station, he might have forgotten the little family he had left behind.

She had a beautiful son, and thanks to her husband, she would not have to worry about having the means to raise him. She should be grateful for all the things he had done for her. What kind of a wife had she been to refuse to accompany her husband? If his life was in Tokyo, she should have gone with him and learned to adjust. She had thought this patch of land held the key to her happiness, but she knew now this meant nothing without Hiro.

Finally, she completed the work in the field and put the ox into the pasture. A farm hand came over to help drag the plow to the back of the house. As she rounded the corner, a powerful fragrance assaulted her. She looked up and froze. From the front of the house to the road, carts pulled by fine horses formed a line, each cart driven by a uniformed driver. In each cart, hundreds of beautiful, fragrant blooms spilled from huge pots. And there, in front of the lead cart, was her husband. He was thinner than she remembered, but still strong, fit, and oh, so handsome. His face crinkled in a tired grin.

"What—what is this?" she finally managed.

"This is my new vocation," Hiro announced, spreading his arms to indicate the wagon loads of blossoms. "I have purchased the farm to the west of us. You can keep growing your vegetables in your fields, and I will grow flowers on the new land. Since you have taught me well, our gardens should be very successful. And our children will benefit."

Hanako felt her cheeks grow damp. Her lower lip quivered, and she sobbed with joy. He had said children—not child. There would be more sturdy little boys and maybe a girl or two. Mindful of the servants' curious stares, she wiped away her tears. Her watery vision suddenly focused on the characters painted on the sides of each wagon.

"Tanaka Farms?"

"Yes, I thought we—" He stopped short and stared at her. "How did you know what it says on the wagons?"

"Reiko-san has been teaching me to read. I'm not very good yet—"

A pair of strong arms squeezed her tightly, cutting her in mid-sentence. "Hanako, this is wonderful! I am so proud of you."

She glowed from his praise. "I didn't want Yasa-chan to be ashamed of his mother."

"That would never happen."

Her husband's conviction warmed her even more. "I will go indoors and prepare a meal for you and your men." She hurried into the house, untied her baby bundle, and set Yasa on the *tatami* mat with some toys in the corner away from the stove. Turning around, she found herself enveloped in a tight embrace.

"The servants will stay outside. I need time with my wife."

Urgent kisses rained upon her forehead, her cheeks, her neck, and her lips. Her knees weakened, and she held him tightly, returning the kisses, fearing the sight and feel of her beloved would suddenly melt away. When he finally lifted his head, he crushed her to him, and she rested her head against his broad chest, relishing the sound of his strong heartbeat.

"You came back," she whispered. "I was so afraid you wouldn't. I was preparing to come to you, if you would accept me. I don't know the ways of a city life, but I would try very hard to learn. I want to be worthy of you."

He leaned back, looking solemnly into her eyes. "My life is here. I want to raise our son and our future children here on this land. I want them to live a peaceful life, surrounded by natural beauty, not golden castles and silk draperies. If you will agree, we will make this farm into a place that will provide comfortably for our family. Of course, we will need to enlarge our home a bit—since our family will undoubtedly grow."

Tears of joy streamed down her cheeks, but she needed to ask, "What of your family? You have responsibilities to them."

He smiled. "My younger brother has agreed to care for our mother. He has a successful business in Tokyo, where *Okaasan* has friends and an active social life. I have relinquished my inheritance rights as the eldest son, but I have not been totally dismissed from my family. She is eager to meet her grandson and daughter-in-law and is making plans to come and stay with us for a while next spring. And after the harvest is complete, I thought perhaps we could visit her."

"But—but I'm not suitable. I don't have the right clothes, or the right manners, or—"

He took her shoulders and shook her gently. "Never defame yourself, my beautiful little flower. You are my inspiration, my reason for living. My family knows you and little Yasa are my life. You have built this farm with your own hard work and determination. As far as they are concerned, you are every bit as brave and strong as a samurai wife should be. I am proud to be your husband and partner." He paused, and for the first time, she heard a thread of uncertainty in her husband's voice. "If—if this is what you want."

Her cry of joy and the tight crush of her arms around his neck gave him the answer he desired.

Epilogue

Tanaka Farms, Hokkaido, Fall, 1879

"I've never seen anything more beautiful."

"So delicate, yet enduring."

"Hiro, you are truly amazing."

Hiro bowed to his admirers in acknowledgement. "It is nothing, really. Without my beautiful wife, this would not be possible."

Hanako gently adjusted the silk fabric wrapped around their latest creation—the Aomori Rose. Through Hiro's diligent study and hard work, he and Hanako had produced a blossom that was snowy white on the outside, with a dark crimson stain inside. He had named it after the place where his friend had been forced to end his life.

Sitting beside his mother, four-year-old Yasa-chan made faces at his little sister, who peered back at him from her perch on Hanako's back. He didn't understand the fuss over a flower. After all, there were lots of flowers just like this in the fields outside their home. But this little creature was different.

She didn't do much except cry and drink, but *Okaasan* and *Otousan* seemed to think she was pretty special. When she'd first arrived, lots of visitors came with presents. Uncle Ginjiro and Aunt Reiko still came often, to help hold the baby so *Okaasan* could rest.

Okaasan said little Michiko would grow like his neighbor, Yumiko. He supposed that would be all right. Yumiko was a lot of fun. She could run almost as fast as he could, and —

Thwak! Yasa nearly toppled from the force of a raw egg hitting his chest and splashing up onto his face. He swerved his head around, searching for the source and spied dark braids trailing the familiar figure as she raced away. Ignoring the sticky ooze trailing down inside his *yukata*, he leapt to his feet, only to be detained by a firm hand on his shoulder.

He looked up at his father, ready to protest. How could *Otousan* expect him to ignore such an insult? But before he could utter a word, Hiro simply looked down and firmly shook his head. *How unfair!* Yasa's lower lip curled, and he felt his eyes grow wet. *Otuosan* wouldn't like it if he cried and made a fuss in front of all these people.

A gentle arm wrapped around him, and he felt his mother's warmth as she wiped the raw egg from his cheek. "Don't worry, Yasa-chan. We all saw what happened. I'm sure Yumiko-chan will receive a suitable punishment."

Yasa scowled, but he knelt again. His sister cooed, and he looked up into her dark brown eyes. They seemed to radiate with understanding.

Otousan had told him the tie between siblings was one of the strongest in the world. "Friends come and go, but Michi-chan will always be your sister," Hiro had told him. "She will look up to you, and you must look out for her and protect her."

The thought of protecting his sister made him sit up straighter. Of course he would do it. He was the son of a samurai. He would protect her with his life, just as his father and his friends had protected the entire village. It was in his blood.

Author's Note

Thank you so much for reading *The Samurai's Garden*. I hope you enjoyed the tale of the Tanaka family. This book was a labor of love from start to finish. It is a reflection of my Japanese heritage, set on the island where my paternal grandmother grew up. She came to America almost a hundred years ago, and never forgot her roots. I remember listening, fascinated, as she told us stories of the place she loved and left.

When I first wrote *The Samurai's Garden*, an agent told me it wasn't marketable because of its shorter length and lack of bedroom scenes. I knew it wasn't like other books out there, but I really didn't want to change it. So I am eternally grateful to Stephanie Taylor and Astraea Press for opening its doors and giving my story a great home!

I plan to continue the Tanaka family saga. Currently, I'm writing Yasahiro's story (Hiro and Hanako's son). In the meantime, please enjoy *The Legacy*, my very first published work at Astraea Press, originally released in July 2011. This is a contemporary short novella about Hiro's great-great-great grandson, Andy Tanaka. Hopefully it will keep you interested in this wonderful family.

~Patricia Kiyono

The Legacy
by Patricia Kiyono
Published by Astraea Press
www.astraeapress.com

This is a work of fiction. Names, places, characters, and events are fictitious in every regard. Any similarities to actual events and persons, living or dead, are purely coincidental. Any trademarks, service marks, product names, or named features are assumed to be the property of their respective owners, and are used only for reference. There is no implied endorsement if any of these terms are used. Except for review purposes, the reproduction of this book in whole or part, electronically or mechanically, constitutes a copyright violation.

To Dad, who taught us the Code of the Bushido through the way you lived. You were a true samurai. I miss you every day.

Chapter One

"Are you reading those ridiculous comic books again? Honestly, you're a college graduate. Aren't you a little old for those?"

"Dad, they're called *manga*. They're different. They're illustrated Japanese stories." Leigh Becker closed her book and stood. Even as the words left her mouth, she knew correcting her stepfather was useless.

"I don't care what they're called. They're not exactly serious literature. You spend half your free time reading those silly things when you should be helping out around the house. Come over here and help me get dinner ready. Your mother will be home soon."

However, as soon as Leigh stepped into the kitchen, Frank Becker left for his study.

"You do a better job of cooking than I do. I'd just get in the way," he muttered.

Leigh didn't mind having the kitchen to herself. Life was more peaceful when her stepfather wasn't around. He hadn't been the same since his company folded. The man who was once larger than life had shrunk physically and spiritually. He spent hours in his home office, staring idly at his computer. He had sent hundreds of letters out, but no one wanted to hire a fifty-year-old former businessman. Lately, he'd been drinking a lot more. Leigh sympathized, but didn't know how to comfort him.

The family wasn't struggling financially. Leigh's mother was a well-known attorney, and Leigh had just started to work for the local newspaper. They hadn't lived lavishly or spent foolishly, so the adjustments they had had to make were relatively minor. Still, it had been difficult for Frank to accept the fact his wife was now the breadwinner. For a short time, he had tried to help around the house, but now he left more and more of it to his stepdaughter.

As Leigh pulled vegetables from the refrigerator, a buzz sounded from her pocket. She pulled out her phone and checked. It was a message from her best friend, Andy Tanaka.

"Found something cool. Can you come?" Andy wasn't one for extra words.

"After supper," she typed back.

"OK," came the quick reply.

She smiled as she prepared the meal. At least she had something more interesting to look forward to this evening. She always enjoyed spending time with Andy and his family.

****

Seated at his desk in his home office, Frank Becker turned on his computer. While waiting for it to boot up, he poured himself a stiff drink. He stared at the screen, his mind blank. What was the use of sending out his resume to more places? No one was going to hire him.

Nobody wanted him. Even his wife didn't want him. She found excuses to be out of town, even out of the country, whenever she could. No errand was too small or too out of the way for Kirsten Becker. Twenty years ago, her ambition was what had attracted him to her. She could do anything—win a case in court, come home and fix a gourmet meal, and then go out and party. It had been such a boost to his ego when she had agreed to marry him. Her cute little five year old had come with her. And now the daughter was looking more and more like her mother. Like her mother had looked. *Except without the cutthroat tendencies.* Leigh was a softer, gentler version of her mother.

Too bad he couldn't have waited to marry the daughter instead.

****

Three hours later, Leigh knocked on the front door of the Tanaka home. The tidy two-story Victorian on the outskirts of town had been a second home to her for most of her life. Since her mother had always worked, Leigh had spent many afternoons and evenings here. Unlike the modern ranch homes in the Beckers' neighborhood, this house had a cozy charm and echoed with the laughter of several generations of Tanakas. On all sides of the house, and in the fields surrounding it, fragrant blossoms grew. Tanaka Farms was one of the largest suppliers of cut flowers in northern California.

She barely had time to lower her hand when the door swung open and a tiny pair of arms encircled her waist.

"Leigh, how nice to see you! Come in, come in." Andy's mom, Lily, stood barely five feet tall, but even at fifty-something she was full of energy and always exuded a warm welcome.

The petite woman took Leigh's hand and led her in. Leigh loved this house. Beautiful blossoms adorned every surface, and the furniture was well worn and comfortable. The entire family was involved in the business, begun by Andy's great-

great grandfather at the turn of the century. Andy had worked there since junior high, working his way up from stocking the retail store to driving delivery trucks. Now that he was a CPA, he spent his time in the corporate offices.

Andy had told her another branch of the Tanaka family ran a similar business in Japan. Every few years, he and his siblings and cousins would go overseas to visit their relatives. She envied him that connection with extended family. The Beckers were not close-knit. They got together at Christmas time—for weddings and funerals—but she barely knew her cousins.

Lily led her to the kitchen. "Would you like something to drink? A snack?"

"Oh no, thank you," Leigh replied. "I just had dinner. Andy told me he wanted to show me something."

"Sure. Go on back." Lily waved toward the back door. "You know the way."

Leigh nodded her thanks and walked outside. Though Andy spent much of his free time with his family in the main house, he lived in what used to be the caretaker's cottage. He had remodeled it to suit his needs—a bedroom, a small kitchen, a bathroom, and a weight room. But she couldn't find him anywhere.

"Andy? Where are you?" The cottage wasn't that large. Where would he be?

"Over here." His voice came from behind the wall. "In the storage shed."

The storage shed was attached to the back of the cottage, but she had never been inside. She retraced her steps and walked around. Andy had left the door open, and she stepped through. She curled her nose at the musty smell hitting her as soon as soon as she entered.

She blinked, adjusting her eyes to the relative darkness. A single bare bulb in the ceiling provided the only light. All around her were dusty old file cabinets. These must contain the older records for Tanaka Farms, she thought. At the back, she finally located her friend, kneeling on the floor, hunched over an old wooden crate. He was still dressed in his work clothes—khakis, a tucked-in polo shirt, and loafers—and Leigh briefly wondered how he managed to keep himself looking so clean and crisp, even inside the dusty shed. He turned toward her, excitement lighting his face.

He motioned for her to join him. Andy didn't speak when a look or a gesture would suffice. It wasn't that he couldn't talk. He had managed to deliver an eloquent, though brief, valedictory address when they graduated from high school. But he said only what he needed to say.

Leigh made her way to him. The crate looked different from anything she had ever seen. It was black, inlaid with delicate gold flowers. Though it was covered with a thick layer of dust, she could tell it was a treasure. Inside were some old Japanese clothes, a scroll, and two swords, one long and ornately decorated, the other shorter and plainer.

"I wonder how your family got these."

"Dad says we had a samurai ancestor."

"It would have been over a hundred and forty years ago. The samurai were outlawed in 1870."

Andy's hands stopped. He sat up and stared at his friend. A single raised brow communicated his question.

She shrugged. "I read about it."

His eyes crinkled and his lips curved. "Your manga?"

Andy was the only person who didn't tease or belittle her about her passion for the manga comics. "Yeah, I guess so. They teach a lot of history."

They looked back at the items in the crate. "This stuff is super old." Leigh mused. "Seems kind of a waste to have it rotting out here. Let's bring it in the house so we can look at it closer in better light and show it to the rest of the family."

They replaced the items in the box and hauled it to the main house. As they put it on the kitchen table, Lily came in, staring curiously.

"I thought I heard a lot of bumping and thumping coming from out here. What have you got?"

Andy simply gestured toward the wooden box.

"It's a cool chest Andy found way in the back of the shed." Leigh often finished Andy's explanations. Maybe it was because they had spent so much time together, but she felt they knew each other as well as they knew themselves.

She fingered one of the gold flowers on the lid. "This looks like a family crest."

Lily grabbed a dishtowel and wiped at the dust. "I think you're right. It could very well be the Tanaka family crest. I've seen it on old documents, as well as some of the traditional ceremonial clothing we have stored upstairs."

Leigh opened the crate and took out the faded scroll. "This probably explains everything, but we can't read it."

His mother opened the scroll and peered at the document. "I can't either. I recognize some of the characters, but I don't know enough of them to make any sense of it."

She looked up at Andy. "Your dad knows even less than I do. Why don't you take this upstairs to your grandfather? He's spent a lot of time in Japan, so maybe he can read enough to tell you what it says."

****

Ten minutes later, Kenjiro Tanaka removed his glasses and rubbed his eyes. He sat back in his easy chair. His rooms on the second story of the house were furnished with comfortable old furniture that suited him. Pictures of his family, past and present, covered the walls. Several shelves housed his collection of books. Grandpa Tanaka was a well-read man who had once harbored a dream of studying English literature.

"I'm sorry, Andy and Leigh, but I can't read this." He set

his glasses down on the side table and sighed. "My parents spoke Japanese to us, but my brothers and I went to American schools so our main focus was learning to read and write in English. I know just enough to get around when I go to Japan, but a lot of these characters I'm not familiar with. Why don't we go and see Mr. Kimura? He should still be awake."

****

"Kimura-san," as his acquaintances called him, was a close friend of the Tanaka family. He had come to America from Japan in the late 1960s as an instructor of *ikebana*, the art of Japanese flower arranging. He quickly became close to the Tanaka family through their mutual work with flowers. Even now, Andy's family included him in their holiday gatherings. Mr. Kimura lived in a retirement home close by.

"*Kon-ban wa*—good evening, Tanaka-san. Andy, what a nice surprise. And Leigh, too. What brings you out here this evening?"

"*Kon-ban wa*, Kimura-san." Kenjiro, Andy and Leigh bowed and offered the traditional Japanese greeting.

Leigh eagerly gave the explanation for their visit. "Andy found an old chest in his parents' storage shed. This scroll was inside, and we wondered if you could translate it for us."

"I will try. It has been so long since I have done any reading in Japanese, I have probably forgotten many characters. Let me find my reading glasses, and I will see what I can do."

Leigh helped the older man find his glasses and Andy set Mr. Kimura's wheelchair next to a table lamp. He started to read, but fussed about the lighting, so Andy brought another lamp over and plugged it in. The reading was laborious, and more than once he consulted an old Japanese character dictionary. Finally, the man set the scroll down.

"This is a letter from a man named Hiromasa Tanaka—

I'm assuming he's an ancestor of yours—to his son, Yasahiro. It is a moving letter. I'm not sure of some of the characters, since the letter is faded from age, and it's written in an old style of the language. You may have to check with a linguist to get the exact meaning of some phrases. But I will tell you what I know."

Kenjiro sat in an upholstered chair. Andy and Leigh settled on the floor in front of the old man and waited eagerly for his story. Mr. Kimura regarded each of them solemnly, and then focused his attention on Kenjiro.

"Hiromasa Tanaka was a samurai soldier. He came from a family of samurai. It says here he always knew he disliked fighting, and at the end of the samurai age, he was actually relieved, even though he didn't know what he would do. It wasn't until he met his wife in the far north, that he knew what he wanted to do with his life. He became a farmer, and established a successful flower farm.

"He had been raised with the samurai code of honor known as the *bushido*, and he believed it was this code that helped him to prosper as a farmer and a businessman. He raised his sons with the same ethics. Apparently his eldest son, Yasahiro, came to live in America. He must have been the Tanaka who established Tanaka Farms in California."

Kenjiro nodded in agreement. "Yes, Yasahiro was my grandfather."

Kimura-san continued the story. "Hiromasa was, of course, sad to see his son leave the country, but on the other hand was proud of him for his bravery in going to a new land. Hiromasa had other sons who continued Tanaka Farms in Japan, but he observed the accomplishments of his son in America with great pride.

"The letter says Hiromasa realized he was growing old, and feared he wouldn't have much longer to live. He wanted to give his eldest son his swords and other treasures of his life as a samurai, which Yasahiro was to pass down to his sons when they proved they were true keepers of the samurai code, or the *bushido*."

Leigh's breath caught. What a beautiful legacy! But she saw Andy's grandfather frown. Was something wrong?

"So this would have been passed down from Yasahiro to his son Ichiro, my father," Kenjiro mused. "And Father would have passed it down to my older brother, Michio. But Michio was killed in World War II. I was in college then, and my family was in the relocation center at Camp Amache in Colorado. I wonder when it was put away in the storage shed?"

"It is hard to say," Kimura-san replied. "Perhaps it was stored there before the family went to the camp, and later, in his sorrow, Ichiro didn't think to pass the legacy to you, his second son. It is rightfully yours now."

Kenjiro nodded. "It would seem so."

"Grandpa, are you angry that your father didn't give these to you?" Andy's question echoed Leigh's thoughts.

Kenjiro turned to him, seemingly surprised. "No, of course not. My father was devastated when Michio died. We all were. I can understand why he didn't think to pass them on to me. I'm just sad this is mine because of my brother's death." He took a deep breath, and let it out. "But it is an honor to have it." He looked at Andy again. "This will be yours someday. You are the eldest son of my eldest son."

Andy's chest swelled with pride. But then he had a thought.

"Grandpa, I hope it's not mine for a long, long time." At his grandfather's puzzled look, Andy explained. "It becomes mine when both you and Dad are gone. I don't look forward to that."

Chapter Two

After dropping Grandpa Tanaka off at home, Andy drove to Leigh's house. Leigh had walked to his home earlier, but now that it was dark, he insisted on taking her back. His thoughtfulness was one of the things she liked about him.

Leigh always enjoyed her time with the Tanakas and hated to see the day end, but now she had to go back to her own home, as dysfunctional as it might be. She took a deep breath. Hopefully her stepfather would have gone to bed. He had been drinking heavily during dinner, and she suspected he had continued long after she had left for the Tanaka's home. She didn't need any unpleasantness.

The closer they got to her house, the tighter her chest felt. One never knew about Frank's mood. He had been quiet at dinnertime, but if he had continued to drink…

The house was dark. Hopefully, both her parents had gone to bed. Life was much simpler when she didn't have to talk to either of them. Mom was always so distracted, so focused on her career. And Dad was…unpredictable. Sometimes he was morose, bemoaning the cards he had been dealt. The unfairness, the sadness, the impossible odds he faced. And other times he would lash out, finding fault with everyone and everything. Leigh didn't blame her mother for immersing herself in work. But that often left Leigh alone with—

"It's about time you got home. Did you forget where you lived? Or were you practicing shacking up with that Jap kid?"

Oh no. He was awake, drunk, and mean. Not a good combination. She held on to the door handle, thankful she hadn't come all the way in. Though Frank had never hurt her, she didn't want to find out what he was capable of.

"Where's Mom?"

"Took off on another business trip. I'll bet that 'business' includes some young dude with a fancy suit and an expense account."

Time to go. "I'll be right back, Dad."

Quickly, she scrambled out the door and tore across the lawn, around the thick hedges separating their yard from the neighbor's. She heard her stepfather calling her from the front door. Thank goodness for the darkness. She ran along the hedge toward the neighbor's backyard.

From past experience, she knew there was an opening in the back hedge through which she could squeeze into another backyard and over to the next street. From there, she could walk over to Main Street, and then to the Shadyside Motel. Hopefully Jenna would be working the desk tonight.

She needed to get her own place. Now that she was out of school and working, she could afford it. But she had wanted to pay off her student loans. And Frank had asked her to stay. He needed help around the house, he had told her, especially since his wife was getting busier at work. Until recently he had been pleasant, especially when he was sober. And she'd wanted to help out. But she didn't want to live in fear.

She stepped into the motel office to find Jenna sprawled in a padded chair, snoring. A tiny black and white television was tuned to the local nightly news.

"Jenna, wake up."

The snoring stopped, and Jenna's eyes blinked. A mop of shaggy, strawberry blonde hair shook as she woke up and tried to focus on her.

"Leigh, it's you! Did you get bored and come to keep me company?"

Leigh instantly felt guilty. She and Jenna had been good friends in high school, but after graduation they had gone in different directions. Jenna had married, and had two children in two years. Now divorced and living with her mother, she worked the third shift at the motel to make ends meet. The arrangement allowed her to be at home with her children during the day, when her mother worked.

"I guess I can stay and talk a while, Jenna," she told her friend. "But I'm going to need a room for the night."

Jenna frowned. "Again? Leigh, you've got to get out of there. One of these days your dad is going to force himself on you. You won't be able to get away. And it won't be pretty."

Jenna was the only person who knew about her father's problem with alcohol and had first-hand knowledge of the way Frank took his troubles out on Leigh.

"I'm working on it, Jenna. It's just that Mom—"

"—will be able to take care of herself," her friend insisted. "She's always gone, anyway. There are a couple of apartments open where Mom and the kids and I live. They're affordable, too. It'll be fun, Leigh. Why don't you check it out? Tomorrow."

"I will, I promise." She handed Jenna her credit card. "Here."

"You want just the basic room, right?"

"Yeah, I just need a bed and four walls."

Jenna rang up the charge and waited as Leigh signed the sales slip. She handed Leigh a card key. "Room 104. Right next door. So how are you going to get to work tomorrow?"

"I'll get up early and walk home. Dad should be sleeping by then, so I can change and go to work."

"Grab a suitcase and a bunch of extra clothes. I don't think you should stay there anymore. I'd invite you to stay with us, but..."

"Oh, Jenna, I couldn't stay with you. I love your mom and the kids, but you've barely got enough room for the four of you. I'll find my own place. Tomorrow."

She started for the door but turned back to her friend. "Thanks for everything, Jenna."

Jenna shrugged casually. "Anytime."

Leigh found her way to her room. This was her third stay at the motel this month. At this rate, she should qualify for a "frequent renter" discount. She set the alarm on her phone, made sure it was turned on, and flopped down on the bed.

It had been a long day. It wouldn't take long to fall asleep. She would need to get up early to walk home. She would be wrinkled and rumpled, having no clothes to change into, and no brush for her hair, no makeup, or anything. But she would get through this. She would.

She was in that zone where reality was getting fuzzy when she heard the commotion on the other side of the wall.

"Where is my daughter?"

"Hello, Mr. Becker. What can I do for you?"

"Don't give me that garbage. Where is Leigh? She couldn't have gone much farther than this." Frank was louder than he had been at the house. Not a good sign. Leigh grabbed her cell phone, ready to call the police.

"She must have found someplace else to go. I haven't seen her." Leigh was amazed at Jenna's calm tone of voice.

"You're just protecting her. Let me see your records. I'll find her."

"I can't let you do that, Mr. Becker."

"Sure you can. I have a right to know where my daughter is."

"Leigh is a legal adult. She can go where she wants. You'd better leave, before I call the police."

With shaking hands, Leigh managed to dial 9-1-1. Her friend was tough, but her father was larger, and the alcohol made him meaner. The dispatcher listened sympathetically to her description of the scene and assured her help was on the way.

The conversation was getting louder, but Jenna held her own. When had she gotten so tough? Had motherhood done that to her?

"No, Mr. Becker, you're not coming back here to look at my computer records. This is company property."

"I don't give a hoot about company property. You're hiding my daughter, and I'm going to find her if I have to knock on every door in this flea-bitten hotel."

"If you start doing that, I'll definitely have to call the police."

"I have the right to find my daughter."

"And the people here have the right to a decent night's sleep without someone banging on their door."

"You always were a mouthy little kid. I'm just gonna go look for that girl of mine."

"Is there a problem here?"

Leigh sighed in relief for her friend. The police had gotten here fast. She sat on the bed, frozen in place, and listened to Jenna's explanation to the officer, her father's loud protests, and the policeman escorting him out to the squad car. Good. If they kept him overnight, she wouldn't have any trouble in the morning when she went home to change and get her car for work.

She lay back and allowed the comforting blackness to overtake her.

****

The alarm on Leigh's cell phone chirped in her ear long before she was ready to wake up. Groggily, she turned it off and got up. She had a chilly walk home, and it would take her a good half hour. Better get going. She grabbed her purse, checked quickly to make sure she had everything she came with, and went back through the lobby. Jenna was just finishing her shift.

"Hey, Leigh," her friend greeted her. "I was about ready to wake you. I've got a surprise for you."

"A surprise?"

Jenna held out a set of keys. "I had the police leave your dad's car and his keys here, since they took him away. I told them I knew his family and would have one of them come by to pick up his car, so they gave them to me. Now you won't have to walk all the way home."

"Thanks, Jenna. For—everything. I heard you last night. I don't know how you managed to keep your cool."

Jenna shrugged. "It was nothing. I pushed the security button as soon as I saw his car pull up. They sent someone right away."

"So that's how they got here so quickly! The dispatcher didn't sound surprised when I asked her to send someone here."

"Yeah, well, it's not the first time."

Leigh stilled. "You've had to call them before?"

"Yeah. He came here looking for you last time, too."

"Oh Jenna, I'm so sorry."

"Hey, it's my job. You just make sure you take care of yourself. Pack a bag while you're at home and look for your own place. If not at my complex, then someplace else. You've gotta get out of there."

"I know. I'll do that. Thanks."

She took her father's car home, parked it in its spot in the garage, and went inside to get ready for work. Heeding her friend's advice, she packed a suitcase and grabbed a laundry basket to fill with her favorite personal items. It was going to be a long day.

****

Andy perched on the seat of his bench press, catching his breath after his morning workout. Something wasn't right with Leigh. He couldn't pinpoint the problem, but her entire demeanor had changed during the drive back to her parents' house last night.

More than once he'd opened his mouth to ask her what was wrong, but the words just wouldn't come out. It had always been like that. Ever since the first day of kindergarten when the teacher asked him what his name was, his vocal chords seemed frozen. The teacher had asked again and Leigh said, "This is my friend, Andy." From then on he let Leigh do a lot of his talking. But he couldn't expect her to read his mind. And she was on his mind a lot.

Leigh had always been strong. She'd worked hard and excelled at everything she did—academics, sports, music, and theater. She was always the best. Maybe it was because she was an only child, and her successful parents expected it.

And now he wanted to be there for her. But what could she possibly see in him? He was a wimp, a numbers cruncher, a nerd. He was a loner, working out in his personal gym rather than participating in team sports.

He and Leigh had always been friends. Best friends looked out for each other. But now his caring was starting to move beyond simple friendship.

Was it possible they could become more than friends?

Chapter Three

Leigh dragged herself into the newspaper building, already exhausted. Her car was loaded with her suitcase and several boxes and bags of her belongings. She hadn't packed everything, because she wasn't sure when the police would release her dad. She didn't intend to be there when he got home. Plus, she didn't want to be late for work.

She would worry about missing items later. Right now, she needed to concentrate on her job. Copy editing required focus and a clear head.

But clearing her head was a daunting task. Early in the morning she had called her mother's cell phone, but Kirsten hadn't picked up. She left a voice mail message, but it had gone unanswered. Where was she?

It was midmorning when she noticed it. People walking by offered sympathetic looks, a pat on the shoulder, even an extra cup of coffee. It took a while to figure out why.

Suzy Kramer, the crime beat reporter, came to see her. Suzy had gone to high school with Leigh's mother and was the biggest gossip on the staff. Suzy settled herself into a chair next to Leigh's desk and leaned toward her.

"Leigh, dear, I just spoke to the police chief. You know I have to publish all the department's arrests. Well, I saw that your father was—in residence there at the station. I just wanted you to know that we're all here for you, if you need anything."

Leigh fought back a wave of nausea. Of course. She had forgotten the paper published everything the police did. It was one of the disadvantages of living in a smaller town. Apparently, the first time Jenna had called the police on her dad, they had just warned him and escorted him home. But this time, they'd taken him in. There would have been a written police report.

She nodded her thanks to Suzy. Inwardly, she wondered if Jenna was going to press charges. He did threaten her. But she didn't think he would have actually hurt her. He had never hurt her or her mother.

Not yet.

The day loomed even longer ahead of her.

****

Andy sat at his desk at Tanaka Farms, his elbows propped on the desktop, his head resting in his hands. He hadn't been able to make sense of the numbers in front of him. His mind kept going back to yesterday's discovery. The entire family had grown up with stories of their illustrious ancestor, the fierce samurai warrior and founder of the original Tanaka Farms. Now, they had a tangible, direct connection with him.

But something niggled at Andy's mind. After his initial excitement, his grandfather had grown silent. It was as if something had deflated his enthusiasm. His grandfather had always been a happy man. He'd have to find out what the problem was.

"Problem, Andy?"

Andy turned to greet his father. James Tanaka was a nationally known horticulturist and often appeared on television newscasts as an authority on flowers. With his white lab coat over his tall, muscular stature and his wavy, graying locks, he was the perfect spokesman for the trade. He had his share of adoration from women admirers, but his heart belonged to his high school sweetheart, Lily.

"Sorry, Dad. Just worried."

"Anything I can help with?"

Andy shrugged. Even with his family, he spoke as little as possible.

James turned to go, but Andy had a question for him.

"Dad, did you and Mr. Becker have an argument?"

James was usually an outgoing, open man, but now his face closed. "Why do you ask? Did he say something?"

"No. But you don't see him any more. Leigh says he just mopes around the house all day."

James weighed his words. "Sometimes old friends drift apart. Often, there's no real reason. You get busy, and gradually the things you used to do all the time don't get done. That's life." He shrugged, and walked off.

Andy stared at his father's retreating figure. He hadn't answered the question. It wasn't like him to be so evasive. James was one of the most open and direct people Andy knew.

He worried about Leigh, too. He couldn't forget the way she had taken a deep breath before opening the car door. It was like she'd had to talk herself into going inside her home. Something was up. He'd better check it out this evening.

****

Leigh stood up, stretched, and groaned. She had cleaned every inch of her new apartment. Jenna had come over to help for a little while, but the children had gotten restless, so she had left. The apartment was small, but it was in a nice neighborhood and affordable. She still had her college loans to pay, but she would manage.

Her mother had finally returned her call. She was in New York, and didn't expect to be back for at least a week. She had offered a blithe apology for forgetting to mention it to anyone. Her reaction to Leigh's account of the previous night had been a simple, "Oh, dear." And then, "I'm sure Frank didn't mean to cause any harm. You're all right now, aren't you? I wish I could be there, but this is a very important case for our firm, and I've got to get this witness to testify. But anyway, you're old enough to be on your own. I'll come and see you when I get back."

Leigh had disconnected, feeling lost. When had her mother grown so callous?

She would have to start looking for furniture sometime. Right now she had a sleeping bag and a beanbag. Most of her clothes were folded in the same laundry basket she'd used in college. She'd managed to squeeze it in the back of her car, along with a few other necessities. She'd also grabbed some of her favorite mugs, and some paper plates. It would take a while to furnish this place.

She put down her cleaning rag and headed to the car to get her things. On the way to the parking lot, her cell phone rang. She looked at the readout to see who was calling, and her spirits lifted when she recognized the number.

"What's up, Andy?"

"I wanted to see how you were doing. It was late when you got home last night." Pause. "Is—is everything okay?"

"Yeah, it's fine. Why do you ask?"

"I'm outside your house. Your car isn't here. Where are you?"

"I just got an apartment at Pine Ridge."

Silence.

"It was kind of a last-minute decision."

More silence. Then, "Which apartment?"

She told him the apartment number, and he promised to be there to help. For the first time in several hours, things were looking up. And not for the first time, she wondered why Andy always managed to lift her spirits.

Andy knocked while she was still hanging clothes in her closet.

She let him in after looking through the peephole. She still wasn't ready to face her father. It wouldn't have surprised her if he had managed to find her. He would probably blame her for his incarceration. If she hadn't run, he wouldn't have had to go looking for her. Never mind the fact he had been drinking and had threatened her. It would still be her fault.

Andy came inside, looking at her as if he hadn't seen her in ages. He studied her face, not looking in her eyes, but looking for something. Then he walked around her, looking her up and down.

"Andy, what are you doing?"

Finally, he looked in her eyes. "Are you okay?"

"I was until you stared me down."

"Why did you need to move so suddenly? You've never even mentioned it."

"What makes you think I never thought about it before?"

"Most people, when they move, make plans and ask for help moving their—stuff..." He looked around. "Which you don't seem to have."

"I've got everything I need."

One dark brow rose. "You do? No furniture." He walked into the kitchen and opened a few cupboards. "No dishes, no pots or pans." He stormed into the bedroom. "And no bed."

He planted himself in front of her, arms crossed. "What's going on?"

There was no reason to lie. "Dad had—too much to drink last night. I didn't feel safe staying there, so I went to the Shadyside Motel. Jenna put me in the room next to the office, and I heard Dad come in and threaten her. She called the police, and they took him away. It wasn't the first time she's had to call them. So, I finally took Jenna's advice and got my own place." She took a deep breath. "I stopped at the house before work and grabbed what I could fit in my car."

"Did he hit you?"

"No."

"Did he try anything else?"

Her hesitation was all the answer he needed. "Leigh, what did he do?" He stepped closer. "What did he try to do?"

"Nothing." She hadn't given him the chance to try anything—this time.

"He's tried something, before, hasn't he?"

She couldn't deny it. A few times, when Frank drank, he had confused Leigh with her mother.

"Leigh, why didn't you tell me? You can call me anytime. My family—we'd all help you. Why didn't you come to my house?"

"I—didn't have my car. I didn't want to take the time to get in it and start the motor. I just—ran."

He closed his eyes and massaged his forehead. Leigh had never seen her friend so upset. Finally, he sighed heavily and began to pace.

"Okay, so you're out of there," he said. "What about your mom? Is she in danger?"

"I don't think so. He only gets angry when she's not there. When she's home, he's as sweet as can be, trying to please her. But when she's on business trips, he gets frustrated. He stays more sober when she's there, because he knows she doesn't like it when he's drunk."

"My dad said he offered Frank a job with Tanaka Farms."

"Dad never said anything about it. Did he turn it down?"

"I guess. Dad won't talk about it."

"Did they fight?"

"I don't know. It's too bad. They used to be the best of friends. Just like their fathers were."

Andy shook his head sadly. He looked around her sparse furnishings. "So, let's get some furniture."

"I can't afford furniture right now."

"You can where we're going. Come on."

Two hours later, they returned to the apartment with Andy's younger brother, Craig, and another friend. They'd borrowed two of the Tanaka farms delivery vans and brought a bed, a dresser, a table and chairs, a couch and two end tables. Andy's car was loaded with bedding and whatever else Lily Tanaka could stuff in. Leigh was amazed.

"Are you sure nobody else in your family needs any of this stuff?" Leigh asked for the umpteenth time.

"Nope. I have everything I need."

"I won't need it either," Craig chimed in. He didn't share his brother's aversion to conversation. "I'm living with Grandma and Grandpa Fujimori while I go to school at UCLA. Jenny's married and has her own stuff. So it's yours. Mom was thrilled to have someone use it. Didn't you see her smiling when we hauled it out?"

"I wondered about that. Craig, if you ever want this furniture, let me know. Eventually I'll be able to save enough to buy some of my own."

"Will do. But I doubt it." Craig turned to his brother. "Nick and I will get these vans back to the farm. See you at home, Andy."

With a quick goodbye to Leigh, he and his friend were gone. Leigh turned to Andy.

"I'd like to do something to thank your parents for their generosity." Leigh couldn't imagine her parents giving anything away and not expecting at least a tax deduction for it.

Andy paused. "Well, there is one thing…"

"Name it."

"Mom says Grandpa refused to come out of his room today. He wouldn't talk to her except to grunt. Something's wrong. Will you go with me to talk to him?"

"Of course! Your grandpa is a sweetie. Do you want to go now?"

Andy checked his watch. "No, it's late. He's asleep. Tomorrow?"

"No problem. I've got the whole evening open, now that I don't have to look for furniture."

"Okay. I'll call you after work. We can pick up something to eat."

"Just come over. You usually work later than I do. I'll pick up a pizza on the way home."

"Sounds like a plan." Andy backed toward the door. His hands were in his pockets, and he wore a pained look.

"What's wrong?"

"Huh? Oh, nothing. I just—"

Before she knew it, she was in his arms and being kissed within an inch of her life. He held her tightly, and yet his hands cradled her as if she were a priceless treasure. The kiss deepened and time stood still as she melted into him, matching each of his caresses with one of her own.

And then, just as suddenly, she was released and alone. She blinked, wondering whether or not the last few minutes had been a dream. Through the foggy haze in her mind, she heard the door slam, and the car start as he drove away.

What had just happened?

****

Andy drove home on autopilot as he scolded himself. What had he done? How could he have been so stupid? Just because he'd always dreamed of kissing Leigh like that didn't mean he should act on it.

He'd been so angry when he'd found out about Leigh's stepfather, he had wanted to shake her. How could she have kept this from him? Why couldn't he have known about Frank's drinking problem? Surely Dad wouldn't be friends with a man who would abuse his own stepdaughter! He was torn with anger for her, her stepfather, and himself. But mostly he wanted to hold her and keep her from danger.

So he had grabbed her like a maniac and kissed her like he'd always wanted. Nice going, Einstein.

The kiss had been like every fantasy he'd ever had. He'd felt like the hero in every old-time movie he'd ever watched with his grandparents. He'd never felt so alive, so powerful, so—masculine. Had he overdone it? No, it seemed she had been as involved as he. She certainly hadn't protested.

He breathed a happy sigh. Maybe there was hope.

Chapter Four

Leigh put the pizza in the oven to keep it warm. She put a few bottles of cola in the refrigerator and made sure the ice cube trays were full. Then she went into the bathroom to freshen up. For some reason, she was warm all over, and it wasn't necessarily because of the weather.

She hadn't been able to get that kiss out of her mind. She and Andy had been best buds since they were small. They had known each other forever. They'd been there for each other when one or the other had experienced bad dates and broken relationships, and he'd even filled in as her homecoming escort when her jerk of a boyfriend got a cheerleader pregnant. But last night was—different. It was like the start of something new. And she liked it. A lot.

After washing her face, she felt better. But then decisions had to be made, and even the simplest task took forever. Should she put on makeup, or would that seem too much? Should she tie her hair back or let it hang loose? Should she change her clothes? Agh!

This was ridiculous. It was just Andy, for heaven's sake.

Good old Andy. So he kissed her. He was probably just relieved she was all moved into the apartment. Just a housewarming gift, sort of.

On the other hand, a kiss like that would be worth moving several times a week.

She finally settled on a T-shirt and jeans, and tied her long hair back into a comfortable ponytail. Nothing unusual. Just a little mascara, no other makeup, no jewelry. There. Decisions made.

Where in the world was that guy?

Andy often worked late. As the future CFO of Tanaka Farms, he was in on all the financial planning of the business, and whenever there was a problem, he was expected to be there. There was no telling how long he would be held up. Maybe she could unpack some more of her things.

At his knock, her heart jumped into her throat. She reached for the doorknob, but remembered to look through the peephole first.

It was Andy. However, her usually impeccably dressed friend looked a mess. She threw open the door.

"Are you all right?"

Her question caught him by surprise. He blinked then stared at her. "Sure. Why?"

"Your hair is standing straight up, your shirt is half untucked, your tie is crooked, and—" She looked down and choked back a laugh. "Your shoes don't match. I thought you were in a fight or something."

He ran a hand through his hair, making it even worse, and looked down at himself. "Do I look that bad? Maybe I should have gone home first."

"No, no, you're fine. Come on in. I got pizza from DeMarco's. Thick crust, with everything."

He smiled widely and stepped in. "That sounds great. I'm starving." He stopped suddenly. "Was I supposed to bring something? Drinks, dessert, or—"

"Nope. I've got Coke in the fridge."

"Great. I'll spring for dessert."

They ate in a comfortable silence. Since they were both hungry after their long day at work, the pizza was consumed in no time. Andy finally sat back and sighed.

"That was great. Are you up for ice cream?"

"Sure. Why don't we pick up a turtle sundae for your grandpa and bring it over there?"

"Good idea."

They stopped at their usual ice cream shop, getting an extra treat for his grandpa, and brought all the desserts to the Tanaka home. The elder Mr. Tanaka was settled in his recliner, watching *Jeopardy*. He smiled when they walked in.

"Well, what have we here?"

"Hi, Grandpa Tanaka." Leigh answered, as usual. "We brought you a turtle sundae. We know how much you love them."

"I sure do. Pull up a chair and join me."

The three enjoyed their treats, and while Grandpa Tanaka chatted with Andy about the family business, Leigh watched with familiar envy. Her mother's parents were both dead, and her father's parents lived on the east coast. Frank's parents weren't around. She had never had the closeness she saw between the generations in Andy's family.

She also noticed how good Andy was with his grandfather. He didn't get impatient when the elder man asked him to repeat himself, and he willingly got up to fetch things for him. He truly cared about the people in his family.

When the conversation stopped, she looked up to find both men looking at her.

"Sorry. What did I miss?"

"Grandpa asked you about your new apartment. Do you feel safe?"

"Oh! Sure, I feel safe there. I know a lot of the residents there from high school."

"Kids, I'm actually glad you came to see me tonight. Now I can give you this." Kenjiro walked over to his desk and lifted the large wooden box. Andy and Leigh looked at each other, puzzled.

"I think you should give this to your father. And maybe he will decide to leave it to you."

"But why, Grandpa? You just got it!" Andy sat back, his arms crossed, clearly not wanting to take the swords from his grandfather.

"Your father deserves it much more than I do. You heard how Mr. Kimura translated the letter. It's supposed to go to the oldest son when he has demonstrated all the virtues of the samurai. The code called the *Bushido*, or "Way of the Warrior." I've never done anything except sell flowers. There's nothing brave or noble about that. My son has won awards for his scientific discoveries. He's president of the Kiwanis club. He's done a lot more for the business and the community than I ever thought of doing. It should be his."

Andy continued to resist as his grandfather held the swords out to him. Leigh had to step in. She reached out and gently touched the older man's arm. "The chest is yours to do with as you wish, Grandpa. But don't you think you should be the one to give it to your son? It would be silly for him to get it from Andy. This is something that's passed from father to son, not the other way around."

Grandpa Tanaka grimaced. "I suppose you're right." He turned to Andy. "Tell your father I need to see him, will you? I know he's busy—it doesn't have to be right away."

Andy knew his father would make time for his own dad, no matter what his schedule was like, but he just nodded. Wanting to change the subject, he asked, "Do you want to play Scrabble?"

At the mention of his favorite board game, Grandpa Tanaka perked up. Andy found the game, and the three played until Leigh smothered a yawn. They said goodnight, and the couple left.

The drive back to Leigh's place was done in silence. When they got back to her apartment, Andy followed her in, sighing heavily as he plopped himself on her couch.

"Well, now we know what's bothering Grandpa," he began.

"Yes. That's so sad. Why does he feel so inadequate? He's always been such a strong person." Leigh pulled a couple of soft drinks from the fridge and offered him one. He took it absently and took a deep drink.

"So how do we prove to him that he is worthy of the swords?" He got up and started to pace.

"I think we should find a list of the samurai virtues and then find the ways your grandpa has shown them."

Andy stopped in his tracks and stared at her. "That's a great idea! I guess I'll look them up."

Leigh walked over to the coffee table. A shelf underneath held a stack of her manga collection. "I know one of these magazines lists them. But it will take me a while to find it."

Andy finished his drink and set the empty bottle down. "Go ahead. I'll check online. Tomorrow. Right now I'm beat."

"Go on home," she told him, setting the magazines on top of the table. "Tomorrow's Friday, and I don't have plans for the weekend. Or I didn't until now."

He looked at her and gave a resigned shrug. "Looks like we're having a scavenger hunt."

She nodded cheerfully. "Scavenger hunts are fun."

He leaned over and kissed her cheek. "I'll call you after work."

She stood still, staring at the door long after he left. After the previous night's passionate kiss, his peck on the cheek left her wanting more. Was he stepping back? She touched her cheek, remembering his warmth, his gentleness, his scent. No, there was warmth and affection in that short kiss. Much more than the affection he would show for a buddy.

She sat on her couch, absently leafing through her manga collection. For years she had read them, wanting to absorb everything she could about his family's culture. It had been her way of being close to Andy and his world.

Maybe there was a chance he was ready to let her into it.

****

"Okay, we've looked up 'samurai code,' 'samurai virtues,' and 'Bushido,' and got a lot of different sites that list them. The problem is, some list only seven, and others list up to thirteen. We'll have to figure out which ones appear most often and start with those."

The Tanaka family's kitchen table was covered with their research materials. Leigh leafed through the manga books she had brought, while Andy sat next to her with his laptop. They compared lists and narrowed them down to a basic eight: loyalty, justice, courage, benevolence, politeness, honesty, honor, and character. Andy wrote the eight virtues on a clean sheet of paper, leaving space between them for notes.

"What's the first one?" Leigh asked, eager to dig into the project.

"Loyalty."

"That's easy. He was loyal to his family, as well as his country. I've seen the medals he got during the Korean War." Leigh knew almost as much about the Tanaka family history as Andy did, having spent so much time in their home.

They found examples of each virtue in Andy's grandfather's life. He had been an honest businessman, a loyal son, a polite gentleman, and all the rest. After this, surely he would feel better about himself.

They were both hunched over the books, looking for ways they could convince Grandpa Tanaka of his worthiness when James entered the kitchen, strode to the refrigerator and pulled out a can of pineapple juice. It was his go-to drink when he was stressed.

"Rough day, Dad?"

James looked at his son, his lips pressed into a crooked grin.

"Is it so obvious?"

Leigh answered. "Your tie is undone, your hair is standing up because you've been running your hand through it, and you've just guzzled an entire can of juice in one gulp. I'd say you're stressed."

James sighed. "I haven't had such a heated argument with my father since I was a teenager." He pulled his tie off, and sat at the table with them. "What are you two working on?"

"The samurai virtues," Andy offered.

"We looked up the samurai code or *Bushido*," Leigh continued. "We're trying to find a way to convince Grandpa he actually did uphold the samurai virtues and that he deserves to keep the swords, even though his father never officially gave them to him. We thought if we found examples in his life when he exhibited those virtues, he'd realize he's a good man."

James beamed. "That's great! I hope you can figure it out. He sure wouldn't listen to me." He got up and paced again, raiding the cookie jar Lily always kept filled. Andy and Leigh shared a look. James was health conscious, and ate sweets only when he was nervous or upset.

"I've never seen my dad so depressed." James sighed. "He's always been so even tempered, go-with-the-flow. But when I refused to take the swords, he almost bit my head off."

James absently reached into the cookie jar for a second treat. "I ended up walking out on him. I've never done that before."

"So the swords are still with Grandpa Tanaka?"

"No, I took them over to Mr. Kimura. I asked him to hang on to them until we get this resolved. I figured they were safer with a neutral party."

"Good idea," Andy agreed.

"Grandpa Tanaka trusts and respects Mr. Kimura," Leigh added.

"Right." James finally settled at a chair next to Leigh. "So what have you found?"

Andy handed the list to his father and sat back. "I guess I can understand how Grandpa feels. I wonder if I could ever earn the right."

James lowered the paper and regarded his son curiously. "Do you think you don't qualify?"

"I'm not particularly strong. Or courageous. You and Mom have taught me about honesty and justice. But as for the rest—I think Craig is more in line with those."

"Your brother is fearless, but he can also be reckless. He was a powerhouse on the football field, but he spent more time in the doctor's office than anywhere else."

Andy laughed at his father's description of his younger brother.

"So he had a few broken bones. As an accountant, the worst injury I'll get is a paper cut or a staple in the finger."

James chuckled. "Well, if you can convince my dad he deserves to keep the swords, you'll be a hero in my book." He rose and disposed of his empty juice container. "I'm tired. Guess I'll call it a day. Good night, Leigh. Thanks for helping out with this project."

"It's my pleasure, Mr. Tanaka."

****

When they reached her apartment, Leigh felt in her purse for her keys then thanked Andy.

She skipped up the step, keyed her way into the building then climbed the stairs to her third floor apartment. But as soon as she opened the door and stepped into her living room, she knew something was wrong. Very wrong. The windows, which had been closed against the cool spring breezes, were open. An open bottle of Scotch and a half-filled glass sat on her coffee table. And her prized manga books lay in a torn heap on the floor.

"So, you finally decided to come home," a voice behind her growled. She heard a boot connect with the door and it slammed shut. She froze. She knew that saying or doing anything only made things worse.

Her stepfather circled around her until he came to a stop in front of her. He'd been drinking so heavily she could smell it even before he spoke. His eyes were bloodshot, and he was breathing heavily.

"You've been hanging out with that Jap family again, haven't you? Whassamatter, our German heritage isn't good enough for you anymore? You wanna be Asian, or somethin'? Ha!"

Leigh fought to avoid cringing from the spittle coming at her. Slowly, she backed up toward the door. If she could just get to it...

"Don't even think about leaving," he warned.

His face got closer to hers. His lips twisted in a sneer, and his eyes shone with anger. She closed her eyes and forced herself to stand still.

"So now that you know what he's like, maybe I should show you what it's like with a real man," he growled.

Her eyes opened wide. "Dad, no!"

The acrid smell of whiskey assailed her as dad's mouth came toward her. She turned her face away and his lips nested in her hair. His arms entrapped her like steel bands. He'd forgotten who she was again, crooning Kirsten's name over and over. "I'll show you what you've been missing. You think I don't know how to be a good lover. I'll show you, I'll show you..."

One hand was at the hem of her blouse now, stroking her

skin. She tried to push him away, but he was stronger, and determined.

The knocking jolted them both. The steel bands loosened, and she turned toward the door.

"Leigh? You left your cell phone in the car."

Leigh turned to her father. "I have to answer it," she told him. "He knows I'm not asleep yet, because he just dropped me off."

Without waiting for an answer, she pulled the door open. She would have stepped outside, but a sharp tug on her belt from behind kept her in place. She had to get help without alerting her stepfather.

"Hi Andy," she greeted him. Her eyes pleaded with him for help. "Thanks for bringing my phone back." She brought her hand to her mouth. "I don't know what I would have done if you hadn't told me where I left it!"

Andy stared at her a moment, and his eyes widened. He nodded. "Sure, Leigh. No problem. I would have been worried too."

He backed up slowly. "I'll—I'll see you soon."

Leigh was yanked back into the house, and the door started to close, but Andy wedged himself in the opening. With a roar, Frank swung his fist, connecting with Andy's cheek with a sickening crunch. Leigh tried to reach him, But Frank lifted the younger man and bodily and tossed him outside, slamming the door and locking it.

He spun around and grabbed Leigh's arms. Large, beefy hands enclosed her wrists like shackles.

"Stupid, obnoxious kid," he growled. First the father ruins my life, and then his rotten kid has to shack up with my daughter!"

Leigh bit down on her lower lip. She wanted desperately to ask what James Tanaka had done to ruin Frank's life, but there was a better chance of finding out if she kept quiet and listened. She wasn't disappointed.

"I worked my tail off to build a business that would support your mother's lifestyle. How was I supposed to know the bottom was going to fall out of the automotive industry? But everybody buys flowers. Valentine's Day, Mother's Day, weddings. All those things made Jim Tanaka rich. So rich that my own wife preferred him over me."

Leigh wanted to cover her ears, but Frank held both her hands in an iron grip, and she couldn't move them. Her mother and James Tanaka? It couldn't be. It had to be the alcohol talking, putting ridiculous notions in his head.

Leigh closed her eyes. There was no way she could overpower him, but she had to try. Her jacket was torn from her body and she shivered, not because of the cool spring air from the open windows, but because she knew what he intended to do. She twisted, trying to get away, but he held her fast. Sloppy kisses rained on her face and neck and she cringed, reciting every nursery rhyme she could remember. Anything to get her mind off what was happening to her. Help had to arrive soon.

She winced at the hard slap across her cheek. Her eyes opened involuntarily.

"Don't do that!" His eyes were filled with rage.

"You never want it from me! I can't help it that nobody wants to hire me. But it's worse when my own wife doesn't see me as a man."

He pushed her down on to the couch. A moment later, he landed on top of her, knocking the breath out of her lungs.

"I'll show you what a man is," he groaned. Unsteady hands groped at her blouse and tangled in her hair. Finally, he grabbed at the neckline and ripped it from her.

He was reaching for her jeans when another knock came at the door. She opened her eyes again, as her father swore.

"Open up! Police!"

Leigh groaned as her father froze, effectively putting dead weight on her. The knocking continued.

"Open up in there!"

"What in blazes are they doing here?" He scrambled up and peeked through the peephole. Leigh rose and grabbed the afghan off the couch to cover up.

"It's that stupid Jap again," he whispered. "You make one squeak and you're dead."

He looked at the afghan wrapped around her and leered. "Kinda late for that innocent little maiden act, isn't it? I know you take it all off for your boyfriend out there. You could go running outside right now, and he wouldn't see anything he hasn't seen before."

Leigh's eyes widened and her jaw dropped. But she closed it again, knowing she would just irritate him more if she tried to reason with him.

The police knocked again, and Frank growled.

"Well, I'll deal with you later. I'm getting outta here." Frank padded back to the bedroom and opened the window.

Leigh realized what her father intended to do. She ran after him. "Dad, no! We're on the third floor! It's too high!"

Two things happened at once: the police broke through the apartment door and Frank Becker, in his inebriated state, slid out the window and dropped to the ground below.

Chapter Five

"Oh, honey, what an awful, awful thing for you to go through! You can stay with us for as long as you like." Lily fussed about the Tanaka kitchen, getting refreshments for everyone, and then running off to prepare the guest room for Leigh.

Kirsten Becker had been contacted and was booked on the next flight back from New York. She had promised Leigh that Frank would get the counseling he needed, and tearfully apologized for not taking Leigh's claims more seriously.

"I'm so sorry, Leigh," she had said through her sobs. "I've been so caught up in my work and avoiding Frank, I forgot to be a mother to you. I promise you, it won't happen again."

"It's a good thing Andy figured out you were in trouble," Craig remarked. "How were you able to warn him?"

Leigh smiled tiredly. "Back in junior high, we took a summer workshop on lip-reading. We used to practice it in school when we wanted to communicate without being heard." She looked at Andy, who sat beside her with an ice pack on his bruised and swollen cheek. "I counted on you being able to read what my lips were saying rather than what was coming from my mouth."

Andy nodded, but said nothing.

James shook his head. "Frank will be in the hospital for quite a while, I'm afraid. Then he'll have to face the court. Even if you don't press charges, he's in trouble. Apparently he was seen driving recklessly, and threatened one of the other tenants into letting him into the building."

He looked into Leigh's eyes. "I am so sorry you had to go through this," he said. "I know your father was angry at me, but believe me, I did nothing to ruin his business." There was a brief pause before he added, "And I *never* had anything going on with your mother."

"I know that, Mr. Tanaka." Leigh assured him. "I think everyone knew that, even Dad. But he wanted to blame someone, and I guess he decided it was you." She sighed. "At least maybe now he'll get the help he needs."

Lily came back into the kitchen. "All right, Leigh needs to get some rest. Honey, I've got a nice, hot bath going. There are fresh towels and one of Jenny's nighties on the guest bed. Let me know if you need anything else."

Leigh nodded her thanks and headed toward the guest room. Hearing footsteps behind her, she turned to see Andy right behind her. She raised a brow, but said nothing. He followed her into the bedroom, watched as she gathered the things she needed and then followed her to the bathroom door, stopping only when she turned to ask if he planned to watch her bathe.

"Sorry," he mumbled. He backed out and closed the door, but she didn't hear his footsteps walking away.

She undressed and slid into the hot, soapy bath, indulging herself in the blissful warmth for a moment, and then scrubbing herself down. She needed to wash away all memories of the night. Then she toweled herself off with one of the fluffy towels Lily had set out for her and put on the borrowed nightie and robe. Combing out her wet hair, she looked at herself in the mirror.

A stranger looked back at her. This was not the face she saw this morning when she got ready for work. Sighing, she pulled open the door and walked out.

And stepped into a solid wall of muscle.

"You've been waiting here all this time?"

Andy nodded. "I couldn't leave. I had to make sure you were okay."

"Andy, I was just taking a bath."

Andy took a deep breath. "This whole—deal—with Grandpa and his dad made me realize that I can't just put things off. Not when they're important. I always thought you were the strongest person I knew. You knew what you wanted and went after it. I always knew I'd work here at Tanaka Farms, and it was just a matter of finding out how I would fit in. I never thought I could be a person you needed. But the thing is, I need—you. You've been my best friend all my life. But that's not enough any more. I want you to be—more than my friend. Would that be okay with you?"

It was the longest speech she had ever heard Andy put together. And it was her turn to be speechless.

Andy fidgeted. "Um. So, you're not saying anything. Is that a bad sign?"

Leigh lips curved. "No, it's a good sign. I'm looking for the right words to tell you how happy I am. I want the same thing. I feel the same way about you. You're my samurai. You've always been there when I need you, and like your grandfather, you always do what is right."

Andy's sigh of relief met her sigh of happiness as they held each other tightly.

****

Andy drummed his fingers on his steering wheel as Leigh climbed into his car. She said hello to his grandfather in the back seat, and then turned to Andy.

"Where are we going?" she asked.

"To the nursing home. Mr. Kimura said he wanted to see us all right away."

"Why? Is something wrong? Is he sick?"

"He didn't say. He just said to get there as soon as possible."

Grandpa settled back in his seat with a frown. Andy couldn't help the unease in his stomach. The call from Mr. Kimura had been short but firm. Get your grandfather and Leigh and bring them to the nursing home immediately. There was something important Kenjiro needed to hear, and he wanted everyone there.

He pulled up to the home's entrance and turned to Leigh. "Why don't you go inside with Grandpa while I park the car?" She nodded and complied. Andy took the time alone to compose himself. Kimura-san was like family. Hopefully the news wasn't bad.

He walked into Mr. Kimura's room to find everyone there. Mr. Kimura looked healthy and was smiling. Andy's anxiety must have been evident, because Mr. Kimura chuckled.

"I see I have worried you, too, Andy. I apologize for that. I wanted you all here because I wanted you to meet Mrs. Samuelson." He gestured to an elderly woman seated beside his wheelchair.

All the Tanakas and Leigh murmured their greetings, then turned their curiosity back to Mr. Kimura. He continued his explanation.

"Mrs. Samuelson is also a resident here. Last night I discovered she was a nurse, often giving care to the terminally ill." He turned his gaze to Kenjiro. "She took care of your father in his final days."

The woman went to stand in front of Kenjiro and reached out to touch him, but paused and brought her arm back to her side. She bowed her head when she spoke.

"I am so glad to meet you," she whispered. "I was a young nurse when I took care of your father, and I didn't understand anything about the Japanese culture. So when he talked to me, I didn't realize how significant his words were to him.

"He kept talking about swords. He said he had to give them to his son. I didn't find any swords in his room, so I didn't know what he was talking about. Your mother and younger siblings didn't know anything about swords, either. I thought he was having a flashback to when he was younger. Anyway, he talked a lot about his son. He said his son was a good man, and he had fulfilled all the virtues of the bush—bush—"

"*Bushido*," Mr. Kimura supplied.

"*Bushido*," she repeated. "I had no idea what that meant. I just thought he was reliving the past. But he kept talking about all the wonderful things his son had done, and how he had never acknowledged them. I just told him that I was sure his son knew how much he meant to him. But he wouldn't calm down. He said he needed to get the swords from storage and give them to his son."

Kenjiro's face darkened as he spoke. "I was in the army, stationed in Korea when he died. I tried to get a leave so I could get back as quickly as possible, but this was in the 1950s, and it took a long time for me to get back.

"By the time I got home, he was gone, and the funeral was over. My mother was a wreck and all my energy was devoted to keeping the business going. Tanaka Farms had taken a big hit during the Second World War, when the family was "relocated" to the internment camp in Colorado, and we were still rebuilding, so I never gave the swords a thought. I knew about them, and I'd seen them once or twice, but it never occurred to me there was a story behind them.

"My father was a stern man, and I had trouble pleasing him. That was one of the reasons I enlisted when the Korean War broke out—I wanted to prove I was as patriotic and as courageous as my older brother. But I worked a desk job there. I didn't see combat. I never felt I lived up to his ideal.

"When Andy found the letter, I realized that if my father had wanted me to have the swords, he would have given them to me."

"Don't you see, Grandpa?" Andy stood, his hands outstretched, begging his grandfather to understand. "You've shown every single one of the *Bushido* virtues in your life. And what Mrs. Samuelson says proves that your father truly believed you were worthy of the legacy. So you have the right to these things. They are yours."

"He's right, Dad," agreed James. "Grandpa should have given them to you after Uncle Michio died. But he didn't. He probably couldn't, if the swords were in storage at the house and the family was in the relocation camp in Colorado. Plus, he was probably too much in shock, overcome with grief. He probably forgot about the swords until he knew he was dying, and then he was unable to give them to you."

"But I still have trouble accepting the virtue about courage. I never did anything courageous. My brother was the warrior—he was strong and had the courage to fight for his country. I was a scrawny kid who went to college. There was nothing courageous about that."

"My friend, I think you've forgotten the *Bushido* definition of courage."

All talking ceased, and all heads turned toward Kimura-san as he wheeled his chair closer to Grandpa. The swords lay across his lap.

"Courage can be seen as a virtue only if it is exercised in the cause of righteousness. In other words, courage is simply doing what is right." He paused until his friend met his eyes.

"When your brother died and your family needed you, you came home from college and took care of them. You gave up your college life to work and help your family survive. And when your father died, you took up the reins of the family business and kept it going. That, my friend, is courage."

Kenjiro finally allowed his gaze to rest on the swords. "You really think so?"

Mr. Kimura picked up the long sword with both hands and presented it to his friend. "I know so, Tanaka-san," he replied gently.

Kenjiro sighed. "I guess I've got a wall somewhere these can hang on."

He turned to his son. "But some day, soon, they will hang in your home."

James nodded. "Not for a long time, I hope. But someday."

Andy and Leigh looked at each other with contentment. The legacy had been passed to its rightful owner.

About the Author

During her first career, **Patricia Kiyono** taught elementary music, computer classes, elementary classrooms, and junior high social studies. She now teaches music education at the university level.

She lives in southwest Michigan with her husband, not far from her children and grandchildren. Current interests, aside from writing, include sewing, crocheting, scrapbooking, and music. A love of travel and an interest in faraway people inspires her to create stories about different cultures.

Made in the USA
San Bernardino, CA
08 July 2019